If I'd Known

A novel written by:
Paige P. Horne

We only get one life.
Be happy in everything you
do. xoxo

Paige P. Horne

Dedication: For my mother-in-law. May everyone find a love as deep and true as yours and Lloyd's. For there wasn't a time I saw you happier than when your hand was in his.

Published: Paige P. Horne 2018
Pgpeacock13@gmail.com
Editor: Paige Maroney Smith
Cover design: Cover design © Arijana Karčić, Cover It! Designs
Proof Readers: Julie T, Crystal, Julie V and Monica

Also, written by Paige P. Horne

Close To Falling

Chasing Fireflies

Chasing Ellie

Prologue

June 2006

Shades of fiery orange, glowing red and smooth yellow, paint the boundless sky as the sun settles. The wind shifts, blowing a lock of hair against my neck and out past my shoulders. Shivering, I cross my arms and rest my hand over my mouth as I gaze out. Tears of agony fill my weary eyes and sting as they chase one another over my wind-chapped cheeks.

Endlessness lies ahead of me. As far as the eye can see, nothing but deep blue. The ocean is a wonder. It holds secrets with no way to tell them. It's where one can find peace or where one can get lost if they choose to or not. It holds life and death; tears and laughter. It captures moments from long ago, grasping onto time like only it can.

It's calm and soothing like a mother as she rocks her newborn. It's vicious and volatile like a cancer. Comparable to life itself, the ocean can tear you to shreds.

Here I stand at the edge of it all as the warm water washes over my bare feet, wave after expected wave. Shutting my eyes, I let sweet memories take over my vision, and my breathing becomes uneven, because it's not fair.

"It's not fair!" I scream out. I clench my fist and dig my nails into the palm of my hands as blood pumps wildly through my body. My knees, after standing so strong, buckle and I fall to the ground. I beat the sand with my fist repeatedly.

I plead with God like it could change a thing, and painfully, I bring my hand to my heart, bunching the fabric of my shirt.

"It's not fair," I whimper as I look at the sand through blurry tears. Shaking my head, a raw, gut-wrenching sob releases from my chest, moving up my throat, and I cry. I weep uncontrollably, unable to do anything else.

Rubbing over my eyelids, I'm torn between praying my frail heart can survive all this unbearable pain and praying that it won't. My chest shudders, and my hands shake as I scrub them down my face. I wipe the tears from my jaw as I blink my eyes open and look ahead.

Still… there's the ocean, unaffected, yet my whole world has changed.

Chapter One

Present day

Strumming clear polished nails on my small kitchen table, I watch as the aspiring journalist sets her baby pink helmet on the table before she grabs a notebook and pen out of the bright pink polka dot bag she carried in here. A long necklace with a blue pendant dangles around her neck, and every finger has a ring on it. She's got fire in her eyes and determination on her pursed lips.

This child has been after me for weeks because she's heard around this quaint beach town that I hold in my heart a tragic but beautiful tale about true love. I'm going to get my friend Maggie. I tell her things in confidence, and the little gossip has betrayed me.

Cynthia Rose is one of the most persistent things I've ever come across. She's been following me around everywhere on that little baby blue scooter of hers—Dollar General, the grocery store. Hell, she's worried me to death. Now here I sit, with years behind me and more memories than enough time to tell them.

"So," she starts, looking across the table at me. She's pretty, quirky, and very young looking. "You were how old when you two met?" she asks with bright green framed glasses and purple streaks in her dark hair.

Kids these days can't decide on one hair color. But secretly I like it. I'd never tell her, though. I want to get this over with and let her move on with her life so I can move on with mine. Which consists of sitting at home mostly, unless I need to go out and get things. Not much of an exciting life, but one would say I've had enough excitement. I'm content.

I shrug. "I'd presume a little younger than you are now."

"You were in your twenties then?" She lifts her brow and tucks her bottom lip in.

"You're in your twenties?" I ask, surprised.

"Yes, just turned twenty-one."

"Oh, I stand corrected. We were sixteen," I say.

The buzzer on my pot-bellied pig timer goes off, and I stand and slide my oven mitt on. Warm pound cake smells like heaven, taking me back to my mama's kitchen, and my mouth waters to try a piece.

"Sixteen. That was a long time ago, wasn't it?" she says.

I turn back to look at her, and she lifts her brow in question. Most people would think that's rude, but she's telling the truth. Sometimes it seems like a lifetime ago, and other times it seems like just yesterday. My eyes go to the lighthouse calendar hanging on the wall.

"Forty-four years to be exact," I say melancholy.

Time sure does fly. One minute, you're a little girl playing with kittens off an old dirt road out in the middle of nowhere. The next, fifty years have flown by and here you sit, in your kitchen, with an aspiring journalist who for some reason wants to write about you. Cynthia clears her throat and pushes her glasses up her nose.

"Did you feel a spark?"

"A spark?" I question as I set the pan down on top of the stove and remove my mitt. I twist my wrist and look at my watch, knowing I must let the cake sit for at least ten minutes.

"Yeah, you know, like in books. There was a spark of electricity in the room, or when our hands touched, it was like a current shot through us," she says sarcastically, adding an eye roll.

"Not a romantic?" I ask.

She shrugs. "I just don't believe two people who don't know a thing about each other can fall in love at the drop of a hat."

I chuckle. "Well, I hate to prove you wrong, but we did," I say. "And there was a spark. Static electricity to be exact."

Cynthia laughs. "Well, that's a bit different, isn't it?"

"Is it? People feel all kinds of things. Who's to say when someone meets the love of their life they don't feel some strong connection, like a shock or a spark for that matter?"

Cynthia shrugs again. "Maybe," she says as she scribbles something down on her notebook. I reach up and grab Mama's glass cake holder from the top of the fridge. Setting it down on the counter, I look over at the TV as *The Andy Griffith Show* starts to whistle its famous tune.

Leaning against the counter, I rest my hands behind me and look at the girl who wants to write a story about something that happened long ago. It's difficult bringing up all those memories.

"Why do you want to write about this, Cynthia? I mean, you don't seem to be someone who cares for romance, and I'm sure there are tons of other great stories you could write about."

She looks up at me from her notebook and rests her pen on top. "Because it's true," she says. "And people relate to the truth."

I look away from her and peer down at the floor. My story is tragic and unfair. I still question it. After all this time, I still ask *why? Why me? Why us?* I'd like to think I wouldn't do it again if I had the chance. That the pain is just too hard to bear, but deep down, I know I would.

The love, laughter, and the feeling of being utterly and blissfully complete when he was around me—how devastating it would be to have never felt those things. Travis Cole was made to love me and I him.

I look back at her. Cynthia Rose is nothing but tenacious. She's been unshakable these past few weeks. I've told her no more times than a person should have to, but she's relentless, refusing to accept my answer. I'm a very private person, yes, but she's grabbed a ladder and climbed herself right over my walls. Besides, I think I like her.

"Okay." I sigh.

She smiles.

"Grab us two saucers from the top left cabinet over there." I point as I look down at my watch, seeing I still have a few more minutes.

"You're into old movies?" she asks me as she looks toward the TV.

"Well, it's old, but it's not a movie. Tell me you know what *The Andy Griffith Show* is?" I say.

"I didn't watch too much TV when I was growing up," she replies.

"You do know who Elvis is, right?" I ask intently.

"Yes." She grins as she places the plates onto the table.

"Good. I was getting worried." I grab the wet dishcloth and wipe the excess sugar off the countertop. "So, what's the deal with this job you've been talking about for weeks now?" I ask her as I lay the dishtowel on the edge of the sink.

"Well, like I've said, it's for *The Sea Harbor Journal*, which is currently hiring for a writing internship. They've set up a competition for the town. Whoever sends in the best story before the end of summer, fiction or non-fiction, will win the internship, and that can then turn into full-time with them. Also, the winner's story will be printed on the front and second page, and depending upon how long it is, the third also."

"That's what you want to do with your life?" I ask. "Be a writer?"

"Yes," she replies.

"Are you in school?"

"I took a few writing classes at the local college here. What about you? What were you before you became a beach bum?"

I laugh. "I wouldn't say I'm a beach bum. Forever ago, I was a daughter, then an accountant." I take a seat at the table. "Eventually, I became a wife and a mother. Then one day, I wasn't a daughter anymore, so I focused all my energy on being a good wife and mother to my son. I went to work, did my job the best I could, and took care of my family the best of my ability. But the day came where I was no longer a wife, so I concentrated on my son and work. And then I became sort of a caretaker, but that eventually changed, too," I say sadly. "My son married and moved away to start his own life, so in due course I retired and moved here." I rub the side of my neck and smirk because it's as if for the first time I'm realizing I no longer have a title. Sure, technically, I'm still a mother, but I'm not raising my son anymore. That job is done. I'm not doing anything anymore.

"What?" Cynthia asks, looking bemused at my smirk.

I shrug. "I no longer have a title," I say.

"So, beach bum it is." She grins. I laugh and stand up. Walking over to the stove, I pick up the grease pan and tilt it upside down onto the cake stand. Tapping the sides, I slowly pull it up, hoping the cake doesn't stick. Once it's separated from the pan, I place the dirty dish into the basin. Grabbing a butter knife, I press it down into the cake. It glides down smoothly. The cake is perfect. Sliding out the pieces I cut, I put them onto the saucers and hand her one along with a fork.

"There's milk in the fridge if you'd like a glass," I say, knowing most people would probably prefer milk over tea with cake, but not me.

"Yes, I would." She smiles. "Where are the glasses?"

"Beside the plates," I reply as I take the milk and tea out. After she pours herself some milk and I make a glass of sweet tea, we sit down and taste what I've baked. Cynthia makes a sound and closes her eyes.

"This is the best pound cake. I've never had homemade before."

I look over at her. "Never?"

"Never," she confirms.

"Your mother doesn't bake?"

She shakes her head. "My mom worked a lot," she says, trading her fork for her pen.

"Worked? Is she retired?" I ask, thinking she must be too young.

"No, she and my dad were killed when I was seventeen."

"Oh," I say, shattered for the girl. I search her face with narrowed eyes. She said that so nonchalantly, which I find very odd. You'd think a girl who lost her parents only a few years ago would show more emotion, but Cynthia Rose shows none.

"So, let's talk about this great love story. How did you two meet?" She changes the subject from herself.

I look at her over the rim of my glass before I set it on the table and clear my throat. Running a thumb across the side, I cast my eyes to the floor.

"It was the summer of 1972," I begin with a small smile on my lips. "I was a skinny thing, with the deepest burgundy hair. Had a handful of freckles spread out across my cheeks and shoulders from too much sunshine and not enough sunscreen. The June summer was hotter than ever, and till this day a box fan in an open window takes me straight back to it. I remember the smell of honeysuckles drifting through my screen into the roaring fan and covering my room with its sweet, sweet scent." For a moment, I close my eyes at the memory before opening them again, seeing Cynthia penning away, and I wonder why she doesn't have a laptop like most of the kids these days.

"All my summers before that one had been the same," I continue. "School-free, old dirt roads, and not enough stray animals to make me happy. *But that summer.*

"God…that summer was the day my life changed forever. The day my heart latched onto another's so severely it was as if they'd become one."

Cynthia looks up at me from her writing.

"You read stories and watch movies about a love you think could only exist in a made-up world. But, my dear," I say, looking at her, "I lived it."

Like a rewinding movie displayed on a projector, my memories flash in front of my eyes. Quickly, every big moment and the sweet small ones in between, until golden rays shine behind my closed lids and the sound of my mama's voice rings in my ears, putting a smile on my face and a warmth in my heart that hasn't been there in years…

Chapter Two

June 1972

Bright sunshine beams through the window of the singlewide trailer my mama and I share, and I blink my eyes open. I squint as I begin to hear her voice calling my name from down the hall and stretch my arms out in front of me. My door opens, and she stands with a dishtowel in her hands.

"Your cousin's here," she says.

"Really?" I ask excitedly.

"Yes. Get up. I need your help in the kitchen." I toss the covers off me and dart across my carpet-covered room out into the hall. Jesse and I have always been close. He used to live in Georgia, too, but now he lives in Florida, where I wish I lived. I haven't seen him in a year. I open the door and walk out onto the small porch. It's early morning, but the Georgia air already feels sticky, instantly making my clothes cling to me.

"Hey, Jesse!" I call out as I rest my forearms on the rail and lean over.

He looks over the hood of his car and says, "String bean!"

I smile, but roll my eyes at his stupid nickname for me. Then someone else catches my attention.

I believe there's a special compartment in our brain that holds onto precious moments. It saves every detail so you can always go back and replay it, and this moment right here is something I know I'll never forget. Before he even speaks to me, a feeling that can't be explained rushes through my chest. My heart skips, and my pulse quickens. I forget how hot it is outside, or that my cousin is here. I forget everything. I often wondered how people knew when they met *the* one, and now I no longer have to.

"This is Travis Cole," Jesse says. "We met working at a small garage back home." With mid-length, dark brown hair and no shirt on, Travis looks over at me from the water hose. Droplets of water fall from his face, and soap covers his hands before he rinses them and then shuts the water off. I watch, almost like it's in slow motion, as he pulls a towel out of his back pocket, wipes down his face, and dries his hands.

He starts to walk my way, and my innocent eyes descend to the small amount of hair on his chest, his happy trail, and on down to the black denim jeans that cover his legs. *Jesus*. My eyes shoot back up as Travis reaches his hand out and smiles the boyishness, boyish grin I've ever seen. *Holy dimples.*

"Nice to meet you," he says. His brown eyes dart down to my body, and the left side of his lip quirks. I wonder why, until I remember I'm in baby doll pajamas. I feel heat crawl up my neck, and I struggle to not clamp my eyes shut.

"You, too." I hardly breathe as I put my hand in his, and static electricity causes both of us to snatch our hands back. He chuckles.

"Sorry," I say with a bashful smile, staring at his beautiful lips as they stay in a perfect crooked position, still grinning at me. *Where did this boy come from?*

I look back up at his eyes as the sunlight reflects in them, and I see small gold flakes and tiny, tiny wrinkles around the edges from his smile. He looks bemused by me, and I feel like I'm caught in a trance until Mama shouts, "Charlotte, ask Jesse if he wants something to eat!"

"I'm guessing you're Charlotte," Travis says as his eyebrows raise and he tilts his head slightly, giving me a look of curiosity.

I smile. *You can call me whatever you want.* "Y'all hungry?" I ask. *Please be hungry, I want more time with you.*

"I could eat." Travis shrugs. "What about you?" He turns to my cousin who shuts the hood of his car.

"You gonna go put some clothes on first?" Jesse asks me.

I roll my eyes. "Duh." I look down at Travis again and bite my bottom lip before walking back to the door. I feel his eyes on me and I get chills as the door slams behind me after I enter. I head through the living room to the hall.

"They're eating," I call out before I shut the door to my bedroom and press my back against it. I look to the ceiling and smile. Heat covers my body, and when I turn my sight to my mirror, I see that I'm blushing. I should be embarrassed by my appearance, but that's not what's got me hot and red, and I have a feeling it won't be the last time Travis Cole does that. I put my face in my hands and shake my head. God, I haven't even brushed my teeth. I throw off my pajamas and head to the closet.

I take a little too long getting dressed, desperately trying to erase Travis' first impression of me in nightclothes and bed hair. I try on four different outfits and go over my hair with the iron at least five times, making sure there are no waves and almost burning myself in the process. My room is a mess, and I'm afraid they're probably done eating by the time I come out, but oddly as I walk into the kitchen, they walk through the door and my eyes go to Travis, seeing he has on a white shirt now. He runs both hands through his hair as his eyes land on me, and this time there's no crooked smile, but something else, and I can feel it everywhere.

"Y'all grab you a plate," Mama says. Jesse walks over to the sink and washes his hands while Travis and I make our way to the stove. I stand beside him, watching as he loads up his plate. I breathe in, noticing he smells like summertime air and grease. He hands the spoon to me, and I brush my hand against his, just to feel it one more time. I look up as his eyes dart down to me, and I can't help the smirk that spreads across my lips.

We all sit down, and Jesse eats like he hasn't in years. My attention turns to Mama as she says, "So, tell us about yourself, Travis."

"She asked him every question possible, and I soaked it up like a sponge. I found out he was from Virginia, but his mom remarried when he was thirteen and they moved to Florida. He had two older brothers, one half-sister, and two full sisters. I also learned we were the same age; he was just one month older," I tell Cynthia. "I remember looking over at Mama as she kept asking Travis everything. The wrinkles around her eyes grew more noticeable every day. She was well into her forties when I was born, but I don't think age was the main thing making those wrinkles deepen. I believe it was from the stress of raising a bunch of kids. Thirteen to be exact."

"Thirteen kids?" Cynthia asks with wide eyes.

I chuckle. "Yes, thirteen."

"So, she was in her forties when she had you?" Cynthia looks skeptical.

"My family's history is very complicated," I reply. "The woman I called Mama was actually my grandmother."

"Your grandmother?" she asks curiously.

"Yes. My real mom was Beverly and at the time she had me she wasn't able to raise me, so the woman I called Mama and the man I called Daddy adopted me. Beverly ended up moving to Indiana, got remarried, and had another child a few years later. I was close to all of them, even though we didn't live near each other.

"Daddy had a heart attack and passed away when I was young, so it ended up being just Mama and me and whichever kid or kids she was keeping at the time."

I look down. "Cynthia, as I tell you the rest of this story, you'll have to understand, the older I got, the more I realized if it wasn't for Mama, there's no telling where I would be. It was just us two for so long and I was grateful for her."

Cynthia gives a small smile. "Tell me about her."

I take a deep breath. "Carolyn Bailey had silver gray hair that was always pulled back. She'd ask if you wanted something to eat every time you stepped into her house. 'It's called good manners,' she'd say, and I guess it was. You never left hungry from a visit with her, and I've lived by the same rule. She was an early riser, way earlier than me.

"One of her famous quotes was 'God didn't give us another day to waste it.' She made each day matter, and to her that was by getting up early, cooking breakfast, and watching all her daughter's kids while they worked. That meant I had my little nephews and nieces constantly driving me crazy. I remember wishing Mama wasn't so helpful," I say. "And back then I really hated it, but if I've learned anything about time, it's that the more of it that passes, the more you learn to appreciate the small things as they are happening."

Cynthia looks up at me and something flashes in her eyes, but before I can place it, she looks back down.

"You and Travis met because he was friends with your cousin?" she asks, getting back to him.

"Yes, he was," I answer.

"So he came from Florida, and you lived in Georgia at the time?"

"That's right."

"Georgia, where the weather is fickle and the mosquitos will terrorize you."

I laugh. "You've been?" I ask as I take up our dishes and place them into the sink. I put the stopper in and turn the water on.

"No," she replies. "Someone I used to know told me about it."

"*Used* to know?" I question as I grab the dish detergent and pour a little into the sink.

"Just an old friend."

"You're too young for old friends." I turn to look at her as I shake my hand under the water, making bubbles appear.

She shrugs her shoulders. "Would you say it was love at first sight?" Cynthia asks, once again taking the conversation off her and back on me.

"Travis and me?" I ask.

She nods.

"Of course, I wasn't madly in love the moment he looked at me," I say. "Even though it did happen pretty fast, but at first I was more intrigued I guess. He was the best-looking boy I'd ever laid eyes on. I knew I wanted to know everything about him. I wanted to know his thoughts, his personality. His heart." I turn the water off and let the dishes soak. Walking to the bar, I grab the remote and flip the TV off.

"Falling in love is one of the best feelings in the world," I tell her. "It's something you can't buy, yet sometimes it does come with a price."

"Did falling in love with Travis come with a price?" she asks.

I look off again and slowly exhale before I say, "Yes, it did. One that I'm still paying, I'm sad to say." I feel her looking at me, but when I turn, she looks down at her notebook and puts the end of her pen to her lips.

I clear my throat. "After the day we met, I couldn't stop thinking about the boy with dark brown hair and chestnut eyes. Those dimples could get him any girl he wanted, but for some reason, that boy only had eyes for me. And let me tell you. We had some pretty cute Georgia boys in my school, but none of them could hold a candle to Travis Cole. I'd already wanted to move to Florida because of my cousins and the ocean, but now, I was determined to convince Mama it was the best idea ever."

"And why is that?" she asks knowingly.

"We had a family-owned house up on a hill, a little walk from the beach, and the best part…well, Travis Cole," I say with a girlish smile. Realizing I haven't smiled like that in a long time, I take in that feel-good feeling. The lightness in my chest and the stretch of my lips. I move and take a seat back at the table.

"It was late summer, and family was visiting from Florida before my senior year started. I remember kids running around everywhere, and Mama had supper on the stove. The smell of cabbage boiling in a stockpot smelled the house up terribly, and the sound of hot grease sizzling from her cast iron skillet still rings in my ears. It was a chaotic day, but looking back, I'd give almost anything to relive it again."

August 1972

"Get outside and play," Mama says to my younger cousins. The screen door slams shut, and I know what's coming next. "And stop slamming that door!" she yells after them. Jennie, Jesse's sister and my closest friend, is up from Florida and we sit on the edge of our bathtub with the water running as we shave our legs.

"Have you seen Travis around?" I ask her casually, like I haven't been dying to know ever since he left in Jesse's souped-up car.

"Like almost every day," my cousin says, taking the razor and running it up her leg. "He asked about you, you know?" She gives me a sideways glance.

"He did?" I say, trying to rein in my excitement, but failing miserably because Jennie sees it and she grins.

"Yeah, he did."

"And?" I respond with wide eyes and a squeakier than normal voice. All cares of showing excitement have exited the bathroom.

"And what?" she asks.

"And what did he say?" I turn to give her my full attention.

"He just wanted to know if you were dating anyone."

"What did you say?"

"I told him no."

"Is he?" I ask, hopeful.

"Nope," she says, all matter-of-fact.

I bite my smile as I stare down at the water.

"I've got to tell you, though, Charlotte. He isn't the best guy."

"What do you mean?" I ask, a little alarmed.

"I mean, he gets into trouble. He smokes grass and drinks."

"So does Jesse."

"I know, but Jesse hasn't been arrested."

"Arrested?"

"Yeah, Travis got arrested a few weeks ago for fighting outside a bar downtown."

I bite my lip and look down.

"Cut that water off when you're not using it," Mama yells from the hallway. I turn the knob off and lower my voice.

"Does Aunt Evelyn know about it?"

"Yeah, you know Mama and those women she has over like to gossip."

I sigh. "I'm sure Mama knows by now then."

"I'm sure Mama B does, too," Jennie says, like that's too bad.

I turn my attention back to shaving. Cutting the water back on, I rinse my legs off before I turn around to get out. My little cousin Mikey stands in the doorway watching us.

"What are you doing?" I ask him.

With dirt on his cheeks and no shoes on his feet, he shrugs and grins.

"Were you listening to us?"

"Travis and Charlotte kissing in a tree!" he yells to the top of his lungs and I jump up to grab him, but he takes off running through the house, still screaming. I follow, sliding with my wet feet but managing to stop as he runs smack into Mama.

"What is that you're yelling about?" she asks him as she grabs his shoulders.

"Charlotte loves Travis," he says, looking up at her.

"Shut up," I say to him.

"Charlotte, don't tell your little cousin to shut up," Mama scowls. "What is this mess about Travis?" she asks me with a lifted brow. I peer down at Mikey, wishing I could make him disappear.

"Nothing. He's just being annoying."

Mama narrows her eyes at me. "I don't want you to have anything to do with him, Charlotte. He's troubled."

My stomach sinks. "Why is he troubled?"

"I've heard it from Evelyn. She says the boy can't stay out of trouble."

I look over at Jennie, who's standing in the hallway, both of us realizing her mama told mine.

"I mean it. You are to stay away from him," Mama says, grabbing my attention.

"Mama, how can I have anything to do with him when he doesn't even live here?"

"Never you mind. Just listen to what I say. Now, go dry your legs off. You're getting the floor wet. Mikey, go wash your hands and face. It's time to get ready for supper."

Mikey runs back down the hall, passing Jennie as she comes up beside me with a towel. I take it and lean down to dry my legs.

"Mama, why don't we move to Florida?" I ask her again. I've asked her several times since Travis left a few weeks ago, and she keeps brushing me off.

"Florida?" she asks, looking back over her shoulder at me, like she hasn't heard me say this the last ten times I've said it.

"Yeah, I'll be closer to Jennie," I say, smiling over at my cousin. "Plus, we won't have to pay rent."

Mama stops once she is in the kitchen and crosses her arms.

"I mean, we've got that house just sitting there." I shrug. "It's hot as heck here in Georgia." I put the towel on top of the washer.

“It’s hot in Florida, too,” she says, turning around at the stove.

“I know, but at least we’ll have the beach.”

She sighs, which means she’s thinking about it. I smile and look over at Jennie again.

“This doesn’t have anything to do with that boy, does it?” She flips the chicken onto its other side and grease pops, causing her to stand back a little.

“What boy?” I ask, feigning innocence. She eyeballs me, and I try to keep a clueless face.

“Don’t you want to live at the beach?” I ask, changing the subject as I jump up onto the counter and look over at Jennie, who gives me a hopeful smile. I dip my finger into the pot of potato salad beside me.

“Moving is a big job,” Mama says, walking over and swatting my hand before taking the bowl away.

“But we have family to help. I mean, look at all these kids,” I say, signaling outside. “Might as well get some use out of ’em.”

Mama turns her head and gives me a look.

I grin and shrug. “What? They drive me crazy.”

“One day you’re going to miss having them around.”

“I doubt that,” I say under my breath.

She moves from the stove and grabs the sweet tea pitcher from the counter. Opening the refrigerator door, she puts the full pitcher onto a rack and shuts it behind her. “Get off the counter and set the table, please,” she says, lifting her brow.

I jump down and grab the plates from the top shelf. Turning around, I see Mama's eyes dart from me to my cousin and then back to me. With her arms crossed, she taps her red fingernails against her skin and leans back against the counter. I hold the plates to my chest as a slow smile spreads across her lips.

She sighs again in defeat. "Let me think on it, Charlotte." Jennie and I squeal and Mama laughs. "I said *think*, not yes."

"I know, Mama." I put the plates down and walk over to her. I give her a kiss on the cheek before Jennie and I walk out.

"Plates," Mama calls after me.

"Mama did say yes," I say to Cynthia. "A year after I met Travis and a short time after graduation, we had the car packed up and were saying goodbye to our friends and family. I remember looking back in the rearview mirror as we drove away, thinking *this is going to be the best summer ever*. How little did I know that it would not only be the most memorable summer I've ever had, but it would be the summer that changed my life forever…"

Chapter Three

June 1973

"I'll be back later," I call out to Mama as I maneuver around cardboard boxes.

"What do you mean, you'll be back?" she says with the bottle of Windex in her hand.

"I'm going to say hey to Jesse before he has to go to work," I tell her. I push open the screen door and put one foot out.

"Charlotte, we have to unpack all of this stuff."

"I'll be right back." I let the door shut before she has a chance to speak any more and walk the small distance to Jesse and Jennie's house. A cool breeze blows across my face as I walk off the porch, and I hear a boat horn in the distance signaling for the drawbridge to be let up. I turn back, seeing Mama cleaning one of the eight enormous windows in the front of the house, and I give her a wave as I take off down the road.

The smell of saltwater and summertime puts a smile on my face, and I breathe in deeply. I can't believe this is my life. Just last week we were stuck in that small town in that tiny trailer. Now we're in a real house that's only a little ways from the beach and close enough to Travis for me to see him hopefully every day. I hear music before I hear the car. I turn and see a royal blue GTO slowing down. I stop and look at the driver who happens to be none other than Travis. My heart starts hammering against my chest in excitement. He turns the knob on his radio, shutting the music off, and smiles. *Those dimples.*

"Charlotte, right?" he asks me.

"Yep," I say, smiling back.

"Hop in. I'll give you a ride," he says as he leans over and opens the door for me.

I bite my lip, look back toward my house, and before I can think any further into it, I say, "Okay."

"Where are you headed?"

"Jesse's," I say, getting in. The smell of leather seats and grease fills my senses, making me feel giddy, and I blurt out, "But I don't really care where we go."

He smiles. "Okay then. Let's ride."

He drives down to the stop sign and turns onto the highway. I reach up and turn his radio back on. He shows me those beautiful dimples and that crooked smile as he presses the gas, making us go faster while the Doobie Brothers sing about a sleepy little town.

The next day I can't wait to see him again, and as I'm walking into the kitchen, the telephone rings from the hall. I run back and snatch it up right before Mama can. I laugh as she shakes her head at me.

"Hello," I say in a singsong voice.

"Hey," Travis replies in a deep, cool voice. My heart smiles, like literally grins.

"Who is it?" Mama asks.

"It's just Jennie," I lie, turning away from her.

"Jennie?" Travis questions.

"Um, nothing," I say. "What's up?"

"What are your plans today?" he asks me.

"The beach in a bit." I twirl the phone cord around my finger and keep an eye out for Mama.

"Which one?"

"Pepper Park."

"What time?"

"In about an hour."

"I'll see you there," he says before hanging up.

Putting my key into the ignition, I roll the windows down and head over to Jennie and Jesse's house. The sound of seagulls flying over the white powdered sand and the waves crashing against the shore confirms I'm just a street over from endless, blue, blue water.

A few minutes later, I'm pulling up in front of her yard. I blow the horn and run my hands over the steering wheel. I hear a lawnmower in the distance, and as the wind blows in through my open windows, I smell fresh cut grass. My mind drifts, thinking about Travis and riding around with him yesterday. His sun-kissed skin, the way his dark brown hair falls carelessly midway on his neck.

I jump when the passenger door opens and Jennie climbs in. She's wearing a blue, white, yellow, and red striped bathing suit with short shorts.

"Scare you?" she asks me with a smile.

"Yeah, I was in deep thought I guess."

"Let me guess. Was it about a brown-haired, dimple-faced boy?" She tosses her towel in the back and I press the clutch and shift my car into first gear. I press the gas and lift off the clutch. We jerk a little, but I don't choke.

"Maybe," I say with a smirk. We pass a few people riding their bikes down to the beach and others caring lounge chairs and big striped towels.

"I went riding with him yesterday," I tell her.

"You did not. Your mama would never let you."

"She didn't know and doesn't still," I say as a matter-of-fact.

She grins but says, "Don't let that boy get you in trouble."

I have nothing to say to that, and unbeknownst to Jennie, that boy is meeting us in just a little bit.

Once we arrive, I put the car in neutral and pull the brake up.

"It's been too long since I've seen the beach," I say, squinting my eyes from the sun.

"You'll get used to it," Jennie says with a shrug.

"Nah, I don't think I'll ever get used to living here," I argue as I get out. I pull the seat up and grab my beach bag.

With our hands loaded, we walk across the hot pavement and climb the steps leading up to the wooden walkway. The summer sun beams down on my shoulders, and I know tomorrow I'll have fresh freckles and tender skin. Our feet stomp loud across old wood that's been lightened by overexposure to the sun, and my flip-flops sink as soon as I hit the white sand.

I adjust my bag on my shoulder and slide my shades down over my eyes as I look out toward the ocean. The sand is thick and I peer down the beach, taking in the view of huge umbrellas and sky blue tents.

Once we're close enough, we put our things down, kick our shoes off, and shimmy out of our clothes.

"Let's go get our feet wet," I say to Jennie as she lays her shorts down on top of her bag. We tread into the water, and I see tiny fish scatter as I take a few more steps forward. The waves come in, brushing against my shins and crashing onto the shore behind us. A few kids have boogie boards and moms and dads build sandcastles with their kids far enough away from the rushing tide.

A boombox plays music from a blue and white blanket surrounded by other teenagers like us. They have red Solo cups filled with beer, I'm sure. I also get a whiff of grass, which is probably coming from them, too. I look down the beach at the lifeguard who sits up high on his post watching the people who are on floats and swimming. A few joggers pass by, leaving shoeprints in the compacted sand, and I lower down into the water, wetting my shoulders and lifting my hair to keep it dry.

After we've had enough of the water, we walk back to our towels, and I lather on some sun protection and sit down. A cool-warm breeze blows my brown straight hair across my face, and I close my eyes and drown out everything but the calming waves.

"Hey, there's my brother and Travis," Jennie says.

I open my eyes and follow her gaze. Travis and Jesse walk with a beer can in their hands and no shirts on. I swallow when my eyes land only on Travis. A lit cigarette rests between his lips, and he removes it to take a swig from his drink as they make their way over here. My heartbeat picks up, and I smile when he looks at me. I've only met this boy twice, but the feeling I get when he looks at me… it's like I've known him forever.

"You two wanna come to a party tonight?" Jesse asks as he takes a seat on his sister's towel.

"I don't think I can," I say as Travis sits down on my towel, causing my heart to pump even faster. He bends his knees up and rests his elbows on them.

"Why not?" he asks, taking a drag from his smoke before he puts the glowing butt out in the sand. I watch his lips as he blows heavy smoke up and away from my face.

"I don't think Mama will let me go to a party." I roll my eyes and play with the fringe on my towel, feeling like a child.

"Let's tell her we're going to a movie," Jennie chimes in, surprising me. I look over at her before looking beside me at Travis. He doesn't speak, just searches my face waiting for me to respond, almost daring me with his eyes to say yes.

"Okay," I say to Jennie. "That'll work."

Once the summer sun sinks, I drop Jennie off and head home to get ready for the movies aka party. Walking into the house, I notice Mama has been busy this afternoon, and the living room is looking somewhat organized. I hurry past it to my room and change out of my bathing suit. I grab my brush to try to remove the tangles the beach wind caused before twisting open my mascara.

I put a little on my eyelashes and run some lip-gloss against my lips. I spray some hairspray on top to keep the flyaways tamed before sliding some platforms on with a pair of my high-waisted bell-bottoms and a blue halter-top.

I notice that my shoulders already have that pink sun-kissed glow, and I grab my perfume and spray a little across my neck. Giving myself a once-over in the mirror, I smile before I run out and turn into the kitchen as Mama walks out of the pantry.

"Going somewhere?" she asks me.

"Well, depends," I say as I walk to the fridge and grab a glass bottle of Cola. Popping the top against the counter, I toss it into the trash and take a sip. It burns going down, and I wince.

"I'm waiting," she says as she watches me with an amused expression.

"Do you care if I go to the movies with Jennie?"

"The beach wasn't enough?" she asks.

"Not really," I reply with a grin.

She sighs, and I know she is going to say yes.

"When will you be home?" she asks me.

"As soon as the movie is over, I'll drop Jennie off and head back."

"Okay, but don't make it too late."

"I won't," I reply as I walk over and give her a kiss on the cheek. "Thanks, Mama."

"Remember, come straight back once it's over."

I can't help but roll my eyes. This woman babies me to death.

"You're going to look real cute when your eyes get stuck like that," Mama calls out as I walk out of the kitchen and head toward the door.

After Jennie gets in, I hit the gas and head to where she directs me. Cars are parked on both sides of the road, and I pull mine over before we get out.

"This house looks empty," I say to her after I shut the door.

"That's because it is," she replies.

"So where is the party then?"

"It's down at the beach. This way," she says as she starts to walk, and I see a small path big enough for one person. "Everyone likes to have it here because no tourists are around."

"Oh," I say as we follow the path up a hill and around the house. Once we hit sand, I slip my shoes off, and she does the same. We climb down the hill of sand, and I see the fire by the water. There's a breeze coming off the ocean, and it sweeps over my slightly sunburnt arms, giving me chills. I hold my shoes as we make our way down, and I notice Travis sitting in front of a piece of dried up driftwood.

"Hey, girl," he says as we walk up.

"Hey," I reply with a smile.

"Jennie," a girl calls out from down by the water.

"I'll be back," she says to me. I watch her run toward the girl.

Travis says, "Come sit down here."

I nervously bite the inside of my cheek but go and sit down beside him, placing my shoes in the sand.

"Your mom think you're at the movies?" he asks me.

"Yeah," I say.

He nods. "She strict on you or something?"

Shrugging, I reply, "I guess. My real mom was a wild child, so Mama is extra worried I'm going to be the same."

"Your real mom?" he asks me, taking a sip of the beer in his hand.

"Yeah. Mama is actually my grandmother."

"Oh," he says. Jesse comes up and sits down beside Travis. I smell grass and see the joint in his hand. He takes a hit and passes it to Travis. I watch as Travis brings it to his lips and inhales deeply. He holds the smoke in his lungs and offers me some. I shake my head no.

He shrugs and takes another hit before giving it back to my cousin. I look down at the beach and see Jennie laughing with the girl who called her.

"You want a drink or anything?" Travis asks me.

"No, thanks," I reply.

"So you don't smoke and you don't drink. What do you do?"

"I like to bake."

"Bake?" he asks me.

"Yeah," I reply.

"Think you could bake me something one day?"

I look over at him as he blows smoke from his lips. His eyes shine, and the fire reflects in his pupils.

I smile. "Yeah, I think I could do that."

He grins and looks ahead. "All right," he replies with a cool nod.

"We spent the rest of the evening together, talking and laughing until I realized what time it was. I grabbed Jennie, and we hurried out of there. The interrogator asked me a million questions because I was late getting home, but I went to bed that night with a smile on my face because I knew I really, really liked Travis Cole, and I was pretty sure he really, really liked me, too."

Cynthia leans back in her chair, giving me a small smile. She sighs and closes her notebook. "I do believe you are one of the rare ones," she says.

"What do you mean?" I ask.

"Finding your true love at such a young age."

"Yes. I guess I am."

She puts her notebook into her polka dot bag and stands up. "I'm going to go home and work on this. Can we meet back up the day after tomorrow for lunch?"

"I'll be here," I reply.

Cynthia walks to the door and turns the knob, but before she steps out, she turns back to me, looking slightly uncomfortable. "Thanks for doing this. I know it wasn't an easy thing for you to agree on, being it took you so long to do it." She lifts her lip. "Anyway, I just want you to know I'm grateful that you're letting me tell your story." She adjusts her bag on her shoulder and clears her throat. "I'll see you later," she says before she disappears.

I sit at my kitchen table, staring at the closed door, processing everything we've just talked about.

"Just wait until you hear it all," I murmur.

Chapter Four

Walking along the shore, I reach down and scoop up a faded pink and pearl white seashell. Seagulls scurry across the compacted sand, and if you stare out, you can see dolphin fins as they swim in the distance.

With the bottoms of my jeans rolled up, I let the rising tide run over my feet while I toss the shells into my bucket. I look behind me when I hear my name being called. Cynthia Rose drops her bag onto the ground and slips her sandals off. Holding them with two fingers, she makes her way over to me.

"I thought you were coming at lunch," I say, remembering our conversation from two days ago.

"Marty woke me up early because she's taking off to Austria. We had coffee together, and once she left, I decided a walk on the beach would be nice." She smiles and shifts her shades up onto the top of her dark hair. Her bright pink toes glow against the white sand, and I can't think of the last time I painted mine.

"Who's Marty?" I ask her.

"She's my aunt. I've lived with her since my parents died."

"Oh," I say. "And she took off to Austria?" I question.

"Yes. She's a flight attendant. She travels all over the world."

"Oh, what an interesting career."

"Yeah. It is," she says as she looks out at the water, and I do the same. "It's peaceful this early." Way out, someone sails a boat, and there's a cargo ship that looks like an ant from here.

"Yes, this is my favorite time of the day, before the beach gets too crowded," I reply.

We don't speak for a moment, both just enjoying God's creation. But then my stomach growls and I realize I haven't eaten yet.

"Have you had breakfast?" I ask, looking over at her.

"No, I wanted to see if you'd like to go to Seaside's with me?"

"Seaside's?" I ask her.

"Yes. You know, the place people eat at." She lifts a brow.

"Okay, smarty. I know what people do at Seaside's."

She grins. "Well, you wanna go?"

"I usually just fix myself some cheese sausage and toast here."

"Umm, okay," she says slowly. "I was really craving some of their coffee, though. It's like the best. Can you do the cheese sausage and toast thing tomorrow?"

I sigh. "I guess, little girl."

"I'm not a little girl, Charlotte. I'm twenty-one years old."

I laugh. "That's what you keep telling me."

We make our way back to the house, and I see her scooter in the driveway. "Is that all you drive?" I ask.

"Hey, don't hate on my Vespa. It's a classic."

I chuckle. "Not hating, just wondering. I'm not sure we'll both fit on it, so we can take my car to eat."

"That's fine with me. Let me put my helmet and bag inside."

We sit at the rustic diner in a booth toward the end of the bar. Life preservers hang on the walls, along with nets and signs that read *Beach life is better*. The waitress places Cynthia's coffee down and sets my sweet tea in front of me. The pale blue walls and white leather seats make this place feel like it should—North Carolina beachy.

I tap my straw against the table and pull the wrapper off. With purple streaks and pink toes, Cynthia takes the sugar container and tips it upside down.

"You want some coffee with that sugar?" I ask her.

She smiles. "Don't judge."

After five creams, she seems to be happy with her caffeine. Reaching over, she slides her notebook out of her polka dot bag. I take a sip of my tea and look out the window at the sailboats resting by the docks. A man and woman walk with a kid between them. His hands are in each of theirs, and they lift and swing him high in the air.

"Did your parents ever do that with you?" I ask as I look back at her. She turns her attention to the window and puts a stray piece of black-purple hair behind her ear.

"No," she says. She stares off at them, seeming to get lost in her own mind. And it's at this moment it really sinks in. She's had something taken away from her, too, and I don't think I'm the only one with a story here.

"How old is your aunt?" I ask her.

She looks back at me and clears her throat. "She's twenty-seven."

"Wow, y'all are that close in age?" I ask.

"Yes, she's my dad's younger sister and the only family I have. Like your mom, my aunt saved me as well. I wasn't easy to deal with for a while," she says.

"I can't picture you being hard to deal with," I say to her.

She shrugs. "Well, I was." She turns away and looks back out the window. The family has moved on, and I see something haunting show on her pretty face, but when she looks back at me, it disappears.

Cynthia lifts her cup to her lips and hums as she takes a sip. Today she has on bangle bracelets, each one a different color, covered in glitter. She reminds me of a sparkly rainbow after a long summer shower. She puts down the cup and grabs her glasses case from her bag. Sliding them on, she grabs her notebook and pen, obviously ready to get down to business.

"So tell me more about Travis," she says. I grab my heart-shaped pendant on my neck and toy with it as I think about the boy who stole my heart so many years ago.

"Travis Cole had a heart of gold. I knew that as a girl, but I really got to know his heart later in life." I move my straw around, stirring my ice.

"Regardless of his golden heart, though, Travis Cole was a bad boy."

"A bad boy?" Cynthia gives me a sly grin. "Look at you, Charlotte Harris."

I scoff and feel my cheeks pinking. "Hush, now." I dismiss her with my hand. "Anyway, he got into some fights and drank a little too much, and smoked grass and cigarettes as I've already told you. It's just where he came from and how he grew up. He had a few alcoholics in his family and they all smoked grass."

"There you go saying grass again," Cynthia says.

"Well, what would you have me call it?" I ask with a lifted brow.

She shrugs as she reaches for the sugar container for the second time.

"Loud, Jazz Cabbage, I dunno," she says as she adds a little more sugar and twirls the spoon around in her coffee.

I cover my mouth to keep from spitting my tea out. "Jazz Cabbage?" I repeat.

"Hey, I didn't make up these names," she says. The waitress walks over with our plates, and I grab the salt.

"So, he smoked Jazz Cabbage as you call it." I smile as I trade out the salt for my strawberry jelly pack. "I remember one time Jennie and I were riding in his car. Travis and his brother, Mason, were smoking. She leaned over to me and said, 'Don't breathe it in or you'll get high.' I got as close as I could toward the cracked window."

Cynthia giggles.

"We were so naïve," I say, shaking my head.

"Regardless of Travis' bad choices and your mother's feelings, you couldn't stay away from him?" she asks.

"No, I couldn't. Travis Cole became my reason to get up every day. Knowing I would see his handsome face was everything to me."

Cynthia chews on a piece of bacon.

"Our relationship happened quickly," I tell her. "The next weekend we hung out again at Taylor Creek Bridge, which was the local hangout for all the teenagers. It was a medium-sized bridge that no one used anymore. Had a creek running under it. Some railroad tracks and an embankment set off to the side of the flowing water, and an enormous strangler fig tree was already latching onto the bridge twirling its vines around the railing…"

———

June 1973

With the sun at our backs, Jennie and I sway our feet over Taylor Creek Bridge. Jennie blows the biggest bubble with her Bazooka gum, and I poke it, causing it to pop all over her nose.

We both laugh as she takes the gum out of her mouth and tries to get it off her face. A boy she kinda likes calls her down by the fire, and Jennie grins at me.

"Did I get it all off?" she asks.

"You're bubble gum free," I tell her as she pops it back into her mouth and stands up. Her ruby red hair sits in a high ponytail, swinging in her face as she slips her shoes back on.

"Wanna come down, too?"

I look behind her, seeing Travis walk up. She follows my gaze before turning back to me.

"I'm good," I tell her.

She gives me a knowing smile.

"Mind if I take your seat?" Travis asks Jennie as she walks by him.

"It's all yours," she replies.

I watch as he holds onto the railing and sits beside me. Butterflies take flight inside my stomach, and my skin tingles.

"How you like living here?" he asks.

"I guess we could live somewhere worse."

He chuckles. "That good, huh?"

I laugh and look down, putting a stray piece of hair behind my ear. "No, I love it. I love the beach."

"Yeah?" he asks, taking a sip of his drink.

"Yeah, it's cool," I reply indifferently.

"It's cool," he mocks softly. I hit his shoulder with mine.

"Hey, Travis. Come shotgun a beer with me," Mason says. He looks down.

"You go on ahead. I'm good, man."

"What, you don't wanna shotgun a beer?" I ask, playfully acting shocked.

"No," he says, looking over at me. "I wanna hang out with you." The boy I'm already addicted to shows me dimples, and my hearts starts pounding—blood rushing and pulse pushing hard against the skin on my neck. He sets his beer down beside him and pulls his soft pack from his front pocket.

"You seeing anybody here?" he asks as he pats a smoke out.

"I thought you already asked Jennie that." I kinda smile as I watch him place the cigarette between his lips.

"I asked her if you had a boyfriend in Georgia. I haven't asked her since you moved here."

"I'm not seeing anybody," I tell him, biting my lip.

"Good," he replies, cuffing his smoke and striking his lighter.

"Why is that good?"

"Well, I was hoping you'd wanna go out with me." He looks over, slightly narrowing his right eye to keep the drifting smoke out of it.

I shrug and look away from him. "I'll think about it."

He chuckles, looking amused. "Okay, you think on it."

"Yo, Travis. Let's go," Mason yells from the embankment. "This guy right here thinks he can beat your GTO." I look down at Mason and the guy standing beside him.

Travis looks over at me with a smile. "Wanna come?" he says.

"Sure."

He stands and reaches for my hand to help me up. I like the feel of his skin on mine, and he must, too, because he doesn't let go until we get to his car.

"You're riding with me," he says.

Adrenaline pumps through my veins as I stand on the side of Indian River drive and watch the boys get in their cars. Travis looks laid-back cool, and I don't see how. Jennie stands in the center of the cars and holds up her hands.

"Ready?" she calls out.

Travis nods, and the other guy revs up his motor. She counts loud, and when she gets to three, both cars take off down the road and all I see is headlights in the distance as Travis takes the lead. I look over at Jennie as she cheers, and Mason laughs. "That dumbass," Mason says. "He knew he couldn't win against my brother."

The sun falls in the evening sky, casting its golden rays over the bridge. With his hand in mine, we walk down, coming to a stop at the spot we were seated at before he won fifty bucks from racing.

I go to sit, but Travis says, "Hold up." He looks down below at our friends before tugging on my hand, pulling us away from their sight. I bite my lip as he smiles at me.

He grabs me closer and places both his hands against my cheeks. I swallow as he leans in, searching my eyes, and I look down at his lips as they grow nearer to mine. When he kisses me, tingles crawl up my back. I feel everything. His hands—rough from working, his lips—soft, yet firm, the brush of his tongue against mine, and my heart as it beats fiercely against my ribcage.

"I can still remember the way he smelled after the golden rays disappeared and the bright moonlight took its place—like grass and summertime air," I tell Cynthia as I breathe in. "Everything disappeared when we kissed. Our friends below the bridge, Mama's fear of me being with a boy who wasn't perfect to her but what perfect meant to me. Nothing mattered or existed except for us. I was completely gone after that. Being around Travis was fun and exciting, but kissing Travis…" I look down, slightly embarrassed to be talking about this with such a young girl, but I feel as though Cynthia is older on the inside. I look up at her and see a small smile on her lips and recognition in her eyes. This girl has been kissed like that, too.

"Go on," she says encouragingly.

"Kissing him was my new favorite thing to do. And boy, did we do a lot of it." I laugh. "I landed a job at a small furniture store doing their books not too long after we got settled. My lunch breaks consisted of very little eating and a whole lot of Travis."

June 1973

I giggle as we round a building downtown. Travis has my hand in his, and as soon as we are out of sight, he pushes me up against the cement wall. His lips find mine, and his fingers go to my hair. My hands move to his biceps and grip for dear life, like my hold is keeping me on the ground.

The sky is bright above us, the clouds spreading out in just the right places. The sun's beaming down, warming us on the outside, but he's warming everything on the inside.

He pulls back and searches my eyes before he looks down at my lips.

"You gotta go back to work?" he asks me.

I frown. "Yes."

He places his forehead against mine, and we say nothing for a moment, just breathing each other in, but then he says, "I like you, Charlotte."

I smirk. "I like you, too." If that's what you want to call it. *Like.* I look down at our shoes, feeling his small breaths against my face as he grabs my hand and brings it to his lips. He kisses each finger softly, gently.

"I mean, I *really* like you." He moves his head back, and his eyes dance over my face.

I swallow.

"Kiss me," he says, and I don't hesitate. I kiss him with everything inside of me. I hand him my soul right here in this alleyway. He exerts passion and makes me feel alive, like I'm the only thing that matters.

Later that night, I walk into my house and hear Mama talking with some friends of hers.

"Is that you, Charlotte?"

"Yes." I make my way to the kitchen, still tasting Travis' lips. After work, I met back up with him. We left our friends and parked his GTO in a parking lot near the beach.

We walked barefoot across the sand and threw a blanket down before we got lost in each other. We talked about everything—his mama and stepdad. He told me he didn't like him, and they didn't get along for shit. His words, not mine.

We had to keep a watch on time, though, because movies only lasted so long. In between talking, we kissed and explored—boy, did we explore. And I was falling more in love every moment we were together.

"Did you have a good time with Jennie?" Mama asks, pulling me from my thoughts. I reach up and grab a glass from the cabinet.

"Yep." I fill my glass with water from the sink and take a few sips.

"What's on your neck?" Mama asks with a wrinkle between her brow. I put my hand up to my skin and rub. Flashes of me all over him in his car make my insides warm, and I try to control the blush rising from my chest.

The hot, humid breeze passes through the windows of his GTO as my bare legs dig into the leather of his seat. My shirt is sticking to my skin, and sweat slides down my back. He controls my lips and consumes my mind. Every emotion possible fills my chest, and I'm hot and needy as I straddle his lap. There are too many clothes, not enough room, and not enough time to do what I'd really like to. I pull back, and he notices.

"You okay?" he asks, a little out of breath.

"I gotta go in."

He moves, and I feel how I make him feel between my legs. He runs a hand through his hair. "Yeah, I guess so."

"I don't want to," I say. "But I'm pretty sure if Mama found me parked down the road in your car, she'd never let me leave the house again."

He smirks and opens his door. I climb out and breathe in as the wind cools my hot skin.

"I'll see you tomorrow?" I ask as he grabs his pack of smokes.

"If not before then," he says, giving me a crooked smirk. He pulls my arm, making me lean down and kiss him again. His mouth opens, and his tongue touches mine. I pull back.

"I gotta go!" I laugh, thinking if we start that again, I'll never get home.

"Your loss." He winks, and I shake my head, thinking how right he is.

"Bye," I call out as the car roars to life. He shuts the door, and I hurry down the road, hearing his tires screech as he guns it at the stop sign.

"Jennie was straightening my hair and accidentally burned me with the iron." I come up with the lie so quickly I surprise myself.

"You two need to be more careful. Let me get you something to put on that." Mama stands up from her chair, and I see her friends eyeballing me a little closer. *Nosy bitches.* Mama takes the top off and goes to put some ointment on her finger.

"I can do it," I say, taking the tube from her hand.

"Okay," she says like I hurt her feelings. I feel bad, so I give her a smile and kiss her cheek before I put my glass down.

"I'm going to take a shower, and then I'll put this on. Goodnight, ladies."

"Night," they all reply slowly as if they're trying to figure me out.

"That girl sure has been going to the movies a lot," one says. I stop and listen.

"Well, there's not much else for a teenager to do," Mama replies.

"But four or five times in a week?" another says. I wanna walk back in there and tell them to mind their own business, but instead, I walk away from the room and toward mine. With a deep sigh, I close the door behind me and toss the medicine onto my bed. I can't help the smile that takes over my face and the giddy feeling I have in my chest.

"Charlotte Harris, you got a hickey?" Cynthia puts her coffee cup on the edge of the table with a grin.

"I got plenty of hickeys," I say, rolling my eyes.

"And your mom really thought you burnt your neck on an iron?"

I take a bite of my toast and shrug. After I chew, I say, "She wouldn't have any reason to think I was lying. I was a very good kid."

"Until Travis came along."

I narrow my eyes and look out the window. "I guess you could say that, but it was never him making me lie. He hated it. He wanted nothing more than to pick me up from my house. To walk up to my door and ask Mama if he could take me out. But that could never happen. Hell, every time he called, she'd take the phone from me and hang it up."

"She really disliked him that much?" Cynthia asks as she puts salt in her grits.

"Yes, she did. Those friends of hers filled her head with so much bullshit, she couldn't see the forest for the trees."

"I know you hated that."

"I did," I reply. "But it didn't stop me from seeing him every chance I could..."

June 1973

I'm lying on the bed with my feet propped up on the wall, listening to my records when I hear something hit my bedroom window. I turn to look and hear it again. Twisting around, I plant my feet on the floor and stand to walk over. I grin when I see it's Travis. His hands are shoved into his pockets, and he looks bad boy sexy. Looking back, I make sure my door is closed all the way and I let my window up.

"What are you doing?" I ask.

"I wanted to see you. Come out."

"I just saw you a few hours ago."

"So?" he says it like *what the hell does that matter*. I shake my head at his smirk and think for a moment. Mama's been asleep for a little while now, so maybe she won't notice.

"Jump. I'll catch you."

"Seriously?" I mean, it's not that high, but I could break something.

"Yes. Don't you trust me?"

"I don't know, Travis Cole. You're not really one of the good guys."

He pretends to be offended. "I'd never do you wrong," he says in all seriousness.

"Okay," I reply before I throw my leg over and sit down on the windowsill. "Ready?" I ask, looking down at him.

He nods and holds out his arms. I push off, and when I land in his arms, he loses his balance and falls, landing on his back as I land on his chest. I giggle as he groans and kinda laughs.

"Fuck."

"Didn't go as planned, did it?" I say, sitting up.

He flexes his hips. "Oh, it went exactly like I wanted."

I slap his chest playfully, and he sits up, pressing his lips to mine. His hands go in my hair, and he brings me closer.

"Let's ride before your mom wakes up," he says, pulling away.

"We rode until the sun came up that night. I hated leaving him. It was like pulling magnets apart to get us away from each other."

"Wow," Cynthia says, looking at me. "You two had it bad."

"We really did." She lifts her second pair of eyes up onto her head, causing her hair to go back with it. I tilt my head, noticing a deep scar on the side of her neck.

"That's some scar you've got there."

Her hand goes up. "Yeah, I went all Evel Knievel when I was a kid and tried to jump a ramp on my bicycle. Didn't end well," she says, shrugging it off.

"Ahh," I say, but I'm not sure I believe it. "So, you were an only child?"

"Yes, it was just me, and whatever nanny or housekeeper they hired."

"Where did you grow up?"

"California," she replies.

"Wow, how did you like that?"

"I loved it until my parents died, of course," she says bluntly.

"I'm sorry."

"It's fine. I mean, I'm digging into your life," she says, putting her fork down.

The waitress places our ticket on the table, and after we pay it, we walk out and make our way over to the pier. It's warm today, but the breeze from the ocean keeps me comfortable. I watch as a seagull dives down into the water and then another does the same. Fishermen have lines thrown over the side of the pier, and a few kids are running around as they wait for their nets to fill up with crabs. Cynthia takes her long-sleeved shirt off and ties it around her waist as we make our way down the pier.

We take a seat at the end, and I breathe in deep as we watch the people around us. Cynthia grows quiet as we people-watch, and I wonder what the girl is thinking. On the outside, she looks like any other young woman. A little quirkier maybe, but I can tell there's a whole lot more going on with her on the inside, and I want to find out what secrets this child holds onto so tightly.

Chapter Five

Maggie Joe has been living in Sea Harbor since she retired. I met her when I first moved here. She was walking her little white poodle, and he took a shit in my yard. I saw it through my window, and the woman just kept on going. I ran out of the house with a paper bag and some napkins and flagged her down. I've never seen a woman's face so red and the kicker— she was mad at me. We've been friends ever since. After all, how else am I going to find out about the town gossip?

"Who is it?" she yells when I knock on the door. I feel it's unlocked so I turn the knob.

"It's Charlotte."

"Why didn't you say so? Come in."

"I did say so," I reply, shutting the door behind me. "Well, my God." I put my hand over my mouth as I take in the view. Rear end in the air and arms behind her calves, she's a sight to see.

"Why don't you put that away?" I tell her, chuckling behind my hand.

"Oh, you act like you've never seen an ass before." She looks at me through the gap of her blue tight-covered legs and huffs before she stands back upright.

Now, I'm in my sixties and this woman is close behind, but I tell you she's in great shape for our age. Me? Not so much. I do good taking my morning walks on the beach. The TV plays with a lady and a few others doing some more crazy exercises. Maggie walks over to the remote and shuts it off. With a white active wear headband on her head and a hot pink tank top, she looks like she stepped out of the eighties.

"You like bending over so much, why don't you bend over and pick up your dog's shit?" I ask her as she wipes the sweat from her brow.

"I told you I was sorry about that, Charlotte. Geez. Archie was having a bad day, and it was years ago."

I roll my eyes. "You do this every day?"

"Of course, I do. How else do you think I stay like this?" She runs a hand down the side of her body.

I chuckle. "I figured this community had a gym or something."

"They do, but there's always a bunch of old people in there." She scrunches her face.

I laugh. "Maggie, what the hell do you think we are?"

"Finely aged, Charlotte. We are finally aged. You need to start doing this with me. You know what they say, 'You never slow down, you never grow old.'"

I look over at the kitchen when Archie comes walking out. He's got a blue bandana around his neck, and he looks recently groomed. He strolls over to his dog bed that's got a window view of the pond behind her house.

"Yeah, whoever says that ain't old," I reply dryly.

She laughs and rolls up her yoga mat. "What brings you over?" she asks as she walks away from me.

"There's this person who's been following me around town for a few days." I lean against the doorway as she bends down in front of the fridge.

"Oh yeah?" she asks, grabbing a water bottle.

"A girl with purple streaks in her hair. About five two, I'd say."

Maggie looks up at me from over the fridge door.

"She's been worrying me to death about writing a story." I lift my brows.

Maggie stands up with guilt-ridden eyes, and I narrow mine.

"My story," I say.

"Now, Charlotte, before you get all bent out of shape…"

"How could you, Maggie?" I ask, crossing my arms. "I told you that as a friend, as my best friend."

She rests her hand on the door. "Look, I'm sorry. I was having a few drinks down at Jim's Crab Shack, and I saw her sitting there by herself. So, I went over just to see if she was okay. You know, a young girl sitting alone is kinda worrisome. Anyway, she told me about the paper and job potential. I asked her if she had any ideas, and she looked at me sadly and said no. Now, like I said, I had already had a few drinks. Your story just kinda came up." She shrugs.

I shake my head and scoff. "Just kinda came up, huh?" I turn out of the kitchen and head for the door.

"Well, yeah, it did." I hear her follow me. "Charlotte, just wait a minute now."

I touch the knob.

"Charlotte. You can't tell me that if you saw an opportunity to help someone you wouldn't." She's hands on her hips now and giving me a stern look.

"It wasn't your place to help her, Maggie. And it damn sure wasn't your place to tell her something I told you in confidence."

She frowns and tilts her head. "I'm sorry, okay?"

I roll my eyes and twist the knob.

"Hey, I mean it." She reaches out and touches my arm. "If I'd known you'd get this upset, I would have kept my mouth shut." She slides her headband off and tosses it onto the table. "But it's a story I think needs to be told. The love you two had and the years…" She stops talking, and I look down at her shaggy rug. "It's just a beautiful story, but you're right. It wasn't mine to tell."

My eyes shoot back to her.

"Can you forgive me?" she asks.

I can see she feels bad about it. I guess I can forgive her. After all, she's my only friend in this town, and that's no one's fault but my own. I'm a loner. I keep to myself and like for everyone else to do the same. Now I've got a persistent purple-headed girl wanting to know all about my life, and it's this woman's fault. Regardless, I know she meant no harm. I run a hand over my forehead and point my eyes to the ceiling. "I guess." I sigh.

She smiles and clasps her hands together. "Good. Wanna go check out the golfers?" She wiggles her brows. "I just bought a new golf cart and she's ready to ride."

I laugh and roll my eyes. "I'd rather not. I've got to get going. There's a girl who wants to write a story about me."

"Are y'all meeting up now?" she asks.

"As a matter of fact, we are."

"Oooh, can I come? I would love to hear details."

"Seriously?" I say, deadpan.

"Yes, seriously. It's my drinking time anyway. Let me get out of these workout clothes and into something else."

"We're going to the beach."

"Oh, good. I need to work on my tan. I'll just be a minute," she says, walking away from me. I step back inside and shut the door behind me.

"Guess I'll wait here," I call out.

I sit under my big umbrella with Cynthia and Maggie as the waves crash against the Carolina shore. Maggie's all oiled up and Cynthia doodles in her notebook as she asks me questions about the good old days.

"Parties were a part of the seventies," I say, responding to her question about what we did for fun. "Smoking grass or Jazz Cabbage," I point out with a smirk.

"Jazz Cabbage?" Maggie questions. "Is that what kids are calling it these days?"

"Seems so," I reply. "Anyway, smoking, drinking, and being a free spirit was in, but I wasn't a follower. I did what I wanted when I wanted to do it, and Travis was okay with that. He never pressured me to do drugs or drink, and that's just one more thing I loved about him."

"So, let me get this straight." Cynthia sits up and crosses her legs. "You grew up in the seventies, supposedly the best years ever, and you didn't smoke weed?"

"What you're telling us is, you were lame," Maggie says.

"I was not lame," I reply to her. "I did smoke occasionally… later and I've had my fair share of drinking…also later."

Maggie shakes her head. "You missed out, woman. Man, I would have fit in good with your Travis and his friends. I really enjoyed my teenage years." She sighs and rests her forearm over her forehead.

"I can imagine," I reply, looking over at Cynthia who smirks. I dig my toes into the sand and scan the beach, noticing a turtle nest is blocked off so people won't step on it. It reminds me of a time so long ago, yet still so fresh in my mind, putting a smile on my lips, and Cynthia notices.

"What are you thinking about?" she asks behind aviator sunglasses.

"Just something that happened forever ago," I answer.

"Well, tell us," Maggie jumps in as she reaches for her drink. At that exact moment, her chair flies forward, causing her to bend in half. "Oh!" she yells, and I burst out laughing. "Good God, would someone help me here?" she whines.

Cynthia giggles and gets up out of her seat. "You're going to have to get up," she says, reaching for Maggie's hands.

Maggie stretches her arms out. "Pull me."

With a pretty side braid and her glittery bangle bracelets, Cynthia digs her heels into the sand and tries to pull Maggie forward. It's trial and error because Maggie falls back twice.

"Pull harder," she says to Cynthia.

"I'm trying. You've got to push up."

Maggie groans and Cynthia yanks, causing her to fling forward and stumble. Cynthia lands on her bottom, and Maggie almost lands on top of her. I laugh even harder, and my eyes start to water.

"Good thing I do yoga," Maggie says to Cynthia as she holds herself up by her arms. "Or you'd be squashed."

"Well, you need to work on strengthening those legs," Cynthia says as Maggie stands upright.

"Nothing's wrong with my legs. I was just in an awkward position, and I may be a little tipsy."

"May be?" I say.

"Oh, hush," she says to me. "And hand me another can from the cooler. I spilled mine."

I reach over into the cooler.

"These flimsy ass chairs," Maggie grumbles as she takes the drink from my outreached hand and carefully sits back down. Her towel pops off the beach towel clip, and she groans.

I wipe under my eyes and shake my head. "You do put on a show, woman."

"I'm glad I could entertain you," she says before popping the top and taking a huge gulp of her margarita in a can.

"So now that that's all over," Cynthia says. "Tell us what you were thinking."

"It was late June, and my bad boy was sitting in jail for breaking into an empty house with some of his dumb friends and his brother Mason. I hadn't spoken to him in a few days because there was no way he'd call my house while being in jail," I tell them.

Late June 1973

I dip my foot under the oven door and lift it so the door slams closed. Walking over to the sink, I turn the water on and rinse the sugar and dough off my hands. Mama and I are baking pies to sell at the festival tomorrow, and that was our last one because we are out of fruit.

"You know they set up the vegetable and fruit part of the festival yesterday. Wanna go and look at some of the shops after we buy more fruit?" I ask her as I dry my hands on the dishtowel she handed me.

"I don't want to leave the oven on with no one here."

"Aw, come on, Mama. It'll be fine," I tell her as I untie my apron and pull it over my head. She sighs and scratches her fingers over her left palm.

"It'll have to be quick, Charlotte."

"We will be."

She bites her lip. "These do still have over forty minutes."

"Ugh, just come on," I say with an eye roll.

She huffs. "Fine. Let's go. I guess it'll be good to get out of the house."

I smile "There you go." And then someone knocks on the front door. "I'll grab it," I say as she takes her apron off, too.

"Hey, girl," Jennie says through the screen.

"Hey," I say, pushing the door open.

"It smells delicious in here," she says, walking in.

"Yeah, Mama is entering into the bake sale at the festival tomorrow."

"I'm sure she'll win. Save me a piece, Mama B," she calls into the kitchen.

"Will do," Mama says, walking out. "And I'm glad you're here. Ride with Charlotte to the festival, please. I really don't want to leave this oven. My luck the thing will catch on fire."

I shake my head and kinda grin at the worrier she is. "We'll be back," I say.

"Be safe," she replies in a happy tune. "Love you."

"Love you, too," I reply as I grab my keys off the table beside the door and step out onto the porch.

"You cool with coming?" I ask her.

"Are you kidding? I've been bored all day," she says as a train flies down the tracks behind our house and rattles the windows.

"So, guess what I heard?"

"What?" I ask as we make our way to my car. We hop in, and I press the clutch and turn the key.

"Travis is out of jail."

"Really?" I smile. "How did you find out?"

"Jesse," we both say.

"I can't wait to see him," I say, more so to myself. Rolling my windows down, I turn the radio up as the Eagles croon sweet lyrics about taking it easy. I think about Travis as we sing along and the wind tosses our hair about. *I can't wait to see him.*

Shifting my car into neutral, I apply my emergency brake once we make it downtown. I open my door and follow Jennie to the tents alongside the sidewalks. People make their way into the souvenir shops, and others pick up baskets to buy fresh produce. I scoop up a basket myself and start toward the peaches.

"I'm going to go look at the mood rings," Jennie says, walking toward a shop door.

I nod as I pick up a peach, bringing it to my nose and inhaling. You can almost always tell a good peach by the way it smells. I place some into my basket and move along the road to the other tents. Out of nowhere, I'm pulled off to the side of a souvenir store.

I notice his smell first, and then I look at his handsome face as he smiles at me.

"God, I fucking missed you," he says, kissing my lips. I kiss him back before I realize I should be mad at this boy. I push against his chest. "What's wrong?" he asks, looking concerned.

"I'm mad at you."

"Mad at me," he says.

"Yes," I reply, walking past him back in between the rows of tents. He follows and dips his hand into my basket, pulling out a peach.

"You gonna eat all this fruit or are you baking me something?" He cracks a teasing smile before he bites into the peach, and I bite something less sweet to control my grin as I look over the blueberries. He leans against the table with a sly smile on his kissable lips.

"You're supposed to wash those before you eat them, jailbird." I turn away from him, trying with everything in me to act mad, because damn him for getting in trouble again. I walk on ahead.

"You gotta pay for that," a guy warns from behind me. Indifferent, Travis pulls out his wallet and tosses the guy a few bills. I keep going, looking for bananas, but my troublemaker steps in front of me.

"I wanna show you something tonight," he says.

"Well, I don't wanna see anything," I reply all matter-of-fact as I sidestep him. I hear him take another juicy bite.

"Why are you mad?" he asks, walking beside me.

I roll my eyes and stop to look at the flowers. He turns, resting his back against the table. I ignore him and decide I'll buy some white daisies to make a bouquet to go on my vanity. He leans over in front of my face.

"You gonna tell me, baby?"

I look at him through squinted eyes. "Why would I be mad, Travis? I mean, you didn't do anything wrong," I say, lifting a few lavender flowers out of the tall galvanized bucket beside the daisies.

"I feel like this is a trap," he says.

I ignore his comment.

"It's not like you broke into a house or anything." I move and make my way over to some pretty daylilies. He follows. "And, of course, you didn't get caught breaking into that house." I grab a handful of the lilies and lay them in my basket before picking up some baby's breath. "You definitely didn't get arrested and go to jail for breaking into that house." I glare at him.

He lifts his brow. "Get to the point."

I stop and stare at him. This boy drives me crazy. He doesn't even show remorse for what he's done, but regardless, I still want to be around him every minute of every day.

What's wrong with me?

You love him, my inner conscience says.

Yeah, but he doesn't care that Mama will find out everything, and it makes it harder for us to see each other, my reasonable side cuts in.

But you love him, my no-good inner conscience repeats and she's right. Damn her.

I hear him sigh. "Yeah, I fucked up. It was dumb. It's over. Can we move on?"

"Can we move on?" I reply unbelievably. "Do you even realize that Mama knows what you did? She's told me I can never see you again, Travis."

"It's not the first time," he says, annoyed.

I shake my head at how blithe he is being. "Do you want to be with me?" I ask, looking over to face him.

"Of course, I do," he says, his boyish grin disappearing.

"Then why do you keep doing dumb stuff? Mama says she's embarrassed for your mom because you can't seem to get right."

"Frankly, baby, I don't give a shit what your mom thinks, and I don't want to be with you on her terms."

"Don't you see? That's the only way we can be together. I need her acceptance, Travis. She's my mom. She's done everything for me."

He exhales loudly and roughly runs a hand through his hair. I put my hand on my hip.

"Are you going to be a delinquent for the rest of your life? I need to know."

Taking his smokes from his front pocket, he slides one out and puts it between his teeth. "I was just having a little fun, Charlotte. Of course, I'm not going to do this for the rest of my life. I'm going to be with you, remember?" He smiles and lights his cigarette, showing me those irresistible dimples and obviously trying to make light of the situation.

He just pours his boyish charm out at me like I won't be able to resist, and he's so damn right. It should make me sick, but it doesn't. It makes me all kinds of things, but sick isn't one of them.

"Now let me show you something?" he asks again so nicely. "Wait till she goes to bed and sneak out. Meet me down at Taylor Creek."

I sigh. "Travis Cole, you're going to drive me crazy one of these days."

"But you love me," he says lightheartedly, and we both realize what he's just said. We stare at each other, my eyes slightly narrowed, and a smile playing on my lips as he presses his tongue up to the roof of his mouth. He clears his throat and slides his hands into his pockets

"So, you cool? You going to meet me?" He's nervous, and it's adorable. I love this boy more than anything; he has no reason to be nervous. He hits his smoke and exhales.

"I do," I say.

He tilts his head sideways, questioning my answer.

"I love you," I say.

He grins. "Yeah?" he asks, lifting his brow.

I nod slightly.

He reaches out and lazily tugs on my arm. Drawing me closer to him, he tosses his smoke, and I swallow as his eyes go down to my lips.

"Me, too, Charlotte, so much," he confesses as he kisses me. He places his hand on the side of my face as he pulls away.

"Meet me, okay?" he says.

"Okay." I nod. He reaches for his peach that's sitting on the table he was leaning on and I watch him walk to the parking lot. I exhale a deep breath before I gather up the rest of the fruit I need, thinking about those three little words and feeling so happy I could float back to our house.

Chapter Six

You know that saying, *It's five o'clock somewhere?* Well, apparently, Maggie lives by that rule. It's not five o'clock; it's just after two, and she's three margaritas in and clearly tipsy. Cynthia and I sit out on the deck and watch her while she dances with the "hotties," as she calls them. They're retired old farts who only come here during the summer.

After our beach trip, Maggie convinced Cynthia and me to play a round of golf in her new golf cart. *"It's the best of its kind,"* she told us. With a Bose, high-performance Bluetooth speaker system, hot pink leather seats, and an extremely furry, baby pink steering wheel. It also has spoke rims and great shocks. Which we got well acquainted with because she was hauling ass over the hills. I thought I might fall out, and I'm sure I have a bruise on my ass.

Anyway, here we sit at the clubhouse now, me babysitting a piña colada while Cynthia drinks a Redd's Apple Ale beer, which she made me try, and it's actually pretty good. I look over at Cynthia as she scrolls through her notes. Today she has on black-framed glittery eyeglasses, and her hair no longer has purple in it, but emerald green. It's quite beautiful, but I do like the purple better. Maggie insisted on French braiding it for her before we got here, and she has loose pieces framing her face.

Cynthia is a pretty girl. I'm not sure why she appears to be such a loner. I'm hoping she's only hanging out with us two old ladies because of the story she's writing.

"How's the writing coming along?" I ask her. She looks up at me with red lips and a wrinkle between her brows.

"I've got a mess going on, honestly. I need to sit down and straighten it out. I just have tons of notes."

"Let me know if I can help with anything," I tell her as Maggie comes over. She's got purple metallic leggings on and a hot pink visor. The woman is a sight, I swear.

"Charlotte, why are you being such a party pooper? Drink that drink!" she says. "It's starting to look like watery mush."

Cynthia picks hers up and takes a sip. "That's the good thing about beer. It can't get mushy."

Maggie unzips her fanny pack and fans out some dollar bills. "I won off bingo last night. What kind of shot do you two want?" she asks, smiling happily and waving her money.

I put my hands up. "Oh, no. No shot for me."

"Aw, come on, Charlotte. Can you tell me the last time you had a little fun?"

"I don't have to get drunk to have a good time, Maggie."

"Well, you need to get something," she replies. "Lookie here." She reaches down into her fanny pack again. "I scored some Jazz Cabbage from one of the boys."

I look at Cynthia, and we both burst out laughing. "Good Lord, Maggie. Put that away." I scowl, rubbing under my eye.

“Come on, ladies. What do you say we go hit this joint a few times out back?” She waggles her eyebrows.

“Maggie, you should be ashamed of yourself being a bad influence on Cynthia.”

“She’s twenty-one years old, Charlotte. Live a little.”

Cynthia looks over at me with a grin. “Why not, Charlotte?” she says.

“Are you two serious?” I ask.

“Serious as that frown on your face,” Maggie chimes in.

I huff.

“Come on,” Maggie says, grabbing Cynthia’s hand and pulling her off the stool.

My eyes grow wide. “You are not serious!”

“I am, too. Now come on,” Maggie insists again. I look around us, but realize not one person here is looking our way. Groaning, I get up and follow reckless and my interviewer.

Thirty minutes later

I’m covered in flour and tears stream down my face as I laugh at these two idiots who have convinced me to smoke pot. I don’t know why I did it, but honestly, I haven’t laughed so much in God knows when. Maggie stops telling dirty locker room jokes, and I look down. She has flour hand splotches all over her leggings. I roll my eyes as she dips her finger into the brownie mix.

"Probably should have asked this before we stopped at the store, but do you own a coffeemaker by chance?"

"I do actually," I tell her. "It was Travis'. He loved coffee."

"You kept his coffeemaker?" Cynthia asks from her spot on the floor. *Yes, she's sitting on the floor.*

"I kept a lot of his things," I reply. She shrugs and continues to scribble in her notebook with a slight smile on her red lips.

"It's in the cabinet over there," I tell Maggie. Cynthia slides her glasses up onto her head as I step over her and put the butter back in the fridge.

"You know, you never said what Travis wanted to show you," she says to me as I shut the door and carefully step back over her outstretched legs.

Maggie chimes in, "That's right. You didn't."

I grin. "Wipe your face off, woman. You've got flour all over you."

"Where?" she says, looking for a dishtowel. I open the drawer next to the sink and hand it to her.

"It's on your nose and cheek," I say. She takes it from me and rubs her nose.

I laugh. "Now it's on your lip."

She sticks her tongue out and licks it.

"Eww," Cynthia says, giggling like a little schoolgirl. More like a stoned schoolgirl. She reaches for Maggie's hand, and with a grunt, Maggie helps lift Cynthia up from the floor.

"How long on the brownies?" Maggie asks, setting the coffeemaker up as Cynthia takes her seat at the table. I twist my fat pig timer.

"Twenty minutes," I answer, putting it back on the stove.

"Oh hell, that's twenty minutes too long," she says, taking her pink visor off and flopping it down on the table.

"Quit your griping, woman," I reply, grabbing the carton of eggs from the counter.

"Tell us about Travis," Cynthia says. I shut the fridge door after I put the eggs up. Reaching down, I grab her pen and notebook she neglected to take with her.

"In case you want to take more notes," I say, putting them on the table. We hear a loud boom, and the windows rattle in the kitchen.

"I didn't know it was supposed to storm today," Maggie says, looking out the kitchen window. I look also and see that it's grown darker outside, and I hear my wind chimes on the porch.

"Me either," I reply, walking over to the TV remote. I flip to the local news channel, and we three watch as the weatherman tells us we are under a severe thunderstorm warning.

"I hope the power doesn't go out or we won't get any brownies," I say, turning the volume down. "Just in case, let's get the storm candles out. They're all in my hope chest." I walk out of the kitchen. "Travis bought a crap load of them once when we had bad weather coming. Luckily, our power didn't go out then, so I've kept them just in case. They've come in handy several times. In his old age, Travis was way more cautious about things." I laugh, thinking how odd that is. My bad boy turned into a cautious man, but with age comes wisdom. Cynthia and Maggie follow me to my room. I walk over to the chest and lift the top.

"Is that a photo album?" Cynthia asks, looking over my shoulder.

"There are several in here," I tell her as I move some things to the side to get to the candles. "That's the thing about young people. You upload all your photos on these social media sites and on your phones. I like the surprise of running across an old photo and looking at the age on it," I say, spotting the candles.

"I agree," Maggie says.

"Can I see it?" Cynthia asks me.

I shrug. "If you'd like." I lift it and hand it to her, and then I grab the candles and holders. I set them down on the bed and tell Maggie, "Grab the matches over on the dresser."

"Let's go sit outside on the screened-in porch," Cynthia says.

"I think that's a great idea," Maggie says. "But first coffee!"

After the girls get their coffee and I pour myself a glass of sweet tea and check the brownies, we walk out onto the porch and take a seat on the patio couch and chairs. Ominous clouds show in the distance, and luminous lightning brightens the dark sky.

The smell of a match fills my nose when Maggie strikes one and begins burning the candles, setting them all around us on the porch as she does.

Cynthia flips open the photo album.

"This is your son?" she asks me.

"Yes, and that's my mama and daddy." I point to show her. I continue to tell her who people are as she flips the pages over, landing on one that makes me smile.

"That's Travis?" she asks, like she already knows.

"Yes, it is." He stands beside me. One arm around my waist, pulling me close to him as he kisses the side of my hair.

"Wow, your hair was beautiful," Cynthia says.

"I do miss how thick it was," I reply as Maggie takes a seat.

"He was a looker," she says, giving me a wink.

I smile at her. "That he was."

We flip through more of the photo album until the timer goes off and their coffee needs warming up. After I walk inside with them behind me, I take the brownies out and let them sit for a few minutes.

"I'll go put this back up," I say as I take the photo album from Cynthia and walk to my room.

On my way out, I hear Maggie, "I'm not sure if you have any idea what you're doing, kid, but I've never seen this woman step out of her shell like this."

I stop and step back a little.

"I'm not doing anything," Cynthia says in return.

"You're doing more than you know," Maggie replies. "I've known Charlotte for years now, and she always turns me down on doing anything out of her comfort zone. You come in the picture, and she's like an open book. She's smoked pot, had a drink, and laughed more than I've ever seen with my own eyes."

Cynthia sounds uncomfortable. "Well, the weed was all you, Maggie." She laughs a little, trying to get the attention off herself it seems. "Anyway, I haven't been around her that much."

"You followed her around for weeks before she agreed to this. You've been around," Maggie says. "I think she's forgotten what life is about. Maybe that happens when you lose a piece of you, I don't know," she says sadly. "I'm just glad she's found someone to help put her back together."

I shut my eyes for a moment and, surprisingly to me, tears fall down my cheeks.

"Yeah," Cynthia murmurs.

Quietly, I walk back to my room and into my bathroom. I shut the door and look at my reflection. With a slight shudder, I grab a tissue from my vanity and blow my nose. I toss it into the trash and look at the age on my face. I still feel like I'm in my forties, but the person looking back at me is surely not.

Wrinkles are inevitable. I used to use those fancy creams to try to stop them, but with every new day, time assures more appear, and time is uncontrollable. I run a hand over my pinned-up hair. I've tried to keep the gray contained over the years, but eventually, I grew tired. I look down at my body. Gravity sure has done its worst, and I haven't done a thing to help. Truthfully, I've let myself go. I'm not sure when this happened… That's a lie. I know exactly when it happened. When the love of my life left, I thought, *why try?* No one else cares what I look like. The one person who mattered is no longer around. But maybe that's not true.

Maybe it doesn't matter to anyone else what this old lady looks like, but it should matter to me. I *should* matter to me, and I'm going to try a little harder.

The evening sky has turned dark from the storm. With a plate full of brownies, we sit out on the screened-in porch and listen to the waves as they crash angrily down at the beach. The ceiling fan twirls above us, and a gust of wind comes through every so often, making the candles flicker. Shadows show on the wall, and thunder booms over the ocean. A huge bolt of lightning strikes, and the ceiling fan slowly stops turning.

"There went the electricity," I say as I bite into a brownie.

"Well, at least these delicious things finished baking," Cynthia says with her mouth full. Crumbs fall out when she speaks, and we all laugh.

"Here's the rain," I say as I hear it begin to fall. It starts small and soon comes down in sheets, surrounding us completely. My back porch is very cozy, and it's one of the things I love most about my house. With plenty of comfortable sitting space and an enormous ottoman for feet propping, it is the go-to spot for stormy days. I set my plate down onto the tray and get up to pull the shades down on the sides so rain won't come in on us.

"So, can we finally hear more about Travis?" Cynthia says as she wipes her mouth.

"Yes, let's," Maggie says, smiling. She kicks her sandals off and props her feet on the ottoman.

"Okay," I reply, taking my seat. "Where was I?"

"You were buying fruit, and you and Travis just said I love you for the first time," Cynthia says, grinning.

"Oh, right." I smile. "After Travis left the farmers' market, I paid for my things. I headed straight home so I could help Mama finish with the baking. After we were done, I remember looking at the clock, and I swear the damn thing wasn't moving. Mama noticed and asked me if I had somewhere to be. I lied, of course, saying I just wanted to get to bed early because Jennie and I were going to watch the sunrise in the morning…"

July 1973

I see it's almost nine, and I sit in the living room staring at the TV waiting on Mama to say she's going to bed. I know that means she'll take a shower first, so I'll have to wait a good hour still before I know she's fast asleep.

The light goes off in the kitchen, and Mama stands at the doorway, untying her apron.

"I'm going to head on to bed," she says, hanging it up on the nail that's in the wall.

"Okay," I reply with the beginnings of a fake yawn.

"Goodnight," I say, stretching my arms out. I'm laying it on thick, I know.

"Goodnight. You better go, too, if y'all are getting up that early."

"Huh?" I ask.

"You and Jennie," she says.

"Oh yeah. Sorry, I was thinking about something else."

She narrows her eyes at me.

"Goodnight," I say again.

"Goodnight, crazy girl." I watch her as she makes her way down the hall, exhaling once her door shuts. I ball my hands and drop them to my thighs, running my fingernails over my jeans. My eyes go to the ticking clock, and I bite my lip as the big hand moves slower than a slug.

Bright moonlight beams down on the road before me, and I can hear the waves as they roll onto the sand one after another. The wind blows through my open windows, tossing my hair around my neck, and the taste of sea salt is on my tongue. Butterflies swarm inside my stomach as I grip the wheel and turn off the main road.

As I near Taylor Creek, I see Travis resting back against his car. After parking the car, I let the windows up and kill the ignition before I step out.

I bite my lip, trying to contain the excitement I feel. He grins and shows me dimples that make my knees weak.

As if on cue, he pushes off the front of his car and walks toward me. Long dark hair rests behind his ears, and it curls slightly at the bottom. He wears jeans and a matching blue jean button-up that's half-tucked into the front of his brown belt. My heart kicks up as he nears, and my legs move on their own to meet him. I jump into his arms and link my ankles behind his back.

He laughs. It's deep and makes my stomach flip. "I was starting to think you weren't gonna show," he says before his lips crash against mine. He walks us a few steps back, so I'm pressing against my car. I bring my hands down to his arms, trying to keep my balance. Hands with permanent grease stains touch my cheeks, and I grip tighter as he deepens our kiss, making me want more…so much more.

He slowly pulls back and rests his forehead against mine. Opening my eyes, I see his staring back at me.

"I'm sorry, baby," he murmurs. "I know I don't make things easy for us." He gives me a quick peck, and I put my feet back on the ground. "Come on," he says, grabbing my hand.

We take his car and head toward the beach. Once he parks it, we both get out and he grabs a blanket and a cooler from the back seat. He takes my hand again, walking us up the stairs that lead to the beach entrance.

At the bottom, I slip my sandals off, and once we are where he wants us, he tosses the blanket down and we both take a seat. The moon is bright above us, so I can see everything. We are alone, nothing but two beating hearts and an endless ocean.

"What did you want to show me?" I ask him.

"Patience, girl," he says, smiling at me. He reaches over and opens the cooler. Grabbing a beer out, he offers me one.

I shrug. "Why not?" I say, taking it from him and popping the top. I take a sip and scrunch my face as I swallow.

"That bad?" he laughs.

"That bad," I say, putting it down beside me. After he opens his, he takes a big gulp and rests back on the blanket. I lean back on my hands and kick sand off my toes with my others.

We sit in silence for a while, enjoying each other's company, as he sips his beer and the wind slowly moves the spacious clouds above us to reveal the millions of stars. "What do you want out of life, Charlotte?" he asks me moments later.

I look over at him and study his face before I turn my attention back in front of me. With a deep sigh, I reply, "I don't know. What does everyone want?" I shrug. "A good, long life surrounded by people who love you and you them. A job that doesn't make you dread going to it every day and a nice house to come home to."

"Yeah," he says, nodding his head. "That's probably what a lot of people would want, but what about you?" he asks.

"What about me…" I say, thinking out loud. I smile and take my bottom lip between my teeth.

"I'd like a little house with the ocean as my backyard," I answer, waving my hand out at it. "A porch that I can sit out on and enjoy a cold glass of sweet tea in the evenings, maybe while reading a good book with only the waves as background noise." I move my hair behind my ear.

"I'd like a couple of babies, maybe a dog, and a cat, too," I say with a shrug of my shoulders. I look over at him. He wears a small grin and searches my face with wonder.

"What about you, Travis Cole? What do you want out of this life?" I smile and hit his foot playfully.

He answers without thought, "To give you everything you just said."

I stare at him, and my smile fades as his eyes never leave mine. He leans in and lifts his hand to the side of my face.

"I love you, Charlotte, and I'll spend my whole life making sure you know that." He kisses me, and my eyes fill with tears as he pulls back.

"I love you, too," I say with a small smile.

"I know," he says, showing me those dimples, and then I see something. I look harder as I see tiny somethings moving.

"Travis," I say, looking past him. His head follows my gaze, and I move a piece of my hair from my face.

"What is that?" I look over at him before I look again at the tiny things.

"Sea turtles."

"Turtles?" I grin.

"Yep, baby sea turtles," he confirms.

"Is this what you wanted to show me?" I ask, standing up.

"Yes," he says.

"Oh my gosh! Travis!"

He stands and takes my hand. "Come on, let's go watch them make it out to sea."

We carefully walk over, hand in hand, as they shimmy their way out from under the sand one by one. Some are already on their adventure, making a beeline straight to the water.

"They're adorable!" I say as they emerge from their nesting spot. I look over at Travis. He's watching me with a small smile on his lips.

"You're adorable," he says as he pulls me to him and kisses me. I pull back slowly and search his eyes.

"I love you," I say to him.

"I know," he murmurs.

Chapter Seven

I sweep the broom across my porch as calmer waves than yesterday's crash against the compacted sand. It was still flooding when the girls left my house last night, but the storm stopped sometime after I went to bed.

Resting against the handle of the broom, I stare out as gray clouds swirl above like smoke from a drifting fire. Earlier this morning, I found myself watching videos from long ago like I do every time this year. Sweet moments that at the time I never thought would be delicate memories. How can so many years pass by, yet this heartache doesn't go away? People say time is the only healer, but my wounded heart only scabs over until a memory comes along and rips it away, bringing me to my knees all over again.

Today is *his* birthday, a day I choose to spend crying and feeling sorry for myself. We got cheated. There's no other way to describe it. I see old friends on social media, happy with their partners. Some have been married for over forty years, yet here I am…alone. I can't date because no one will compare, and I honestly just don't have the energy for it. I sigh and rest the broom against the patio couch.

Opening the screen door, I take a seat on the steps and roll the bottom of my jeans up. Resting my forearm across one knee and my elbow on the other, I turn my face into the palm of my hand and let heartbreak pour from my eyes once again.

I'm watching my soaps when I hear a little horn blow outside and I turn to look out the door to see Cynthia and Maggie getting off the Vespa. *Jesus, what a sight.* I almost laugh, but my sour mood forbids it. I'm back in my pajamas and have not a drop of makeup on, so answering the door is not happening. *Maybe they'll go away.* Leave me be, so I can drown in my tears and watch as Victor Newman makes his family drown in theirs also. But the knocking continues, and once I hear my name being called, I grumble and pause the television.

"Open up, Charlotte!" Maggie yells.

"I'm coming," I call back to her in a voice that hasn't been used all day. I clear my throat when I get to the glass door and see the two in birthday hats. *What in the hell?* As soon as I open the door, Tweedledee and Tweedledum place party blowers between their lips and give them a blow, and then they put a damn smile on my face by singing "Happy Birthday" to Travis in the highest pitch imaginable.

Cynthia hollers and claps her hands while Maggie does a little dance holding onto a small cake that reads *Happy B-day Travis.*

I laugh. "How did y'all know?"

"It's on your lighthouse calendar," Cynthia says, walking past me.

"You look like shit," Maggie says.

"Well, thanks." I move so she can walk in, too.

"So, what are you doing right now?" Cynthia calls behind her.

I look down at my outfit. "You're looking at it," I reply, unenthused, as I shut the glass door and walk to the kitchen where they already are.

"What do you think Travis would want to do right now?" she asks with a mischievous grin as she slides onto the kitchen counter, reminding me of myself when I was a girl, but then I think about her question. Younger Travis would want to get into some trouble. Listen to some music, drink some beers, smoke some pot, and hang out with me. Older Travis was more cautious, but he'd still want to listen to some music, drink some beers, smoke some pot, and hang out with me.

"He would want to party," I say.

"That's what I thought." Cynthia smiles as she locks eyes with Maggie. "Come on, you can ride with me on the scooter!"

Oh hell.

I don't know how they talked me into this. I already accepted the fact I wanted to do nothing today but feel sorry for myself, yet here I am, dressed in a lavender top, black slacks, and comfortable dress shoes. My best friend wears a silver glittery blouse, matching wedges, and metallic black leggings. She looks like a damn disco ball. Cynthia said she used hair chalk to put hot pink in her dark hair, and she wears a white and blue striped sundress with a small yellow belt around her tiny frame and blue flats.

Up on the stage, a band plays, and I listen as the lead singer croons sweet melodies about Sweet Melissa. The Allman Brothers were a favorite of Travis' and I know he would have enjoyed this. They've also played some Lynyrd Skynyrd and The Doobie Brothers. The soft glow of the outdoor lights brings a calming feel to the festivities, and the sound of the soothing waves crashing remind me that the ocean is only a few yards away.

I didn't even know this was happening tonight. Everyone in this small town is out and enjoying themselves, and I almost missed out. I blame it on Victor Newman. Yep, has nothing to do with the fact I was having a bona fide pity party.

You mean like you've been doing for the last eleven years?

Shut up, conscience.

My eyes turn to take in the view of the Ferris wheel, and I watch as a few kids try their hand at ring tossing, while teenage boys concentrate hard on winning an enormous stuffed bear for their girl by throwing darts at balloons. I pull in a deep breath of fresh North Carolina air and sway to the music, thinking back on our conversation from last night. I told them about mine and

Travis' first time together, but I didn't go into details—just that it was the best and worst moment of my life. That he showed me more love than I've ever been shown, but I left out the part where I thought about leaving Florida and never looking back…

August 1973

It was the end of August on a warm summer night. My bad boy was parked at a local gas station, and I was trying to sneak out. I had the window up in my bedroom, letting the breeze from the ocean drift through, blowing my curtains and my hair as I sat in front of my mirror doing my makeup. Mama had gone to bed only ten minutes ago, so I had to wait until she got into a deep sleep, which luckily didn't take long.

Once the woman of the house was out, I put my car in neutral and pushed it out of the driveway, a move I was getting good at. I met Travis down at the gas station, and as soon as I reached his car, he grabbed me and kissed me like his lips were on fire and mine were water. My hands went to his dark brown hair, loving the feel of the silk-like strands between my fingers.

"I feel like I haven't seen you in forever," he says as he pulls away.

I'm all smiles, and my stomach is full of butterflies. "I saw you last night."

"I know, but it's been almost twenty-four fucking hours."

I laugh as he places his smoke between his lips and opens the door for me.

"Climb in, baby," he says, but it sounds muffled with the cigarette in his mouth.

I watch as my cool bad boy strides around the car. He hops in and cups his Marlboro Light before he strikes his Bic and then tucks it into his front pocket. With smoke drifting up into the car, he pulls his door closed and pushes in the clutch. Travis starts his GTO, releases the emergency brake, and shifts it into first. A tire squeals when he lets off the clutch and hits the gas. We peel out of the parking lot, and I lean up to control the radio.

He smokes his cigarette and rests his hand on the bottom of the wheel as we ride to a local park everyone has been hanging out at lately.

Moments later, Travis tosses his nicotine. "Open the dash," he says as he blows smoke and points over at it. "There's a joint in there."

I do as he asks and take the joint out of the glove compartment, handing it over to him.

"Hold the wheel," he says as he leans up and digs his lighter back out of his jean pocket. I reach over and grab the wheel, making sure I don't kill us both, because he is going sixty.

He cups his hand around the end of the joint, and I smell that familiar scent after he strikes his lighter. "I got it," he says, putting his hand back on the wheel.

He puffs on the joint and then offers it to me, but like always I shake my head no. He shrugs as he places it between his lips, letting it rest there as he pulls into the park. It's a big piece of land with bushes and woods all on the edge. A few picnic tables are scattered around, and there's a swing set and a jungle gym. A little ways to the left is a camping area, and like every summer, it's packed with people.

Travis parks the car near all the others, and we both hop out. When I walk around the car, he grabs my hand. His smile is lazy now, and his eyes are glossy. He wets his index finger and thumb and presses it to the end of the joint, putting it out.

"I'll save that for later," he says, sliding into the front pocket of his blue jean shirt.

The evening flies by with everyone drinking and passing a joint or two around. I'm standing with Jennie and a few girls by her car. They gossip, but I don't join them. My eyes look for Travis, and I see his are already on me as he stands with Jesse and some other guys. He looks away, and his lips read, "I'll be back in a bit." I watch as he walks toward me, and before I know it, he's grabbing my hand.

"Come on. Me and you need some alone time." I don't question him, and I don't even look at the girls. I let Travis take me wherever he wants. He walks us toward his car and pops the trunk. I grow anxiously excited when he grabs our beach blanket and shuts the trunk, because I know we are going to

make out, and there's nothing I like more than making out with Travis Cole.

He moves us away from our friends and off to a secluded spot surrounded by several impenetrable bushes. The blanket goes down on top of thick grass, and it takes less than a minute before he lifts me up and takes complete control of my senses. Touch, feel, taste, he takes it all, and at the time, I don't know it, but I'm about to give him so much more.

His rough grease-stained hands move down my body to the button on my jeans. My pulse pounds against my neck, and nerves make my hands shake. Softly, he pulls my jeans and panties down my legs, and his head descends.

I feel his lips press against my stomach, and then he places a kiss right at my pubic line. He moves back to his knees, and I feel it when the night air hits between my thighs, causing me to clench them together as he stands up. He makes quick work unbuttoning his shirt, and my eyes move with his hands as they unbutton his jeans.

There's only the glow of the moonlight, and as soon as his pants come down, I see all of him. Every. Single. Part. His knees bend again, and he spreads my thighs before pulling me closer to him. I gasp when he kisses me, and I feel as though my whole body is shaking.

"You're trembling," he murmurs.

"I'm not cold if that's what you're wondering," I whisper.

He chuckles. "Don't be nervous around me, baby."

"Okay," I say softly. He smiles, and I kiss him, bringing him down with me, and as my back touches the blanket, he moves my leg to the side and slowly sinks. My body's natural reaction is to tense up, but he continues forward, and a small sting is all I feel. I close my eyes tight as he moves, and I breathe through my nose.

"You can squeeze me harder," he says. I open my eyes, realizing how hard I'm holding his arms. "You okay?" he asks, apprehension showing on his handsome face.

"Yeah," I say, loosening my death grip on his forearms. "Keep going."

He bites his pouty bottom lip and shifts forward. It still stings, but the more he does it, the less it hurts, and soon the pain is gone, left in its place is bliss—heaven and everything that is good with the world. My whole body sings as he continues, and I cross my ankles around his back.

He kisses me and grips onto my hips while his other arm keeps him from falling. He brushes his mouth against mine, and my teeth graze his bottom lip as he clutches my hip tighter.

Once we finish, I take in a deep, satisfied breath. He moves, wrapping his arm around me, saying, "I love you. You feel so good, baby."

With I love you, too, *on the tip of my tongue, my mind starts racing, and I think about the fact we didn't use protection and how I didn't think this was going to happen. I wasn't prepared. I mean, I wanted it to happen, but I... It feels like it went by so quickly, yet at the time, I felt like we were like that for hours. We stand up and put our clothes on, and I feel something wet between my legs. Concern simmers inside of me as we walk back to the party. Travis goes to put the blanket back up, and I look for Jennie because my stomach is starting to hurt. Oh God, what if I get pregnant? My mama would never forgive me. How can something so beautiful turn quickly in my mind to something horrible?*

"Jennie," I say, walking up to her.

"Where did you go?" she asks? "You and Travis make out?" She smiles but stops when I don't.

"I need to leave," I tell her.

"Why?" she asks, concern in her voice.

I come up with something to tell her. "I think I started my period."

"Oh, well, there's no bathroom here. You want me to take you?"

"Please," I say.

Travis walks up. "What's wrong?" he asks me when he sees my face. I'm sure I look distressed.

"I'm fine," I lie. "It's just late, and Mama usually goes to the bathroom a few times a night. She may check in on me."

He tilts his head. "Are you sure you're okay?" he asks in a low voice, and I know he means with what just happened, but honestly, I'm not okay right now.

"Yeah," I say. "I'll call you tomorrow."

He frowns. "Okay."

On the way home, I ask Jennie to stop at the store to get us a drink. When she walks inside, I put my hand between my legs and pull it up in horror. My heart drops to the pit of my stomach, and my pulse quickens, painfully aching against the skin on my neck at the sight of the blood. I know women bleed when they lose their virginity, but this much? Instantly, I grow more worried.

I jump into the shower as soon as I get home and hand-wash my jeans. With tears in my eyes, I crawl into bed with more worries than a young girl should have. Thinking about pregnancy and blood. This can't be normal. Anxiety takes over my body until I finally come to the decision I'm going to tell Mama I want to go back home to Georgia. After I've made my decision, I cry myself to sleep.

The sound of the train bellowing down the tracks and shaking the house wakes me the next morning. As I stretch my arms and blink my eyes open, last night hits me like a ton of bricks. I'm a woman now, and I'm fucking floating. All my worries disappear, and I think about Travis. I jump out of bed and go to the bathroom to check myself. The bleeding has stopped, and I decide right then—if I'm pregnant, so be it. I love Travis, and I know he loves me. We can get through whatever together.

The smell of bacon drifts through the house as I walk on air into the kitchen.

"Good morning, Mama," I say as I kiss her on the cheek and grab a piece.

"Wow, someone's happy this morning," she replies.

I smile. "What's not to be happy about? I have a great job, I live at the beach, and..." I think about Travis. "Life's just good."

"What are you in deep thought about?" Cynthia asks, pulling me from my reverie.

"Just thinking about our conversation last night," I say to her.

"You mean about losing your v-card?" Maggie asks.

"Yes. Maggie, I was thinking about when I lost my v-card." I roll my eyes. She sure has a way of putting things so they sound impersonal.

"What?" she says. "It's what you were thinking, wasn't it?"

"But do you have to say it so tactless?"

"What other way do you want me to say it, woman? Shit, we all know what v-card means. We're all women here."

I shake my head and take a sip of my piña colada.

"We're going to take a little break now," the singer says. "Be back shortly. Enjoy the drinks and grab some barbeque."

"There's a bunch of cute boys here," I say to Cynthia, trying to change the subject.

She shrugs. "I'm not here for cute boys."

"Oh, to be young again," Maggie says wistfully. "I'd be behind one of these tents here with my tongue in one of their mouths."

I gape at her. "Jesus, Maggie."

"Well, it's true," she says with no shame.

"You know, Maggie. I'd love to know about when you lost your v-card," Cynthia chimes in after she takes a sip of her beer.

"My first time was in the back of a pickup with some lowlife who couldn't figure out where the hole was," Maggie says, exasperated.

Cynthia and I burst out laughing. "Good Lord, woman," I say in disbelief, although I don't know why. Maggie says whatever is on the tip of her tongue.

"It's true, and it lasted about one minute," she throws in. "How about you, Cyn? When was your first time?"

Cynthia looks over at her with blinking eyes.

"Your first time?" Maggie repeats.

Cynthia's expression is blank, and she looks back in front of her and mumbles, "Nothing special."

We both look at her.

"No details then?" Maggie says.

"Nothing really to tell. It happened, and then it was over." She picks at the label on her beer, and I take it she doesn't want to talk about it.

"Was it anyone here?" Maggie asks.

"No one here," Cynthia confirms.

"You're telling me you haven't slept with any of these cuties?"

"Maggie." I scowl. It's obvious the girl doesn't wanna talk about it. How can she not see this?

"Look at her, Charlotte. She's beautiful. How has she not snagged one of these good-looking boys around town? I bet they wanna bang you like a screen door during a hurricane."

Cynthia smirks.

"You really have no filter," I tell her as I try to stifle my laugh.

"I'm just being honest. I remember being young—all those hormones running through you. I know it had to be worse for the boys." She shrugs and crosses her legs. "I'm sure they were jerking that thing several times a day."

I almost spit my drink out as Cynthia leans back, open-mouthed, releasing a fit of laughter. I don't know how this woman ended up being my best friend. We are total opposites.

"So, what gives, honey?" Maggie keeps going. "Why haven't you got yourself a boyfriend? Are you into girls?" Maggie asks. "I mean, there's nothing wrong with that if you are."

"No, I'm not into girls," Cynthia says, trying to compose herself. She wipes under her eye and sniffs. "I lost my v-card to a boy. I'm just not interested in anyone."

Maggie holds her hands up in a backing off manner. "Okay." She takes a big sip of her drink, and then she says, "I just hope you didn't have the no hole finding experience like me. It makes a hell of a difference when it's someone you care about. If I could go back and let it be my Robert in that pickup, God knows I would," she says sadly.

"What happened to your husband?" Cynthia asks, taking the conversation away from her. I don't blame her.

"A heart attack took him a few years back," Maggie replies. "But thankfully, we had many, many years together."

I sigh quietly, thinking how time is so precious to some, yet so unappreciated by others. It's easy to forget how fragile life is, until you know you only have so much of it left. To enjoy the small simple things in life that matter the most, like holding hands and small kisses that mean nothing but everything all at once. The way your loved ones smell…that distinct scent only they have. I can't even remember his smell anymore. I breathe in and try not to cry. Sometimes I miss him so much, it literally pains me.

"Well, shit, I didn't mean to make you sad," Maggie says, reaching over to touch my hand. I flip mine up and squeeze hers.

"You didn't make me sad. If anything, you two have made me extremely happy lately, and I'm grateful you got me out of my house to enjoy this beautiful night." I look up at the stars and sigh. "Travis would have loved this. The only thing missing," I say, looking back at them and making sure no one else can hear, "is the weed."

Cynthia laughs.

"That can be arranged," Maggie retorts. "I know a guy."

"Oh no," I counter quickly. "Once every so many years is quite enough." We all laugh, and I love the way it makes me feel. Sometimes God takes, but thank goodness for those times He gives.

Chapter Eight

"That's cheating," I tell Maggie as she picks up her golf ball and drops it into the hole.

"Well, it's hot as balls out here, and I'm in need of a cocktail."

"This was your idea," Cynthia says as she wipes sweat from her brow.

"I know, but I didn't realize you two sucked and it would take all day." She props her golf club onto her shoulder and walks to the cart.

"You've played with us before," Cynthia calls after her. "You know we suck. You're just upset Frank isn't out here."

Maggie looks back at her. "You're damn right I'm upset he isn't out here. The man said he would be. Why can't men just be honest?" She shoves her golf club into her bag and hops onto the front seat. "Let's go. Happy hour is starting."

I shake my head and grab the golf ball from the hole. Maggie has been seeing Frank off and on now for a few months, and sadly *he* chooses when they see each other. Cynthia and I climb in, and Dale Jr. stomps on the gas pedal.

We're seated at the bar, and I sip on a glass of sweet tea while Maggie and Cynthia have the happy hour special. Cynthia fans herself and moves her hair away from her neck.

“That’s some scar you’ve got there,” Maggie states as she reaches out and rubs her fingers across it. Cynthia pulls away.

“How did that happen?” Maggie asks with a crease in her brow.

I know Cynthia told me it was from a bike accident, but I’m still not sure if that’s true, and when she says, “I don’t want to talk about it,” and drops her hair, I’m even more curious.

“Why not, Cyn?” I counter.

Cynthia exhales and puts her drink down. “Please don’t call me that. My name is Cynthia.”

Maggie lifts her eyebrows at me as Cynthia grabs her polka dot bag from the bar. “I’ve got to go. I promised Marty I’d pick her up from the airport.” She gets off her stool and puts her bag over her shoulder.

“We didn’t mean to pry,” I say. “We’re just concerned, is all.”

“Well, don’t be,” Cynthia snaps. “I’m fine.”

We watch her walk off, both of us staring at her back.

“Wow,” Maggie says. “You had to be nosy, didn’t you?”

I look over at her. “Are you serious? You’re the one who asked.” I exhale, and Maggie huffs. I take a sip of my tea and bite my bottom lip, studying the rows of liquor bottles on the bar. “Something happened to her.”

“No shit,” Maggie chimes in.

“Don’t be a smartass,” I say. “I’m serious. I mean, it’s been more than a few weeks now that we’ve been hanging out, if you count when she was following me around. Don't you find it odd that she wants to spend all of her time with two old ladies? She has no boyfriend, no other girlfriends that we know of."

"Well, she *is* writing a story about you," Maggie points out.

I smirk. "True."

Maggie sighs, and after a moment she says, "Time is a thief, Charlotte. We've reached that age where the big man upstairs takes more than He gives. So if the girl wants to hang out with us, I'm not questioning it."

I hold my hands up in surrender. "Okay."

I lightly knock on the door of the quaint beach house, taking in a dying plant on the front porch and some boards that need a fresh coat of paint as the door opens.

"Can I help you?"

I turn to look at the woman before me. She's gorgeous in gray shorts and a white T-shirt. Her blonde hair is pinned carelessly onto her head, and she wears no makeup.

"Hi, I'm Cynthia's friend, Charlotte."

"Oh, yes, Ms. Charlotte. I've heard a lot about you. Come in. I'm Marty."

"Please, just Charlotte is fine, and I hope it was good." I laugh.

She smiles. "Of course. Can I get you something to drink?"

"No, thank you. I've come to see Cynthia. She left my friend Maggie and me upset yesterday, and I wanted to make sure she was okay."

"I'm sorry. She isn't here now. She did seem quiet last night on the way home, though," she says, grabbing her glass of wine from the counter. "Please, have a seat," she tells me.

"Oh. Well, I'm afraid my friend and I overstepped," I say as I sit down on the comfortable looking sofa.

"How so?" she asks, taking a sip from her glass.

"Maggie noticed a scar on Cynthia's neck that I noticed the other day and Cynthia told me she got it from jumping a ramp as a kid. Now, I don't know, but Cynthia doesn't seem like the kind of person who jumps ramps."

Marty gives a small smile. "No," she agrees. She sighs and rubs her arm. "Charlotte, I wish I could tell you more, but I'm afraid this is something Cynthia herself will have to open up to you about. My niece has been through a lot, and she's very private."

"Seems we have something in common," I say.

She smiles. "I understand she is writing a story about you?"

"She is. I'm a very private person, too, but this girl has come into my life and opened my eyes…if you will."

"Cynthia is a very special young woman."

"That she is," I agree. I scan my eyes over the small living room and notice a photo on the TV stand. It's a man and woman and Cynthia.

"Are those her parents?" I ask.

Marty's eyes follow mine. "Yes. My brother and sister-in-law." She sighs and rubs her finger over her glass. "I didn't get to spend as much time with him as I would have liked to."

"Time is a funny thing," I say. "It doesn't wait for us to figure things out, does it?"

"Sadly no."

"Have you been living here long?" I ask.

"Eh, longish. I used to never stay in one spot, but after Cynthia's parents died and she came to live with me, I had to take some time off work to be with her. Plus, I wanted Cynthia to feel like she had a permanent home, so I bought this place for us to always be able to come back to."

"I couldn't imagine losing my parents at such a young age."

"Me either and she took it hard. We went through some rough patches, but I think she's doing better."

"Yeah," I say, but really, I'm not so sure. Of course, I don't know how bad it got back then, but I know Cynthia isn't the happiest young woman, and I'd bet my life it has something to do with losing them. I rub my hands over my jeans. "Well, I guess I better get going." I stand. "Thanks for inviting me in."

"You're welcome anytime. A friend of Cynthia's is a friend of mine."

Chapter Nine

I park my car after I get home from the grocery store and make my way to the front door. I can taste the sea salt coming off the Carolina shore, and my toes ache to feel the sand. I haven't spoken to Cynthia much over the last few days, only short conversations on the phone when she wants to know more details about parts of my story we've already discussed. I must admit, though, I miss the girl.

Walking inside with an arm full of groceries, I lay them all on the table and take out my ingredients to make a red velvet cake. I turn on the country station on my TV and listen to some music while I go about putting everything together. Mama always baked in our home, and I try to keep something homemade and sweet in my kitchen also.

After the cake is in the oven, I set my pig timer and then change out my shoes for sandals. I make my way to the bathroom to grab my current Janet Evanovich book and snag a Heath bar from the candy dish before I go plug my dying cell phone up. Grabbing my floppy hat from the coat hanger, I push the screen door open, and the phone rings.

"Well, shit. Someone would call now," I huff and let the door slam shut behind me. "Haven't had a phone call all day, but as soon as I'm walking to the beach, someone wants to speak to me."

"Hello," I say after I slide my thumb across the screen and see that it's William.

"Hey," he replies. I smile, feeling bad I got annoyed when it's my son who called me. Moving from the table, I take a seat in my recliner. "What are you up to?" he asks me.

"Oh, I was just about to step out and sit under my umbrella. I got the new Janet book Elizabeth sent me."

"Good. She'll be glad to know it showed up," he says.

"Yes, tell her it's a funny one. Stephanie Plum is at it again."

"Who's that?" he asks me.

I laugh, remembering, unlike his wife and me, my son doesn't care for reading. Elizabeth is actually an author herself, but William has only heard what she's read to him. She doesn't mind, though, because he helps her with the business part of being an author.

"It's the main character in the book, but never mind. Tell me how work is going," I say. My production assistant son tells me all about life on the current set he is working on and complains about Atlanta weather. I laugh, remembering how those hot and humid Georgia summers can be. While he's talking to me, his Great Dane squeaks his chew toy, and I hear Elizabeth tell him to drop it.

"Mom, I've got to go. I just saw Dottie run across the front yard. She's escaped the fence again."

"Oh Lord," I say. "Love y'all."

"Love you," he says before he hangs up. Looking over at the table beside my chair, I smile at the photo of my son and daughter-in-law. They were just married in the picture—Elizabeth with short blonde curls and my son, the most handsome I've ever seen him, with a navy tux and baby pink tie. Those two have had some rough patches, but they always seem to come out stronger in the end. Like Travis and me, they have a rare love that will outstand time.

Exhaling, I push up from my chair and plug my phone back up, leaving it to charge. I grab my pig timer from the counter, and once again, I make my way to the back porch and across it to the screen door leading out to the beach. I step onto the warm sand and look out at my umbrella. It has two seats under it, and one of them is occupied. Turquoise highlighted hair waves in the wind like a flag on a flag pole but prettier. Cynthia Rose sits facing the crashing waves, her toes dug into the white sand. I shut the screen door softly until it clicks and leave my sandals before I make my way out to her.

She turns when she hears me approaching, and I see she has on sunglasses that look like they are wrapped in newspaper.

"Hey," she says softly.

"Hey," I counter. "What are you doing out here?" As I sit down, I notice she has her notebook and pen on her lap. She shrugs and looks out.

I wonder what to say to her. I don't want her to get upset like she did the other day, so I don't mention what happened before.

Instead, I take my hanging eyeglasses from around my neck and put them on. I open my book, flipping to where my bookmark is. I'm two sentences in when she says, "You know, sometimes it's nice not to talk."

I don't look over at her, but agree, "Yes, it is."

"Sometimes it's good to have the silence. To not have to fill an empty void with useless words no one wants to hear anyway."

I don't say yes to this one. I don't make a gesture because I want to hear. I want to hear everything about this girl's past. I remove my glasses and look ahead. My squinted eyes watch as a pelican plunges down into the water after a fish. I wonder about that bird, and in an odd way, it reminds me of our situation.

"Did you see that bird?" I ask Cynthia.

"Yeah."

I nod and close my book. "I'd bet good money that pelican had no idea what dangers were lurking below the surface of that water. He simply knew he had to eat, and his only way of doing so was to go all in, blind or not."

"Um, true," she replies dubiously.

I smirk at her confusion. "We often shy away from things that scare us—moving on, talking about things we don't want to talk about, diving into dark water without knowing what's below," I say. "Because it makes us uneasy or brings up bad memories, or it just fucking scares us," I say plainly. "But the reality is, like that bird must eat, we must heal, and sometimes the only way to do that is to dive in blind."

"And pray to the gods there's no shark on the other side," Cynthia says with a lift of her lips.

I chuckle. "Yeah. That, too."

We are still for a moment, and then I say, "I guess my point is, that for so long, I've kept my past to myself, afraid that all of those feelings from back then would come rushing to the surface, and it would be like I'm reliving it all over again. And it has," I say meekly. "That's why I avoided you at first."

I look down at the cover of my book and run my hand across it in thought.

"But you know what?" I question as I look over at her. "After we talk, sometimes I cry and say every cuss word in the book, and occasionally, it makes me feel a little better. Like a weight has been lifted from my chest, giving me a chance to breathe again." I take in a shaky breath. "I haven't even told my kid some of the things I've told you, and it feels good to talk about it. Because it happened. All the good, the bad, the ugly. It was all real. There's still so much I haven't told you, but I've been thinking about all of it and, you know what? I've lived one hell of a life, and you've made me realize I still have so much more to live. You, Cynthia Rose, made me a pelican."

Cynthia gives a small smirk before looking away, and then she says softly, "My dad used to call me Cyn."

I peer over at her. She looks ahead, still hiding her eyes behind those shades. Her red bottom lip is sandwiched between her top and bottom teeth, and she toys with a tiny seashell.

"In fact, until you, no one else has called me that since. Well, except for one other person," she says mostly to herself. I want to ask her who this other person is, but I don't want to interrupt, afraid she may stop.

"My parents were doctors. They worked too much and lived too little. They spent their whole lives saving others," she says pensively. "But in the end, they're the ones that needed to be saved." Her voice is grave, and my heart literally breaks for my girl. I have so many questions. Who's this other person? Who did her parents need to be saved from? But I keep them to myself, hoping that soon she will be brave and dive in.

Cynthia sighs and tosses the seashell to the ground. "So, how about you tell me some more of your story?"

"Okay," I say, but wanting to keep talking about her. Exhaling, I peer down at the seashell she tossed. "Where was I?"

"You and Travis had just done the deed," she says.

"Oh, yes," I say, trying to think of the timeframe, and then it hits me. "It was the beginning of September," I tell her.

I grow quiet as I stare out at the calming waves, thinking back on that exact moment. His words, the way he looked at me like he had it all figured out. God, how I wish it were that simple, but life isn't simple. It's ugly, and it's downright hard sometimes. I believe occasionally we all go through hell just so we can appreciate that little bit of heaven we get to witness. Travis Cole was my heaven. He was my everything.

September 1973

With the windows down in his GTO and the warm fall ocean breeze blowing around us, we eat lunch quietly, just enjoying each other's company. Still sneaking around behind Mama's back, we had to park in a beach parking lot, away from downtown and her nosy friends' eyes. Last week, Travis' boss at the mechanic shop told him he had to cut back, so Travis got a job in construction a few days ago and he seems restless. With a white stained T-shirt and worn blue jeans on, he tosses his hamburger wrapper into the takeout bag.

He grabs his smokes from his dash beside his tool belt and pats one out. Placing it between his lips, he cups his hand around the end and lights it. I watch him as he settles down into the driver's seat, staring out the window at nothing, enjoying his smoke soundlessly. I look out of mine and listen as the cars pass by behind us and the waves roll repeatedly in front of us.

"Let's run away," I hear his deep voice say. I turn my head quickly in his direction.

"What?" I kinda smile and kinda can't swallow because I know from the look in his eyes and the sound of his voice he is serious, and that both scares me and sends an exciting rush through my blood.

"I've got an uncle who lives in Virginia. We can stay with him until we get on our feet." He takes another drag from his smoke and flicks his ashes out the window.

"I can't run away," I say as I pick up the takeout bag and put my trash in it.

"Why?" he asks point-blank.

Yeah, why? my heart counters.

Because…I…Mama, my conscience tunes it.

Shut up, both of you.

I blink my eyes and just stare over at him, trying to come up with reasons I can't do this. But my thoughts scatter like the ashes he just flicked away.

"We can do this, Charlotte. We can make this work, and honestly, baby, I don't see any other way. She's never going to let us be together."

I swallow and look down at the floor mat, studying a tiny piece of sand. *He's right. She'll never let us be together. Travis is who he is, and she will never accept him.* My heart wins over the thinking, and I hear myself say, "Okay. Let's do it."

"You said yes?" Cynthia asks, her voice full of surprise.

"I did," I reply. "I wrote Mama a letter on the stationary at work."

"What did you say?"

I think back on that letter I wrote forever ago now. The squeaky desk chair surrounded by four nicotine-stained walls, a rotating fan in the corner of the room, and brown shag carpet underneath my feet. I was nervous and sad. Regardless of how Mama felt about Travis, she was still my mama and I didn't want to hurt her, but my heart was made up.

Mama,

Please don't worry about me. I'll be okay. I hate it had to come down to this, but I didn't see any other way. I love him Mama or at least I think I do. I've never been in love before, and you won't give me a chance to find out for sure. You won't give us a chance to find out if we can make this work. I know you just worry, but I am old enough to be able to decide on my own, and I choose him. I'd choose him every time. Travis may not be perfect to you, but he is what perfect means to me. I'll call as soon as we get settled. Again, please don't worry. I love you so much. I'm safe. I trust him with my whole heart.

Love, Charlotte

"Of course, later in life, I realized how that would be impossible for her not to worry. I mean, I couldn't imagine if my son ran away at seventeen. I would have been a mess." I shake my head. "But when you're young, you think you've got it all figured out—that you're invincible."

"Yeah," Cynthia agrees quietly. "Life sure does have a way of showing you, you have nothing figured out."

"It does," I reply solemnly.

She reaches down into her bag and grabs her eyeglass case. As she clears her throat, she says, "I guess I should be writing this stuff down, huh?" Trading out newspaper shades for hot pink specs, my interviewer opens her notebook. "So, how did y'all do it?"

I inhale and rub my neck. "Well, I told Mama I was going out with Jennie and, of course, she told me to be back by eleven, but I already knew I wasn't coming back…"

Chapter Ten

September 1973

"I need you to give this to Mama," I tell Jennie as we stand in her yard.

"I can't believe you're doing this." She looks past me to my car. I look back. Travis stands outside, leaning cool against the driver side door with a smoke between his lips. His hands are shoved into his front jean pockets, and his eyes are on me. He wanted to take my car instead of his GTO because it's been acting up, and he doesn't have the money to fix it if we get stranded. I give him a closed-lip smile and turn back to her. "I love him, Jennie. That's all there is."

"I know," she says as she sighs. "Just be safe. Call me when you can."

"I will."

I hug her bye and walk toward my troublemaker.

"You ready to go?" he asks as he tosses his smoke.

"Ready as I'll ever be."

He grins and pulls me to him.

"I love you," I tell him as I pull back, lazily lacing my fingers with his.

"I know," he says, looking at our linked fingers. "You sure you want to do this?" he asks me. "You can change your mind, you know?" He brings our hands to his lips and kisses my knuckles, gazing at me with love in his eyes. My heart is racing, and on the inside I'm a nervous wreck. I don't know what I'm doing, but I do know I want him. All of him, all of the time, and since Mama won't approve, then this is the only option we have.

"I'm sure," I say. "Where you go, I go."

"We didn't get very far the first night. Only made it to Daytona and we spent the night at a hotel off the interstate. Our room was right across from the pool, and there was a bunch of bikers with beer bellies and leather vests hanging out there. Travis left for a beer run, and I jumped in the shower." I start laughing thinking back on it.

"What's funny?" Cynthia asks me.

"While I was in the shower, an idea hit me. See, it was our first time being alone with an actual bed. I was excited about that, as I'm sure he was, too. So, after my shower, I decided I'd wait for him behind the door, and when he came in I was going to drop my towel. Good Lord." I laugh and put my hands over my face as the embarrassment hits me just like it did a lifetime ago. "It didn't turn out exactly how I wanted it to."

September 1973

With a pounding heart, I stand behind the door. I hear my car pull up, and a few moments later, I hear the key in the lock. As the knob turns, I loosen my towel and let it fall, puddling around my bare feet.

It all happens so fast. Travis yells, "What the fuck, baby?" as I'm being pushed back farther into the room. Bikers whistle and catcall, and with wide eyes, I realize I'm on display for every one of their asses to see.

"Shit," I curse as I feel my face burn, and I quickly reach for my towel. I run to the bathroom and slam the door shut with such force it rattles the hung-up mirror above the sink. I twist the lock on it and lean back against the door, sliding down to the floor.

Exhaling, I wipe my hands down my face, trying to rein in my embarrassment. A light knock sounds on the door, and I grumble, "Go away."

"Charlotte, did you forget the door opened out?" Travis asks with a hint of amusement in his voice.

"This isn't funny," I reply, deadpan.

"It's a little funny," he says. "Come out."

"No."

"Come on, Charlotte."

"I was trying to surprise you and only ended up embarrassing myself. This is horrible," I mutter, putting my face in my hands again.

"You surprised more than me," he says.

I groan and look up when I feel the door open behind me. "That door was locked," I say, moving in front of the sink.

"It's not now," he says.

"Travis Cole, you shouldn't be picking locks." I stare down at a loose string on my towel.

"Look at me," he says.

I dart my eyes to his face.

"It was a good thought, baby."

"Whatever," I pout.

He bends down, and I look over his handsome face as he stares back at me. A slow, crooked smirk spreads across his lips, and he says, "Show me again."

I bite my bottom lip as his smile makes me melt. He gently takes my hands and pulls me up with him. I let the towel fall, and he looks down before his smile widens and his eyes meet mine. He lifts me up, gripping my waist with one hand while the other holds onto my thigh. I link my ankles behind his back as he walks us out of the bathroom.

"A fucking bed," he says before his kiss captures my laugh, his tongue breaking my lips apart. He tastes like breath mints and Marlboro Lights. He smells like fresh linen mixed with sawdust from working. I pull up on the bottom of his shirt so I can feel his skin. He bends down and yanks the comforter off the bed before I feel the coolness from the sheets against my back. The roughness of his jeans rubbing against my naked body sends a shiver down my spine, and he quickly undoes his belt. I help slide his pants down with my feet, and in one movement he is where we both crave him to be.

The headboard slams against the wall, and the fitted sheet pops off the side. He's everywhere, and I hold onto him, wishing we could always stay in this safe little bubble.

After we christen the bed, I lie here, slowly listening to his heart flutter under my ear. I rub my fingers over the light sprinkle of hair on his chest as he smokes a cigarette.

"Is it possible to be happier than this?" I ask.

"I just hope you're always this happy with me," he says.

I look up at him and see his expression is serious and slightly worried.

"Why wouldn't I be?"

"Charlotte, I know you love me, but I also know you love your family just as much, if not more."

"I want to be with you, Travis."

"I know. I just wish there was another way, is all. I want you to have everything."

I sit up on the bed. Bringing the sheet with me, I tuck it under my arms. Travis hits his nicotine, and I reach out and take it from him. Leaning over, I put it out in the ashtray. He blows smoke from his lips as he watches me with narrowed eyes. I put my hands on both sides of his cheeks and stare into his golden browns so he'll know I mean this.

"Travis Cole, as long as I have you, I have everything." I kiss him, showing him once more that he is my whole world.

"We woke up with the sun the next morning and drove straight to Virginia," I tell Cynthia as she pens away in her notebook. "Why don't you have a laptop?" I ask her.

She looks over at me and shrugs. "I guess I'm old school. Marty bought me a typewriter from a yard sale one year, and that's what I use."

"You use a typewriter?" I question in shock. *Who uses those anymore?*

"Yes, I like the sound."

"You are one peculiar child."

She shrugs again. "Maybe I was just born at the wrong time."

I smirk. "Maybe so. Do you prefer landlines also?" I ask because she never has a cell phone.

"Cell phones are a distraction that's destroying people's ability to be social face-to-face."

I chuckle. "I'll agree with that."

"So, you drove to Virginia?" she asks, obviously done with the conversation about technology.

"Yes," I reply. "If we were on a farm, there would have been roosters crowing. That's how damn early we got up the next morning. The weather was sticky, and there was a light drizzle of rain coming down. Travis grabbed a coffee from the first convenience store we ran across, and I stocked up on candy bars and Coca-Colas.

"We filled up the tank, and I mapped out our directions. We were headed north, and we had almost 700 miles to go. It would take us a little over ten hours to get there, but I was so damn happy, I didn't care how far we had to go. I just wanted to be near him.

"I slept, we listened to the radio, and talked about a future we were surer about now than we had ever been. We'd have a big backyard with a place to build fires. There'd be plenty of chairs for all our friends and his family to come and drink, smoke pot, and just enjoy life.

"I wanted a front porch swing and flowers I didn't have to tend to, because God knows I didn't have a green thumb to be found. We'd have a few cats and a few more dogs. Travis would open his own mechanic shop, and I'd get a job doing accounting somewhere. We'd wake every morning side by side, and we'd go to bed every night wrapped up in each other.

"Eventually, Mama would get us. She would see how much I loved him and him me, and then she'd get to know Travis for who he really is. We'd have babies and enjoy watching them grow up, while we grew old together. Life was going to be good. We had it all figured out."

Chapter Eleven

September 1973

Rain falls heavy around us, so thick we can hardly see. The windshield wipers struggle to keep the windshield clear, and thunder booms somewhere in the distance. It's storming like crazy, but I can't keep my hands off Travis, not even caring that he could wreck and kill us both.

I just woke up from a nap in the back seat, and my lips are on his neck as he smokes a joint. He offers it to me, but I decline and continue kissing him and rubbing my hands across his bare chest. He is shirtless and in a pair of jeans. He hits the joint again before putting it out in the ashtray and leaving it there.

He turns his blinker on, carefully getting over. I hardly pay attention as he stops the car and presses the flashers on. I move back, wondering what he is doing before he moves the steering wheel up and turns, grabbing me and climbing into the back seat.

I breathe in, seeing his expression is self-possessed as he lifts my dress up. He undoes his jeans in a hurried, desperate rush and presses his lips to mine, gripping onto my thigh as he settles between my legs. I melt, breathing in love. Cars cruise past us, but the rain is still too heavy for them to see what is going on. For all they know, we just can't drive in this. The windows fog up, and Travis grabs onto the back seat as he kisses my neck and lifts my hips. I close my eyes as he loves me, knowing I'll never forget this—sheets of rain, the feeling of forever, and Travis Cole's desperate love mixed with mine.

It's late when we cross the Virginia *welcome* sign, so we drive a little farther into town in search of a hotel with plans to go to Travis' uncle's house tomorrow. We pull into this dump of a place, and I look over at Travis with slight concern.

"It'll have to do," he says with a shrug. "Come on."

After we check in, I head straight for the shower. There are water stains and rust around the knobs, but it smells like bleach, so I guess it's clean.

I slide my nightgown over my head as I walk out of the bathroom, noticing Travis sitting on the bed with his ankles crossed watching me towel dry my hair. He offers me the joint in his hand. Hanging the towel over a chair, I walk over and lie stomach down across the bed, and this time I take it from his fingers. I've never smoked before, but I've seen him do it enough times to know how. What I didn't know is how bad it would make me cough the first time I hit it. I give it back to him and roll over onto my back.

"Jesus!" I sputter.

He chuckles and says, "You'll be bent now."

I blow my hair out of my face as a feeling of pure calmness takes over my body, and I sigh contently.

"I want you to meet my dad," he says.

"Your dad?" I ask, looking back at him. "Do you know where he is?"

"I'm pretty sure I can find him." He stands up and slides his wallet into his back pocket. "He hangs out at this joint a few miles from here."

"You're leaving now?" I ask.

"Yeah, we gotta get going in the morning, so we won't have time. I'll be back." He leans down and gives me a kiss, grabbing a handful of my backside as he picks up the keys off the table. "Lock the door behind me," he says, walking over to it. "And put some clothes on."

About thirty minutes later, my high has worn off, and a man who kind of looks like Travis walks in the door along with his son. I'm in jeans and a flowy shirt with flowers on it. No shoes and damp hair.

"Charlotte, this is my dad. Dad, this is Charlotte."

"Good to meet you," the man says to me.

"You, too," I reply as I shut the door behind them. Travis' dad walks over to the table and takes a seat.

"Can I get you a beer?" I ask, walking over to the small fridge.

"That'd be nice," he replies. The two pop tops and smoke a few cigarettes as they catch up, and I listen. We share some laughs, and by the time Travis' dad leaves, I'm pretty sure

Travis is feeling right, so I offer to drive his dad back to wherever Travis got him from.

We go to bed when we get back, and the next morning we head over to his uncle's, excited and ready to get the ball rolling on our new planned-out future.

———

The lonely roads of Virginia twist in front of us, and I stare out the window as we pass by changing leaves. Spring is my favorite time of the year. I like to see the flowers bloom, not die, but right now, we could be in the middle of a blizzard and I'd still be happy.

I look over at my troublemaker with a smile on my face. He stares ahead with his elbow hanging out the window and a smoke between his fingers. He looks over at me and only gives a small smirk. He's clearly stoked about all of this, even though he doesn't show it.

Travis turns down a small road no two cars could fit on, and with another turn, we pull up to a house that looks like it's seen better days. The front porch is leaning, and the screen door is wide open. The shudders are crooked and hanging, the roof looks worn from rain, but the land around it is beautiful.

"This is it," he says to me as he kills the engine. "I'm psyched for you to meet everyone." That was one thing about Travis Cole—he always wanted me to meet everyone he cared about, and he always wanted everyone he cared about to meet me.

I get out of the car, and he takes one last hit of his smoke before he tosses it and puts my hand in his. I look over to the left of us and see a big pen with chickens, and around it stands a few goats eating grass.

The front door opens as we walk up the steps, and a big grizzly looking man with suspenders and a full gray beard says in a deep tone, "Travis Cole, you going to jail, boy. You better call Harold Taylor." My heart starts slamming against my rib cage. *Jail?*

See, I told you this wasn't a good idea, my conscience butts in.

Shit, my heart replies.

Shit is right, I agree.

"Why do I need to call my stepdad?" Travis asks, pulling me on up the steps. *Did he not hear the word* jail*?*

"You two got everybody looking for you. Get in here and get on that phone."

Travis looks back at me, but his face shows no concern. I, on the other hand, am scared shitless.

A woman stands in the kitchen at the stove, flipping pancakes, and she turns her head to look at us. "Come on and get y'all some breakfast," she says.

Travis looks at me. "You hungry?"

"No, thank you," I reply because my stomach is in knots. He squeezes my hand, and we take a seat on the couch. Travis reaches over and picks up the phone and dials a number. I don't hear the other end, but I listen to his reply.

"We haven't done anything wrong," Travis says to his stepdad. "Her mom won't let us be together, so we came here." Travis listens to whatever his stepdad is telling him, and afterward he says, "This is bullshit." He hangs up the phone. With a heavy sigh, he says, "Call your mama. They're threatening to take me to jail."

"Take him to jail?" Cynthia asks. "Why would he go to jail?"

I chuckle. "They said because Travis took me across state lines, and I was only seventeen, it was considered kidnapping." I roll my eyes. "The thing is, he was seventeen, too, so it was all bullshit to scare us into coming home. But we were young and naïve."

"What did y'all do?" she asks, looking over at me as she slides her glasses up onto her head.

"I called my mama, and boy was she pissed. I got an earful from her and more threats about sending Travis to jail if we didn't come home. My real mom, Beverly, lived in Indiana with her daughter and husband, and after several different phone calls back and forth and arguments, we told them we would drive there. They wanted to pick us up, but I remember Travis saying,

'That's stupid. We have a car. We can drive ourselves,' so we did."

September 1973

I sit in the car as Travis fills it up. It's a cool morning in Virginia, and I stare out the open window as people come in and out of the small store. A man walks out packing a box of cigarettes against the palm of his hand, and another comes out with a cup of steaming coffee. They're off to work. It's just a normal day for them, but my world is crashing in around me. Just yesterday we had it all figured out, and now… Well, now I'm wondering how we'll ever be together. Why can't we be older? Why can't they accept that we love each other and leave us the hell alone?

Travis opens the door, pulling me from my thoughts. I sigh and roll my window up as he pats his box of smokes against his hand. Pulling one out with his teeth, he tosses the box onto the dash and lights it before pressing the clutch. The car rumbles to life, and we don't say anything as he shifts it into first and pulls out onto the road.

I look out at the trees, all various colors of orange, red, and brown. The sky is gray, matching my mood, and the clouds shift leisurely above us. Some tunes play from the radio speakers, and

Travis slows the car as we come up to a four-way. He unhurriedly rolls to a stop, and I look both ways noticing we are the only ones on the road. I turn to look at him as he sits soundlessly, resting one hand on the bottom of the wheel and the other on the gear shifter with a smoke between two of his fingers. I don't say anything, clearly seeing the wheels in his head turning. He hits his nicotine and looks at me. His golden brown eyes dance between mine, and he bends his brow.

"I love you, Charlotte. No matter what happens, know that. Okay?"

"O…kay," I say apprehensively.

He turns his head to look in front of him as a stream of smoke drifts upward from the cigarette.

"We can go straight." He points his smoke toward the windshield. "We'll be at Beverly's in a few hours." I see his chest rise as he inhales a deep breath. "We can do what they all say and hopefully be together one day." He clenches the steering wheel with his hand, his knuckles turning white as he brings the smoke to his lips and takes a drag. Blowing it out the window, he looks down the road. "Or, we can turn left here," he counters as he looks back at me. "And say fuck 'em all."

Chapter Twelve

"I often wonder about that day, daydreaming on how my life would be now if we would have turned left." I exhale and rub under my chin as my pig timer goes off. "I'm baking a cake. I've got to go check on it," I tell Cynthia as I lift myself out of the chair. I see her grab her bag, then stand, too.

"Did you tell him no?" Cynthia asks as she walks beside me.

"I did." I nod. "I was too worried about the consequences, and I know somewhere in the back of my mind I didn't want to hurt Mama more than I already had.

"Surprisingly, though, when we got to Indiana, Beverly was very welcoming, more so than any of my other family. Maybe it was a guilty conscience for the decisions she made earlier in life. Maybe she was still a rebel and wanted to go against her mom, or maybe she saw that we loved each other and that was enough," I say, shrugging. "Beverly told us they would buy us a trailer. We could live at the end of the property out by the creek at the foot of the mountain, and she would sign for us to get married as soon as Travis turned eighteen. It felt too good to be true."

"Was it?" Cynthia asks.

"Aren't most things?" I say. "Later that day, I got a phone call from my older sister, who was technically my aunt, and boy that phone call changed everything. She lit me up like I was a firecracker on the Fourth of July."

September 1973

"You should be ashamed of yourself," Natalie says to me. "Mama has done everything for you! She raised you as her own. What has Beverly done? Nothing," she barks. "I can't believe you're going to stay there with him."

"I love him, Natalie."

She huffs, "You're only seventeen, Charlotte. What do you know about love? You need to come home. You have stressed Mama out enough. I don't know how you could feel okay about any of this." She talks more, but her voice fades out, and my thoughts run wild.

I know Mama has done everything for me. There's no telling where I would be right now if she wouldn't have kept me. I would have never met Travis. I stare ahead at the door as she rambles on and on about how I should feel terrible and how much pain I have caused our mama.

Her words crawl inside my skin, twisting along my veins, traveling their way straight to my heart and conscience. I blink tears away, because I know this is the point where I must choose. *It's Travis or my family.*

"Let me talk to Mama," I say, cutting her off. *I don't need to hear this crap anymore.* I wipe fallen tears away from my cheeks and sniff as Natalie gives Mama the phone.

"Charlotte," she says.

"Mama, I love him. I don't want to have to choose." I cry, begging her to understand.

She's silent for a moment, and then she says, "You don't have to."

"Huh?" I say in shock.

"You come back to Florida, and I will let you two date."

"Are you serious?"

"Yes, I just want you home."

A smile bigger than Texas spreads across my lips, and I take a deep breath. "Okay."

"She actually let you two be together?" Cynthia asks skeptically.

"Well, that's what she said," I reply. "But she also made us agree to drive on to Indiana where my real mom lived. There, we would wait until she could get off work and could take us home."

"Why not just drive back to Florida?"

"They didn't trust us to. But I wanted that side of my family to meet Travis anyway, so it worked out."

A knock sounds on my front door, and Cynthia turns her head from the counter she's now seated on.

"It's Maggie," she says, jumping down.

"There you two are!" she says, bursting in once Cynthia opens the door. She's got a margarita in her hand with black glittery leggings on and a black shirt long enough to cover her ass that has little white poodles all over it.

"I've been looking for you everywhere," she says.

"Really?" I question. "Was this your last thought?"

I dart my eyes over to Cynthia who smirks.

"Oh, Charlotte. I've come to invite you out, and this is how you treat me?" she huffs and pulls a chair out from the kitchen table. Flopping down in it, she says, "There's a huge party going on at the clubhouse, and I need my girls. Frank will be there."

"Why do you need us?"

"I'm mad at him."

"Then why are you going?"

"Because I'm mad at him! Get with it, Charlotte."

Cynthia looks over at me with a smirk.

"Well, what are you two standing there for? Come on," she says, getting on her feet. "I'm just starting to get a buzz, and I don't want to lose it."

I'd normally argue with Maggie about going out, except for Travis' birthday celebration, but after all that deep talk, it didn't sound like such a bad idea. Who am I kidding? I'm doing this because a certain inspiring journalist is making me feel young again. I'm hoping we can talk about *her* a little more now that her notebook and pen are back at my house.

If I'd Known

She dances with Maggie on the black and white tile squares out in the middle of the spacious room. Disco lights twirl above them, shining glitter on the walls and across their smiling faces. I sit at a tall table people-watching as I babysit my piña colada. Pieces of our conversation from earlier cross my mind, and a deep longing settles heavy in my chest. How I wish he were here with me.

I slide down from the stool, taking my drink with me, walking past people to make my way toward the enormous wall of French bay doors that are all open, letting in the fresh salty air. Outdoor lights droop between the poles of the wraparound porch, and I spot a few vacant rocking chairs that look out toward the docked boats.

The breeze is warm, and the water is calm. The evening air reminds me of campfires down at Taylor Creek Bridge, and for a small moment, I can feel his fingers slide between mine.

The smell of nicotine drifts in the air, reminding me of him, and I look down the porch and see a woman sharing a smoke with her friend. I turn back to the rocking boats and close my eyes, envisioning leaves rustling from the wind and chatter from our friends below us as we sit on Taylor Creek Bridge. Sighing, I open my eyes and lightly kick my foot off the porch to rock.

There were many other times we sat around a fire pit and talked. We used to visit his family a lot when we were older, and I think about those videos I watch on his birthday…

Kids are running around us, and his sister walks out to their brother to help with the grill. His niece sits in a plastic chair across from us, as her cousin sits beside her.

"Uncle Travis, have you ever built a porch?" she asks him.

"Yes, several," he replies.

"Have you ever got arrested?" she asks. He looks over at me with a small smirk, still as handsome as he was when we were teenagers. He will always, always take my breath away.

"Only a couple of times," he replies with a smile. That was one thing about Travis. He never lied, maybe left a few details out from time to time, but never a bald-faced lie.

"Ever raced a motorcycle?" the other one asks Travis.

"Once, and I almost killed myself," he says, chuckling.

"What about you, Ms. Charlotte? You ever raced a motorcycle?"

I laugh as I hold the camcorder. "Can't say that I have."

The kids grow tired of playing twenty-one questions, and they get up from their chairs, leaving behind notebook paper with scribblings and crayons with the wrappers torn off. I do a take around the yard before landing on Travis. He looks at me and smiles, giving me a wink at the same time.

"I love you," I tell him from behind the camera.

"I love you, too," he says softly.

I have several sweet moments like that on tape, but that one is extra special to me because it was an honest, raw moment between two people who were madly, unapologetically in love. We weren't saying it out of habit. It was real. He made me feel like I was the most important thing in the world. He didn't have to tell me he loved me. I could feel it deep in my soul when he was around me. Even in those moments where I'd say, "I love you," and he'd simply reply, "I know," I knew he was saying he loved me, too. If possible, I think I loved him more then than when we were seventeen.

I hear chatter behind me and realize it's Cynthia singing and twirling as she walks toward me.

"You're in a good mood," I tell her.

"That I am," she replies as she sits down in the rocker on the other side of me.

"Where's Maggie?"

"She's with Frank. They made up." She grins. "What are you doing out here?"

"Just wanted to look at the boats," I say.

"You're missing out on the hot action in there," Maggie chimes in as she walks up behind us.

"The only hot action is you," I reply. "You're putting on a show for that old fart."

Cynthia laughs. "She was killing that dance floor."

"I can dance now," Maggie says. "I used to get down all the time in my younger years." She moves her hips and snaps her fingers. Cynthia and I laugh.

"Sit down before you pop your hip out of place," I tell her. She does and rocks the chair back.

"What happened to Frank?" I ask.

"Eh, he was ready to call it a night, and I wasn't."

"Are y'all arguing again?" I ask.

"Not arguing. I'm just finally telling him how it's going to go."

Cynthia props her feet up on the porch railing, and I lean back in my chair.

"Well, good for you," I reply.

We sit in comfortable silence for a moment, and then Cynthia says, "My dad had a boat." Maggie and I look over at her. "We were planning on taking it out together. Just us three and Lit."

"Who's Lit?" I ask.

She looks over at me and gives a small smile. "Just an old friend."

"The same old friend who lived in Georgia?" I ask, remembering one of our earlier conversations.

"Yes."

"The only other person that called you Cyn?"

She nods. "That's the one."

"What kind of name is Lit?" Maggie asks.

"Litton Daniels. He goes by Lit."

"Was he a close friend?" Maggie asks.

"He was a good friend," she replies, her smile slowly fading.

"Can I ask what happened?"

Cynthia looks over at Maggie and bites the inside of her cheek before she turns to look at the boats. "I broke it off."

"Broke it off?" I ask. "He was your boyfriend?"

She nods.

"Where is he now?" Maggie asks.

Cynthia shrugs. "I have no idea. His dad was in the Army, so they traveled a lot."

"Well, that's too bad," I say.

Cynthia shrugs again. "It's what needed to be done."

We don't reply to that, just sit reticent, wondering if this mysterious girl will reveal more about herself, and shockingly, she speaks again. "He took my v-card."

"Oh," Maggie says as she looks at me.

"Have you searched for him on social media?" I ask.

She shakes her head. "I don't know if I want to know where he is or what he's doing."

"Do you still love him?" Maggie asks a moment later.

Cynthia peers down. "I don't know what I feel. I just wish I would have told him thank you."

"For what?" I ask.

"He was there for me when no one else was. Before my parents decided they wanted a relationship with me, Lit was there. After they died, he tried to be there, but I wouldn't let him. I just wish…" She sighs. "I don't know." My interviewer puts her feet down and places her empty glass onto the railing.

"I've got to get home. I need to type up everything we talked about tonight." With that, she stands. "Had a good time, Maggie. Thanks for the dance."

"Anytime, girlfriend," Maggie says. As Cynthia walks by, she slap-clasps her hand with Maggie's.

"We'll talk tomorrow, Charlotte?" she asks, turning back to look at me.

"Yep," I say. "Goodnight."

I turn to look at my friend after Cynthia Rose walks away.

"How did her parents die?" she asks.

"I'm not sure. She hasn't said, and I don't want to pry, but she is opening up more."

"She isn't the only one," Maggie says to me with a lifted brow.

"Why, what do you mean?" I ask, feigning innocence and putting my hand over my chest. Leaning forward, I push myself up as Maggie places her drink onto the railing. I take a sip of mine as she stands.

"You're not sitting at home, are you?" she says because we both know that's what I'd normally be doing.

I place my drink down and look around. "Wait, this isn't my house?"

She grins and slaps my arm. "Come on, homebody. My legs are killing me, and I think I twisted my damn knee dancing with that twenty-one-year-old."

I laugh as we walk away from the chairs and the view of the rocking boats. My closest friend hooks her arm around my waist, and I put mine around her shoulders as I say, "Let's get home, dancing queen."

Chapter Thirteen

"I think we should find him," Maggie says to me as we sit on my screened-in back porch. It's an amazing day out with the perfect amount of breeze coming off the ocean. I sip a cold glass of sweet tea, while Maggie enjoys a Bloody Mary.

"Find who?" I ask.

"Lit."

I look over at her. "Oh no," I say. "I'm pretty sure Cynthia would not be happy with us for doing that."

"I think she needs us to do that," she says, taking another gulp of her drink.

"I think you need to stop drinking," I reply, straight-faced.

She huffs, "I'm being serious, Charlotte. I think it would do her some good."

"Maggie, we don't know what happened between the two of them. We don't know if they ended on good terms."

"There's a lot going out on me in my old age. My bones creak, the joints in my hands ache, and I'm losing hair, but there ain't a damn thing wrong with my hearing, and I heard the sound in her voice when she talked about that boy. Now, I don't know a lot, but I do know love, and she loves him. It's as clear as that sky out there." She points.

I sigh. "I think she was just tipsy, and it's not our place, Maggie."

"Maybe you're wrong; maybe it's exactly our place. Maybe it's the reason our paths crossed, to get your story out and for us to help that girl get some life back in her…and you," she finishes.

I roll my eyes at her. "Maggie, I'll have you know I enjoy my life very much."

"Good. But you can't say you haven't enjoyed it more here lately."

I look away from her. "No…I don't guess I can."

"So help me. We don't have to tell her anytime soon. I kinda just wanna see what the boy looks like."

"How in the world will we know who he is? I'm sure there are plenty of guys named Litton."

"Did you just hear yourself?" Maggie asks me.

I laugh. "Okay, you're right. Maybe there aren't that many."

"Come on," she says before she tips her drink up. She makes an *ahh* sound and wipes her mouth with the back of her hand after she kills the Bloody Mary. "I've got to let Archie out, so we can use my computer. I need you to drive. I think I put too much liquor in that drink."

I sit on Maggie's wicker couch in her sunroom as she walks in from outside with Archie. His red bandana tells me he's been groomed recently, because he always gets a new one when she takes him down to the Clip 'n Dip. *"It's a two for one deal,"* she always says. *"You get 'em clipped and you get 'em dipped."* She unhooks his leash, and he walks over to where I am. He sniffs my feet before dismissing me, going about his business of chew toys and doggie treats.

Maggie sits down beside me with her laptop on her lap. "Okay, so Litton Daniels, right?"

"Yep, that's what she said."

"I wish she would have described his hair or something." She opens her computer and moves her finger over the mouse pad.

"I'm shocked she told us his name," I reply.

"True," Maggie agrees as she bites the inside of her check. "So, how do we search for people?" she asks, squinting her eyes and one finger typing *Facebook* in Google. I look over at the blurry screen.

"There's a search bar at the top," I say, leaning to have a better look. She bursts out laughing, and I give her a sideways glance. "What?"

"God, Charlotte, look at us. How the hell are we supposed to see a damn thing without our glasses?"

"I didn't bring mine," I say with a chuckle.

"I've got more than one pair around here somewhere." She places the computer on my lap and stands up. I look at the screen as she goes to search for glasses. I kinda see she has finished typing *Facebook*, so I click *Enter*. Her page automatically comes up. She walks out of the hallway with two pairs of eyeglasses. One is lime green with hot pink glitter all over it, and the other pair is black and white with square frames.

"Which pair do you want?" she asks me.

"Give me the square ones I guess."

She sits down after she hands them over and grabs the laptop. "How did you say we search for people?"

I point to the search bar, and she moves the mouse up to it. She types in *Litton Daniels* and a handful of people come up.

I sigh. "There's no way we are going to know which one is him."

She clicks on a profile. "Well, my grand boy made me write a description about myself when he helped me set my account up, so I'm assuming Lit probably has one, too. There has to be something in there that gives us a hint it's him."

She scrolls down and clicks on a profile. We look through photos and read in the *About* section. Some of them are private, so we can't see anything but a few outdated photos, and then we come across a young man with a buzzed head. It says he's in the Marines and from Georgia.

"This has got to be him," I say as we look through his photos.

Pictures of him and some other Marines come up. Christmas parties and them goofing around, and one of him with a baseball bat over his shoulder with a few other guys in uniforms.

"It says he's single," Maggie points out with a smile.

"I wonder where he's living now?" I scan over the photos to see any sign of where he may be. Some of them have a location, but most don't. "Go down more," I tell her.

"This one was in California, and this one," she says, toying with her lip as she scrolls down. "He looks younger in these."

"The date they were posted was more than a few years ago," I say.

"Oh my goodness. Is that Cynthia?" Maggie asks as she points to a photo at the bottom. I move in closer to the screen.

The photo is captioned *Throwback.* Cynthia has dirty blonde hair and a small smile on her lips with Lit's arm around her shoulders.

"It looks like they were at school," Maggie says. She scrolls back up to more recent photos. "Oh, look, all of these are in Georgia! That's not that far from here. He's a cutie. I don't know why she'd let a thing like him go," she adds, grinning.

I roll my eyes. "Maggie."

"What, you have eyes just like I do. You can't say this boy isn't good-looking."

I shrug. "He is cute. Scroll down some more," I tell her and she does. "Well, at least we know this is the guy. I think we should let this go."

"Now why would we do that?" she says mischievously.

"Maggie, Cynthia is a private girl. She won't even tell us what happened with her parents. I really think she would be upset about this."

She sighs. "Maybe you're right." She slides her glasses off and shuts the top of her laptop. I take my borrowed glasses off, too.

"I'm glad we got to see what he looks like."

"Yeah, and Cynthia looked so different back then," I say, chewing on the inside of my lip.

"Yes, she did," Maggie agrees. "She seems happier, and more carefree. Whatever happened with her parents changed her. Poor girl. Losing her family so young."

"I couldn't imagine," I say.

"You know what we need?" Maggie says after a minute.

"Oh Lord, I'm scared to ask."

She huffs and stands up, placing her laptop where she was seated. "How come you think it's going to be bad?"

"You don't exactly have a good history with great ideas."

"Tell me one that wasn't good." She's hands on her hips and lifting her right eyebrow. The sun shining in through her windows makes Maggie's sparkly purple leggings glisten. She looks like a purple disco ball.

"Umm, well, smoking pot, playing golf in that racecar you call a golf cart. I still have a bruise on my ass," I tell her.

"First off, smoking pot is not a bad thing. Hell, most people smoke it for medicinal purposes, and it helps me sleep. Second, I wasn't going that fast over those hills. You're just old and have thin skin."

I laugh. "It helps you sleep, huh? And you're not that much younger than me, woman."

"Charlotte, we may be close in age, but I am way hipper than you."

"You *have* more hips than me," I say, reaching out and poking her in the hipbone. I push off the side of the couch and stand up. "I've got to get home. My soaps are recording."

"You don't want to hear my idea?" she asks as she follows me to the door.

"I think we've done enough for the day. Let's try again tomorrow." I open the door and step out.

"Oh, Charlotte, you're no fun."

I laugh. "Bye," I say, waving behind me.

Chapter Fourteen

The springtime sun warms my bones as the tall grass brushes against our legs after we walk off the small porch steps into the yard. He has on his blue jean long-sleeved shirt, and his pants are looser than they once were.

"I need to get out here and cut this," Travis says, pointing to the lawn. "Or maybe we can get the boy to do it later."

"Yes," I say. "William will do it, and I'm sure Elizabeth will help. She's a go-getter."

He laughs. "Yes, she is. She cleaned that boy's whole room and bathroom today while he was at work."

I smile. The air is warm, and his hands are cold. His bones show beneath his pale skin, but I don't mind. I let go, and we get into the car. It's doctor day, which is nothing unusual for us.

"I love you," I tell him after we get our seat belts on, and I turn the heater up to keep him warm.

"I know," he says.

I jump awake at the sound of someone knocking on my door. Sighing, I get up from my bed and make my way out toward the living room. I see it's yet again Cynthia and Maggie.

"Good Lord, do you two not have any hobbies?" I ask, leaving the door open and my girls standing there. I walk to the kitchen to get a glass of tea, with them right behind me, I'm sure.

"Do you?" Maggie calls after me, and I hear the door click shut.

"Yes. Napping," I reply.

"You do nap a lot," Cynthia says.

"Wait till you get my age. You'll wanna nap, too."

"Geez, grumpy much?" Maggie says.

"I'm not grumpy... I'm just…well, I'm grumpy," I say, grabbing the tea pitcher from the fridge. I choose not to tell them I was dreaming about Travis and they interrupted me. I don't pick up my feet as I walk to the cabinet to grab a glass, and my bedroom shoes make a sliding noise across the kitchen floor.

"Maybe we should tell her later," Cynthia says.

I turn around. "Tell who what later?" I ask.

Cynthia chews her dark purple stained lips and looks over at Maggie.

"I guess I'm the who," I say. "What aren't y'all telling me?"

Maggie sighs. "First off, get in a better mood, and second, before you automatically shut us down, listen and think about it first, okay?"

I narrow my eyes. "This isn't about that idea you said you had the other day, is it?"

Maggie stands up straighter. "Actually, it is."

"Oh Lord," I reply as I make my way back over to the tea pitcher.

"Now don't start being all Negative Nancy on us," Maggie says. "Promise you'll think on it first."

I sigh and take a sip of my tea after I fill the glass up, eyeballing the two over the rim.

"Promise," Maggie repeats.

"Okay," I say. "I promise. Just tell me what it is so I can start thinking."

Cynthia smiles. "So, Maggie thought it would be cool to take a road trip. Our destination will be Ft. Pierce, and on the way, we can stop in Georgia where you lived."

"A road trip," I say. "That's a long drive. I don't think…"

"Hush, Charlotte. You promised you would listen and then think. Cynthia isn't finished. Go on, child," Maggie says. I eye her before looking back at Cynthia.

"Go on," I say, taking another sip of my drink.

"I thought it would help me get a better understanding of your story. I mean, to see where everything took place," she says. "I want to visit where you and Travis lived, where you grew up as a child, and where y'all fell in love in Ft. Pierce. I feel like I can write about it better if I can see it all, and wouldn't it be great to go back and see how things are now?"

I peer down at the floor, biting my bottom lip. I haven't been down south in a long time. Here, the only memories I have are videos and photos, but down there… Memories are everywhere.

"I need to get this story written, and I think this is the best way to do it. I want to see the things I'm writing about."

I look up at her and give a closed-lip smile. She's just as eager now as she was when she was following me around to write this story and, unlike before, I'm struggling to tell her no. I've grown to love this girl like my own, and she wants to take a trip with Maggie and me. Two old ladies who will have to stop and pee, stretch our legs, and want to check out the flea markets along the way. "It's a long ride, but a road trip is something I used to love to do." I look between her and Maggie. "I think that sounds nice."

Cynthia squeals, "Yes! We should leave as soon as possible. I've got to get this done before the end of summer. I'm going home to pack!" She turns out of the kitchen and yells back, "I'll see you two dark and early."

I look over at Maggie. "What have you done?"

She scrunches her face. "Who me?"

Cynthia Rose knocks on my door at four a.m. with freshly dyed all over purple hair. I usually crawl out of bed around seven. Normally, I only get up at four to pee. So here we three are—well, make that four. Maggie had to bring Archie because her neighbor didn't want to watch him, not knowing when she would be back and all. At least that's what she told us, but I know better. Maggie loves that dog, and I'm sure she just didn't want to leave him.

We watch the sun come up over the highway, and we stop so Cynthia can get her coffee fix and we all can have some breakfast. Maggie and I pop our daily blood pressure pills and anything else we must take to keep our bodies going. For Maggie, arthritis meds; for me, pills to help keep my blood sugar good. I often wonder if I'd survive if I tossed all these pills into the ocean, but then I think I probably wouldn't. My body is so used to them by now, it wouldn't know how to work alone.

"Oh, look! *The Welcome to Georgia* sign is up ahead. We have to get a picture," Cynthia says. I turn my blinker on and get over, turning into the visitor center. We are now in Augusta, Georgia, and we all hop out of the car. Cynthia goes to the trunk and rumbles through her bag.

"How will we all get in the photo?" I say.

"Sir," Maggie calls out to a young man. He turns around. "Will you take our picture, please?" she asks.

"Sure," he answers, walking over to us.

"Well, that works," I say to her as Cynthia shuts the trunk and hands him an older Polaroid camera.

"Where did you get that?" I ask.

"I've had it for years. I want to put photos from our trip in an album. You know, so I can maybe run across them one day."

"I think that's a great idea." I smile at this girl.

We all stand off to the side of the sign that reads *We're Glad Georgia is on Your Mind*. Maggie has on her hot pink sun visor, and her lime green fanny pack is in place. Archie is on his leash, and he lifts his leg to pee on the signpost. Cynthia's lavender hair is pulled into a cute bun on top of her head, and she wears a baby pink spaghetti strapped sundress. I'm in a pair of jeans and a white and purple flowered blouse. I'm sure we are a sight, different in every way, yet we share one thing in common as we smile for the antique camera. We're friends who accept each other for who we are, and that's rare to find in this lifetime.

———

"I have an idea on where we can eat for lunch," Cynthia says. "Last night while I was waiting for my hair to dye, I looked up some things." I glance over as she pulls her notebook out of her pink polka dot bag. She flips to a page that already has a folded piece of paper in it. I look back at the road as she opens the paper. Darting my eyes over again, I see it's an enormous map with places marked in red.

"I see you've done some work." I smile.

"Yes, have you ever eaten at The Whistle Stop Café?" she asks me.

"Yes, I have. They say they have the best fried green tomatoes."

"They say?" she asks. "You've never tried them?"

"Yes, and I don't like tomatoes," I reply, adjusting my hand on the wheel. Maggie makes a snoring noise, and I look in the rearview mirror. "She's out." Cynthia and I giggle.

"I've never tried them, so I'm excited."

"Well, that will be our first stop then," I say.

"Hey, I have an idea," Cynthia says. "On this trip, we should each do something we've never tried."

"Oh Lord, that'll be hard for Maggie. That woman has done everything."

"I'm sure we can find something. What about you? What would yours be?"

"Hmm," I say. "I don't know. I'll have to give it some thought."

"Okay. When Maggie wakes up, we'll tell her."

"Sounds like a plan."

About two hours later, we're going down back roads through Juliette, Georgia. Pine needles and pinecones are strewn across the pavement, and even though it's late summer, it's still hot as fire.

Cynthia reaches up and turns the radio down. "Since we have some time, why don't you tell me what happened after you got off the phone with your mom."

I nod. "Well, we drove on to Indiana. It was October, and I remember the weather was turning chilly. Like I said before, even though Mama agreed she'd let us date when we came back, we had to wait until Beverly got off work because Mama didn't trust us to drive back alone.

"Travis was to take the bus home, but without Mama's knowledge, Beverly let Travis stay until a week before I was set to leave. She still didn't let us sleep together, though, and I remember Travis saying on the way there, 'Do you think they'll let us sleep together?'

"In return, I'd said, 'We have been. I don't see why not.'" I shake my head. "We were so naïve. Of course, she wasn't going to let us sleep together. For one, we weren't married, and two, she had a daughter she had to think about.

"She had two daughters, Sophia and me. You remember when I told you she remarried in Indiana and had another child?" I ask Cynthia.

"Yes," she says.

"That's Sophia. Now, we've had some good times," I tell her. "I'd love for you to meet her some day. You'd love her. She's a little like Maggie," I look in the rearview and see she's still asleep, "but has cooler style," I whisper.

"I heard that," Maggie says. "If I've told you once, I've told you a thousand times. Fanny packs make sense, and sun visors are meant to be hot colors."

I look at Cynthia and roll my eyes. She giggles.

"Anyway, Beverly was more laid-back, and Travis and I were in no hurry to be back under Mama's watchful eye..."

October 1973

Desperate for some alone time, we sneak away to the back of the property near the creek behind Beverly and Bill's house. Travis holds my hand as we walk through the woods, and once we're far enough from the house, he lifts me up and presses my back against a tree.

His lips roughly kiss mine as I wrap my legs around him. I reach down between us and undo his belt and jeans. My heart hammers inside my chest, pushing my blood feverishly through my veins. I breathe hard through my nose, and Travis grips my thigh with one hand while the other moves my skirt higher. He moves my cotton underwear to the side, and my mouth goes slack once he presses into me.

Our lovemaking is frantically perfect and earth-shatteringly satisfying. He pushes forward and puts his face in the crook of my neck as his hand goes flat against the tree. I clamp my eyes shut as a feeling of pure bliss moves through me, and Travis kisses my lips until we are both nothing but deep breaths of air and wildly beating heartbeats.

We come down from our high, knowing it won't be long before we crave another hit, but we also know we better get back.

"I hate that you're leaving before me," I tell him.

"I know," he says. "But it'll be okay. I'll get back to work and start saving up some more money, so when you turn eighteen we can get our own place."

Even though the thought of having our own place makes me smile, I have an unsteady feeling about how being back at Mama's will be.

"We will be together, Charlotte. Know that," he says to me.

I pull into a gravel parking space near the railroad tracks in Juliette.

"Shit, Charlotte. Y'all had some serious heat between you! I'm surprised you didn't light that damn tree on fire," Maggie says.

I snort. "We had passion, for sure."

Cynthia puts her notebook inside her bag, and we four get out. I breathe in fresh pine, and my eyes take in the Georgia red clay mixed in with the chalky gravel.

"What are we going to do with Archie?" Cynthia asks as he lifts his leg and pees on my tire.

"He'll be fine in the car," Maggie says. "Cut it back on and roll the windows down, Charlotte. Archie's afraid of heights, so he won't try to jump out."

I do as she asks, and we leave the car and make our way up the worn front porch steps. "We missed the crowd," I tell them. "There doesn't seem to be a wait like I remember it." I take in the place. Boy, it's been a long time since I've been here. The Whistle Stop Café was once an old general merchandise store. The owner closed its doors after forty years back in the seventies, I believe, and twenty years later, it became what it is today. A small street is to the left of The Whistle Stop, running up through the quaint town full of souvenir and antique shops. There's also a shop or two that is dedicated to the movie *Fried Green Tomatoes.*

The train tracks line the right, and I can hear the train's rumble as it comes rolling toward us. We open the screen door and walk up to the glass counter.

"Hello. How y'all doing?" the lady asks.

"Hungry," Cynthia replies.

"Then you've come to the right place. Three today?"

"Yes," I reply. She nods and grabs us menus.

"Y'all can have a seat in that booth by the window. I'll be right there," she says.

The all-wooden booth creaks when we slide in, and moments later, the waitress walks up and leaves us with the menus after taking our drink orders. We decide on a plate of fried green tomatoes for my girls, and we each choose our dinner.

"This place is awesome," Cynthia says after the waitress takes our order. "We have to go look in the shops after we're done eating."

"Yeah, I'd like to walk Archie around a bit," Maggie says. I look out the old windowpane and watch as the train goes by. It rattles the glass and vibrates our seats. I scan my eyes over the pictures on the wall and whatnots hung around the café. Cynthia grabs her straw and opens it when our server brings us our drinks. We make light conversation, and I enjoy my Georgia sweet tea as Cynthia sips on Coca-Cola and Maggie has the same. The fried green tomatoes are set down in front of us, and Cynthia picks one up and blows on it before dipping it into the sauce.

"I used to eat these all the time," Maggie says. "So good."

Cynthia takes a bite, and obviously, she agrees with Maggie because she makes a *mmm* sound and goes for more.

"That would be my one thing I've never had or tried."

"Care to fill me in?" Maggie asks, reaching for her napkin.

"When you were snoring, Cynthia said she'd never tried fried green tomatoes before. So she came up with the idea we each have to try one thing or do one thing we've never done."

"Oh, this should be interesting." Maggie smiles.

"What haven't you done?" Cynthia asks.

"Well, there isn't a lot that I haven't done, but I think I can come up with a few things."

"This should be interesting indeed," I reply.

Our dinner is served a short time after, and we enjoy small talk and fresh cooked vegetables.

"I never learned how to cook well," Maggie says. "Which is a shame because I sure do like to eat."

Cynthia laughs. "My mom never cooked, but we always had a chef and I'd sometimes watch him or her."

"What did your parents do to afford a chef?" Maggie asks.

"They were surgeons."

"That's impressive."

"Yeah," she says. Maggie looks over at me as she says, "So tell us more about this Lit fella."

Cynthia picks up another tomato. "Nothing to tell really. He was just an old boyfriend."

"An old boyfriend who you loved and who took your v-card," Maggie says.

"Okay, can we stop saying v-card?" I tell her.

Maggie huffs. "Fine. Your first screw." She looks at me, and I eyeball her. She smiles.

"Why did you two break up? Was it because you moved here?"

"Partially," she says.

"You said you never looked for him?" Maggie asks, and I narrow my eyes.

"What are you doing?" I mouth. She ignores me.

"No. I haven't," Cynthia confirms.

"Would you be really mad if I told you I found him?"

Cynthia stops chewing.

"He lives in Florida," Maggie continues. Cynthia looks down as our server refills our drinks and lays down the check. Cynthia picks it up.

"I'm going to go pay and walk around for a bit." She slides out of the booth and walks to the glass counter.

I look over at Maggie and say, "You didn't."

"I did, and I'm not sorry for it. The girl is obviously missing something in life. She's helping us find our happy; we need to help her, too."

"First off, how is she helping you find your happy?" I ask. "You seem to be happy all by yourself, and second, there you go again, sticking your nose where it doesn't belong. I've said this before. We don't know what happened between the two of them."

"She's helping me more than you know," Maggie says. "And she said it was because she moved away."

"She said *partially*, Maggie. We don't know what the other part of the partially is."

"It can't be that bad. Charlotte, stop overreacting."

I shake my head. "Let's go, so we can get on the road. I'm sure we'll be getting the silent treatment." I pull my wallet out and put some money down on the table before I pull myself up out of the booth. Maggie slides out after putting money down, too, and we walk out to look for Cynthia.

Chapter Fifteen

After we walk around and Archie stretches his legs and pees on everything, we four get back in my car and head to Wayside, Georgia. Cynthia is quiet, just like I thought she'd be, and Maggie is feeling bad. Not about what she'd done, of course, but about the fact Cynthia is upset.

"Cynthia, I got you a pendant to go on your bag," Maggie says, and I hear her take it out of its paper wrapping. "It's a peacock." She sits up and shows her. I look over at the white peacock pendant as it shimmers in the afternoon sun.

"Thank you," Cynthia says, taking it from her. She pins it on her polka dot bag and then sits back in her seat, gazing out the window as we pass by farmland. I look in the rearview mirror, making eye contact with Maggie.

"Apologize," I mouth to her. She narrows her eyes, and then I see her shoulders slump.

"I'm sorry, Cynthia," she says a moment later. "I know I overstepped. I seem to be good at that lately," she mumbles.

I smirk.

"You just seem so sad sometimes, and I wanted to help. That's all."

I dart my eyes over at Cynthia when she doesn't respond. She's picking at the skin on the side of her thumbnail and in her own world it seems.

I turn right onto Highway 11, knowing this road will take me straight to Wayside. The small town I once played with stray kittens in and then Clinton, the place I first met the most gorgeous brown-haired boy I'd ever seen. I haven't been back in a long time, although I know that little green trailer Mama and I shared is long gone, but the memories will live on forever in my heart and mind.

"Where does he live in Florida?" Cynthia asks, pulling me from my thoughts. I look over at her and then dart my eyes to Maggie.

"St. Augustine. On a fishing boat."

"A fishing boat?" Cynthia questions. "How do you know all of this?"

"My husband used to be a detective. I called in some favors from some old friends of ours that used to work with him."

"Oh," Cynthia says. She shifts in her seat to look at Maggie. "What does he do now?"

"He was in the Marines, but it seems he isn't anymore. He runs a fishing business now."

"Really? Lit owns a fishing business." She bites her curious smile. "I can see the Marine part, his dad being in the Army and all." She shrugs. "Guess I can see the fishing part, too. He was always laid-back."

"We can go see him if you want," I chime in.

"No!" Cynthia blurts. "I wouldn't have any idea what to say to him." She turns around and faces the front again.

"I'm sure we can come up with something," Maggie says.

Cynthia shakes her head. "You don't get it, Maggie. I broke his heart. He called me for weeks after I left. I shut him out." She looks out her window and continues working on her thumb. We come into Wayside, and I pull over into the parking lot of a store I used to get candy from as a little girl. It's shut down now, nothing but old red brick and rusted gas pumps left for age to take over. I kill the engine and turn to Cynthia.

"Why did you shut him out?"

"Because…" she says. "He…I…" She takes a breath and looks out the window. "It was too hard. The pain. It was just a text message," she says meekly, sadly.

I look back at Maggie with a lifted brow.

"A text message?" Maggie asks. "Did you break up with him through a text?"

"I was driving. I…" She stares out the window as if what she's saying is playing in front of her eyes. "He sent me a text telling me he missed me, and I looked down. I killed them." Her voice cracks, and I see the shake in her shoulders, realizing she's crying.

"Cynthia." I put my hand on her leg.

"I killed them," she repeats. "I killed them." She brings her hands to her face. Her whole body shudders as she repeats those awful words. I get out of the car, and I hear Maggie do the same. I open Cynthia's door when I make it around.

"It's okay," I tell her as I pull her to me. She gets out and clings to me.

"They're dead because of me," she cries. "My whole life."

I rock her in my arms and look at Maggie with concern on my face. My best friend's brows draw together, matching mine, I'm sure. This poor child. What has she been through?

"Come on," I tell Cynthia. "Let's go sit over here." I move us toward the store, and we bend down and take a seat under the store awning. Maggie unzips her fanny pack and pulls out some tissue.

"Here," she says. "Dry those tears and explain to me this nonsense about you killing someone."

Cynthia sniffs, and her glossy eyes look ahead. Mascara runs down her baby-faced cheeks, and she pulls her dress down over her knees as she hugs them.

"It was the best and worst time of my life," she says. "How can you feel two different emotions when thinking back on a memory?"

I think about Travis and how often I've thought about our time together when we were older with both a smile on my lips and painful tears in my eyes.

"I was driving, and my phone dinged. I looked down," Cynthia says. "The boy I loved sent me a text and I looked down for one second, and in that one second my whole life changed.

The sound of metal and glass. I'll never be able to get it out of my mind." She rubs her fingers over the scar on her neck, and everything falls into place. My eyes widen and shoot to Maggie's. That scar, the reason she and Lit broke up, her parents and why she shuts out emotions when talking about them. They were in a car accident and this girl blames herself, and I think somewhere deep down, she blames him, too.

"Okay, it is that bad," Maggie says to me.

"Cynthia, you know it wasn't your fault or his. It was an accident," I tell her.

"An accident," Cynthia repeats. "An accident is something that happens by mistake. Me looking down was not a mistake. I did that. I chose to look down."

I sigh and realize she has set this in her mind for so long she believes it.

"Sometimes things happen, and we don't understand it. You can get mad, cry, scream to the top of your lungs even, but it doesn't change the fact it happened. I've spent nearly the last eleven years doing that exact thing, and then you came into my life."

She looks over at me with tear-filled eyes.

"Be a pelican, Cynthia." I grab her hand and give it a squeeze. "Don't let the things you can't control, control you. Don't stop living like I did."

Cynthia looks down at the old gravel parking lot. "I don't know how to do that," she says.

After we leave Wayside, we drive on through the city of Gray, Georgia. It's a quaint town with small shops and a railroad track running through it. The timeworn train station is still there, but it's now a feed and seed store. I turn right onto Gray Highway, and we make our way to Clinton, passing by the enormous reddish pink courthouse that has been standing since the early 1900s.

Gray is a stretch of highway with a few fast-food restaurants scattered on both sides and two grocery stores. Enough convenience stores for people to choose their go-to items and a Fred's. At one time, they thought they were going to get a Walmart, but that never took off.

I put my blinker on and turn right past the Old Clinton gas station onto Old Clinton Road. I point toward the small piece of land up on the hill that mine and Mama's trailer used to sit on. There's a beautiful home built there now, no sign that our trailer was ever there. I park in the small park area, and we all get out, Archie finding a spot to pee immediately.

Cynthia wanted to stop talking about her past earlier, so we got back in the car and made our way here. She mindlessly looks around at the place, which isn't much to look at really. Just a bunch of old homes built back before the Civil War and a few fields spread out. She walks up to the history marker and squints her eyes as she tries to read the history of Clinton, and

Maggie takes a seat at the picnic table. She inhales a deep breath and unzips her fanny pack while I walk to the edge of the road. My eyes roam down the street at the unincorporated community I spent a few of my teenage years in. It's insignificant to most, but the memories bring a tear to my eye as a feeling of sweet nostalgia passes over me.

There's an age-old, burned red barn a little ways down the road and houses from the 1800s with white picket fences that still stand. I smell a familiar scent and look back at Maggie seeing she's lit up a joint. I shake my head at that crazy woman, and my mind wonders.

I think back on longish brown hair, that crooked smile, and the way my heart pounded when he looked at me. The first time I met him I was in nothing but baby doll pajamas, so young with my whole life ahead of me. If I'd known then what I know now…. Well, I'm not sure how my life would be. Maybe I could have gotten him help sooner before it went too far. Maybe I'd never have gotten back together with him. Maybe I'd be standing in this same exact spot thinking these same exact things. I've loved him nearly my whole life, and everything has changed but that. Time changes a lot. It makes the green leaves turn yellow, the warm air turn colder. It makes laugh lines deepen and wrinkles appear where smooth skin once was, but sometimes not even time can change the feelings of the heart.

I gaze ahead at the long stretch of road before me. It's late in the evening now, and after our tour of Clinton, we four have driven on to Macon, grabbed some snacks, and jumped on the interstate south bound. Maggie drives, and Cynthia sits in the back seat with her newish baby blue vintage looking typewriter. The sound of the keys echoes through the car as she types away. The one her Aunt Marty bought her stopped working, so she got a travel-friendly lighter one. Maggie yawns, Archie sleeps on her lap, and I look out the window as The Rolling Stones croon sweet lyrics about a woman named Angie, and it takes me back to sitting in a car with tears running down my face.

Early October 1973

We sit in my car with the sun beaming through the windows, shining on his brown hair and showing me strands of natural golden highlights.

"I don't want you to go," I say to him as I rest my head back against the seat. They didn't want us to drive alone, afraid we may take off, but Travis put his foot down. He told them if we were going to run away, we would have never come to Indiana, and so Beverly gave in. I'm glad because I wanted alone time with him before he left me. I bring my thumbnail to my lips and chew anxiously.

"You'll be back in Florida before we know it." He reaches over and takes my hand away from my mouth, linking our fingers together and rubbing his thumb across the skin on my thumb. "And I'll be working, and we'll be saving up for our own place. Your mama is going to let us be together now. There's nothing to be sad about."

"I hope you're right," I say, turning my attention to the front windshield. A slow, small smile spreads across my lips when I see snow flurries begin to fall.

"It's snowing," he says. I look over at him as he peers out the window, and I move closer, hooking my arm with his, resting my head on his shoulder, breathing in his scent—Marlboro Lights and cologne mixed. I feel him kiss the top of my head, and I move back so his face is closer to mine. He kisses me, taking my breath away. I hold onto him because I have an uneasy feeling about all of this.

Once the bus drives up, I unwillingly let go and watch him get out of the car into the bitter cold. He turns back to me, showing me his dimples and that beautiful crooked smile. I crack the window, feeling the icy wind hit my face.

"I love you," I say.

"I know," he replies with a wink. I inhale a deep breath and watch him step onto the bus. I don't leave until it is out of sight, and then I drive back to Beverly's house.

The snow is coming down thicker now, and once I reach her house, I get out and lean back against the car. Looking up to the sky, I shove my hands into my coat pockets. Pieces of white icy flakes fall into my eyelashes and I close my eyes, imagining his handsome face and telling myself it is all going to be okay.

We pull up to a hotel around dinnertime, and after we check in, we scan the area for some quick, simple supper. Spotting a diner a little ways from our hotel, we leave Archie with the windows cracked and head inside. The evening sun sinks in the sky, and once our stomachs are full, we go back to the hotel room. There, Cynthia pulls out her notebook and pen, ready for more of my story.

"Once Travis left, I was so desperate to get back to Florida, I could hardly stand it," I tell them as Cynthia sits cross-legged on the sofa bed and Maggie lies on the bed beside mine with Archie curled up near her. "The car ride was long, and the whole way I couldn't stop thinking about seeing him again." I look down at the comforter at the end of the bed and think back on when we pulled up to our house on the hill. With a deep sigh, I tell the second half of our story.

Chapter Sixteen

October 1973

I jump out of my car, not even looking back at Beverly, who's pulled up behind me in her own vehicle. I still think it was dumb she followed me here. I mean, this is where Travis is. Why wouldn't I come back?

Running up the steps, I smile when I hear the windows begin to rattle from the train coming down the tracks. I've missed this place, and now that we can be together, it's like heaven on earth. Opening the door, I'm hit in the face with the sight of the living room. My eyes scan over the boxes stacked up in the middle of the floor and the now blank walls that once had photos on them. I take a step into the room, my feet echoing throughout the almost empty house.

"Mama," I call out cautiously. I keep walking, making my way down the hall and seeing that the bedrooms are also empty. My heart plummets to the pit of my stomach as realization dawns on me. *I knew it. I knew this was too good to be true.* I shut my eyes when I hear her voice coming from the living room.

"Charlotte," she says. I clinch my fists as I walk out of my vacant bedroom and into the hall, seeing her standing there by the door, alone. She smiles at the sight of me, but her happiness quickly fades when she sees the tears running down my face.

Anger boils inside of me as my hands start to shake and my pulse quickens furiously against my neck. At this moment, I hate her more than I've ever hated anyone.

"Charlotte, this is what needs to be—"

"I hate you!" I yell acidly, cutting her off.

She flinches, and her mouth slams shut. The wrinkles beside her eyes deepen as she narrows them, and I see the pain I've caused set in her expression.

"Be careful with your words. They can be forgiven, but they can never be forgotten." Her chest expands as she takes in a firm breath before straightening her shoulders. "Now dry those tears. We are leaving in the morning to head back to Georgia. We'll stay at your Aunt Evelyn's house tonight."

"You packed up all of our things and are making us move back to Georgia because of him?" I ask bitterly.

"Charlotte, you ran away with the boy." Frustration lines her tone.

"Because you won't let us be together!" I yell, clearly shocking her. "You can't control my life forever, Mama. I love him!"

"You're too young to—"

"Oh, *too young*!" I interrupt her and look up at the ceiling in defeat. "I'm so sick of hearing those words. You know what I think?" I say, looking back at her. "I think you're scared. You're so scared that I'm going to move away with him and never come back."

She doesn't say anything.

"Don't you know I can love you both? Don't you know that by keeping me away from him it only makes me want him more?"

I walk toward her and head for the door.

"Where are you going?"

I look over before I pass her. "I'm going to find him," I say impertinently.

She grabs ahold of my arm. "Don't be out too late." I look at her with a fury I've never felt before, and without responding, I yank my arm away from her hold and walk out the door, wishing we had turned left.

We sit in the back of my car with the music playing low on the radio. I cry as he holds me, telling me over and over that it's going to be okay. We will find a way, but I'm not sure anymore.

"We'll be so far apart, Travis."

"I'll move up there, baby. If you can't be here, then I'll move there."

I look up at him. "You will?" I ask.

"Of course, I will. I love you. I'll do anything for you." My heart feels like a heavy weight in my chest, and the pain of not being able to see him every day slices me in two. Why can't they leave us alone? He leans down and kisses my tear-stained lips, and I savor every touch after and every feeling he gives me because I know it'll be a while before we see each other again.

———

"Holy shit, your mom really did that?" Cynthia asks with a look of shock on her pretty face.

"She did," I say sadly. "There was never a time I was madder at her than I was at that moment."

"What happened next?" Cynthia asks, shifting on her bed.

"Yes," Maggie says. "Tell us more."

———

October 1973

A week passes by without seeing Travis. I get a job at the Bantam Chef up the road from our house, which serves hamburgers and hot dogs, so I spend my time there. To say I'm miserable without him would be an understatement. I'm downright depressed, and Mama notices it. How could she not?

The day that boy pulls up in his GTO she doesn't even tell him to leave, although she doesn't let him in either. I, on the other hand, run out of that house like a bat out of hell.

In worn jeans and a button-up jean shirt, he looks like perfection to me. I jump into his arms and kiss his lips, not even caring if Mama is watching. It's only been a week, and I miss his lips like the moon misses the night.

"Come on," he says to me. "Let's go."

"Mama, I need to grab something from the store. Travis is going to take me," I call back to the house.

She walks out with a dishtowel in her hands, looking skeptical. "Hurry back."

I jump into his car and let him drive us somewhere so we can be alone. We climb in the back seat and rip each other's clothes off, frantically dying to be closer, desperately needing to feel each other. Young love is like a raging fire that can't be tamed. It's addictive and borderline obsessive. Satisfying in every way, yet never getting enough. I'm the flames, and he's the fuel keeping me burning. We are perfect.

"Mama, just let him come in. It's freezing out there," I beg her.

"That boy is not staying in my house. He can go back to Florida if he's cold." She walks into the living room, and before she takes her seat, she calls out, "There are some clean blankets in the closet."

She's unrelenting about Travis coming in so late at night. I open my window, and he climbs inside. We quietly get tangled up in each other's arms and stay like that until the sun starts coming up. Sadly, he later gets a job working nights, so the sneaking in through the window comes to an end quickly, but we figure out other ways to be together.

About a week later, the weather has turned painfully cold, and finally Mama says, “Let him in. He’ll die of pneumonia out there.”

She sits Travis down at the kitchen table with a piece of paper.

“These are the rules,” she tells him. “You break any of them, you’re out. Do you understand me?”

“Yes, ma’am,” Travis says. I hold my bottom lip between my teeth, peering over her shoulder at the paper she has on the table.

Rules:

1. Never go into Charlotte’s room.
2. You two will not be allowed in the house alone.
3. Never go into the bathroom if Charlotte is in there.
4. You will sleep in the back spare room.
5. You will pay rent.

And that’s that. I’m the happiest I’ve ever been. I have Travis Cole living in my house! He has his own entrance and bathroom in the spare bedroom, so it’s nice for him to have some space. He gets a job right away, so he comes home after work and spends time with me until I have to go to work, then he sleeps until I come home. I sneak into his dark room with him sleeping and sit cross-legged with my knees under the bed, so I'm as close to him without being in the bed and Mama freaking out.

"Travis," I say softly. He opens his eyes and always, always shows me that crooked smile.

"Hey," he says. I lean up and kiss him, and we talk until he has to get up and get dressed for work. Life is good. Well, until it isn't…

———

The cold winter wind hits my face as I walk out onto the small porch. Travis is talking with my sister, Natalie's, husband. His hands are shoved into his jean pockets, and there is a slump in his shoulders. We have just finished Thanksgiving dinner, and it's the first time he has really been around my whole family. I know he has to be uncomfortable, but he still has that laid-back look that only Travis Cole can pull off. I watch as they walk and talk until the bitter cold becomes too much and I go inside.

Later, we sneak out together and share the back seat of his car. It's cold out, but I've never been warmer wrapped up in his loving arms. I draw small circles on his chest and listen to the beat of his heart as he lies quietly. Something is off, but I don't mention it, afraid he might be thinking of going back home. I'm not stupid. I know Travis loves me, but I also know he's getting homesick. He gave up everything for me. Dropped it all without question and I love him more for it.

Weeks have passed, and my birthday comes and goes. I'm now eighteen, but still living with Mama. I can't leave her. She has no one else, and the thought of her being alone makes my heart ache. But Travis is getting more restless, and the day finally comes when he's had enough.

It's December, and Christmas is near. Travis has just woken up from his nap, and I got off work a little early. Mama is out, probably thinking I'm still at the Bantam Chef, because she would never leave us alone. I'm in an apron, preparing a cake for us all to eat later, when he comes walking in, barefoot, no shirt on, and sleepy hair. He's the definition of sexy, and just the sight of him makes me want to forget the cake and take him to bed, but I have to control my teenage hormones, not knowing when Mama will walk in.

"Hey," I say as I wipe my flour-covered hands on my apron.

"Baby, we need to talk," he says as he pulls a chair out from the kitchen table.

"Okay." I sit down, too, and he runs a hand through his hair. His eyes narrow, and he searches my face. Concern bubbles up inside of me like a festering wound.

"Back at Thanksgiving, your brother-in-law asked me what my intentions were with you."

"Really?" I ask, scrunching up my face in embarrassment. *Why would he do that?* I run my fingers over my lips, looking down at the table.

"I want us to have a life together…" He pauses too long after he says those words, and I want to scream because I know there's more.

"But what?" I question.

"But…I'm just not sure right now," he says. "Your family will never accept me, and I've tried everything to show them my feelings for you are real." He runs a hand over the stubble on his face and leans up, resting his elbows on the table. "I miss my family, and I know you're never going to leave your mama. I just…I think I'm going to go back home and figure things out."

I stare, dumbfounded, as my heart shatters. Tears immediately spring to my eyes, and I turn my head, glancing down to the floor. My knee starts to bounce as my nerves flare up, and I grab ahold of it, trying to make it stop. The back door opens, and Mama walks in.

"Charlotte, why are you crying?"

I quickly slide my chair back and run to my room.

"Charlotte," Travis calls after me, but I can't think right now, much less talk. Travis is leaving me, and there's really nothing I can do about it.

"Nothing you could do about it?" Maggie says. "You could have left your mama's and moved in with the boy."

"Now, Maggie, you know, just like I do, these were different times. Besides, I was scared and so young."

"But you were eighteen," Cynthia says. "It was clear he wanted you to decide something."

"And do you two think I don't regret not leaving? I think about it every day. What would my life be like if I would have turned left? What would it be like if I would have gotten some courage and taken a chance with Travis? But I'm too old for regrets. I made my choices, and they are choices I have to live with every day." I get up off the bed and make my way to the door.

"Where are you going this time of night?" Maggie asks.

"I need to be alone," I reply as I grab the hotel key and car keys from the dresser. I open the door and walk out onto the sidewalk, breathing in the warm night air. Tears well up inside my eyes, and I let them fall as I open the car door and sit inside.

I grip onto the steering wheel until my fingers ache, and I cry. I cry for missed moments and stolen time. For every stupid choice I made that led me here—alone and brokenhearted.

I cry because life isn't fair, and sometimes I fucking hate it. I sob until my ribs ache and I'm too tired to do anything else. I let myself fall completely apart, and then Mama's words come into my mind. *"Things could always be worse, Charlotte. Count your blessings."*

I sniff and lean back in the seat. Taking in a shaky breath, I look ahead. Things could be worse, and I have many blessings in my life, but sometimes it's hard to care about the good. Sometimes you only want to think about the bad and let yourself sulk, and right now that's exactly what I want to do.

Chapter Seventeen

I shield my eyes from the bright sun and pull my sun visor down. That familiar sound of a beer popping open turns my attention to the driver's seat, and Travis smiles.

"It's beer thirty, baby."

I laugh as he drives us home. Home. He'll be living with me now. William, Elizabeth, and me. I look down at my current Janet book and can't help the smile that spreads across my lips. I turn my head slightly to look at him again.

He rests his hand on the bottom of the wheel like he used to when we were seventeen riding in his GTO. Relaxed and calm as always on the outside, but he's expressed his feelings about meeting my son, so I know he's nervous. He knows if William doesn't like him this can't work, but I know my son will love him, so I'm not worried.

He turns the volume up on the radio and starts singing along to an Allman Brothers' song. His raspy voice croons away, until he starts coughing.

"Damn cough won't go away," he says after catching his breath. He rubs his throat and sets the beer down in the cup holder.

"I guess my niece gave me her strep throat," he says, pulling out his smokes from his front pocket, and I think some things never change.

"I love you, baby," I say to him as he lights his nicotine.

"I know." He smiles that crooked smile my heart has missed for over thirty years, and it flutters fiercely. It's been in a deep sleep, my heart. Waiting patiently for the day it could wake up, and because of him, it finally has. My attention turns to the radio as it starts making a weird, loud vibrating noise. Bzzzzzzz. Bzzzzzz. Bzzzzzzz.

My eyes fly open at the sound, and I see Maggie's phone vibrating like crazy against the wood of the table. I exhale and look at the time. It's early, and the sun is barely peeking its way between the thick curtains. Maggie reaches over and shuts the thing off, and I turn on my back and stare at the ceiling. Flashes of my life play in my mind, and after last night's meltdown, I've come to a conclusion.

I've played it safe nearly my whole life, and look where it's gotten me. Sure, I have a good life, but I've never taken any real chances. I didn't turn left at that stop sign. I drove to Indiana and then came back to Florida, only for Mama to move us back to Georgia. I didn't ask Travis to stay. I didn't tell him I'd move out and we could start a life together. So many things, and time has flown by.

I sit up and look over at Maggie.

"You okay?" she asks.

"I wanna dye my hair," I reply. I look when Cynthia sits up, her purple locks in a tangled cute mess.

"I'm down with that."

I smile and throw off my covers. "That'll be my thing I've never done."

"You've never dyed your hair?" Maggie asks.

"Not purple." I smile.

"Purple?" Maggie says in disbelief.

"Yep. My favorite color."

"We'll be twins!" Cynthia squeals, getting out of bed and stretching. "I'll write down what we need, and we'll get them when we get to Florida."

"Sounds good to me," I say, walking into the bathroom. I shut the door behind me and walk over to the sink. Resting my hands on the counter, I look in the mirror and smile. "Charlotte Harris, you are finally back."

"Sorry I wasn't in town, Mom," William says to me as we ride down the interstate headed to Florida.

"That's okay. I know you and Elizabeth stay busy. Maybe I can swing by on the way back?"

"That sounds good. We'll go out to eat."

"Okay. I love you, son. I'll call when we get to our hotel later on."

"Love you. Drive safe."

I hang up the phone and put it on the charger. Cynthia has her hot pink toes hanging out the window, and Maggie chews on a piece of licorice as she reads my Janet book.

"You didn't tell me this shit was funny," Maggie says, looking up at me. She shuts the book.

"Why are you stopping then?" I ask.

"I'm getting carsick, and I want to hear more of your story."

"Yes!" Cynthia agrees. "So, Travis told you he was going back home?"

I exhale and rub my thumbs over the steering wheel. "Yeah, and he did."

December 1973

We sit at the bus station because the GTO died. It was going to cost too much to fix it, and Travis hadn't had a chance to get another vehicle yet. I stare ahead with blurry tear-filled eyes.

"I can't help but wonder if this is it for us," I say.

"It's not, baby. I'm going to come back and visit. I just need to be with my family right now."

"I thought I was your family," I say, looking over at him. I feel it when the tears tumble down my cheeks.

He grabs my hand in his. "You're everything," he says. "This has nothing to do with you. I just need this. I love you." I look down, but he puts his hand under my chin. "I love you, Charlotte." He stares into my soul like only he can, but this time it crushes me.

"My heart's breaking."

"I'll fix it," he says, pulling me to him and pressing his lips to mine. Our kiss is mixed with salty heartbreak and raw love, sad goodbyes and promises of *I'll be back.* We hold each other until the bus comes, and then I watch him leave me, yet again.

The next few weeks are a blur. I'm as far down as I can be, and nothing makes sense anymore. We had it all figured out. We had everything planned—the white fence and front porch swing. Now my future seems to be blank, and I don't know what to do with myself. I go to work at the Bantam Chef, and I come home. Sadly, I can't even talk to him because it's long distance. I'm devastated. I'm a wreck. I'm hopelessly heartbroken.

I'm cleaning up at work when my friend and co-worker Sam comes walking from the back.

"You gonna come out with me tonight?" she asks like she does every weekend, but I still don't feel up to it.

"Maybe next weekend," I reply.

"Girl, you've got to get over this. You're young, and that doesn't last forever."

"I know. I just miss him."

"He isn't gone, gone, silly. And I'm sure he isn't sitting at home every night."

"What do you mean?" I ask her.

Sam rolls her eyes. "I just mean, I bet he's going out with his friends like you should be." She lifts her purse from under the counter. "I'll see you tomorrow," she says, walking toward the door. "Call me if you change your mind."

"I didn't change my mind that night. But two weekends later, I did. I danced and had a little too much to drink and, believe it or not, I actually had a good time, but nothing compared to the weekend after, because guess who came back?"

Cynthia grins.

"Go on," Maggie says excitedly from the back seat.

I smile and dart my eyes to the rearview mirror. Looking back at the road, I say, "He got a hotel room in Gray, and I lied to Mama and told her I was staying at Sam's."

January 1974

"Fuck, I missed you." He hoists me up onto the dresser and pulls my legs around him. My ankles link behind his back, and I kiss him. Gripping his hair, I pull him closer to me, never getting enough. He reaches down and undoes his belt and pants. I lift up and quickly slide my jeans and panties down my legs, stepping out of them just before he lifts me back up again. The lamp on the dresser shakes and crashes to the floor, leaving tiny cracks of sunshine shining through the closed curtains, our only light.

He places his hand onto the side of my face and completely takes over my lips, mind, body, and soul. His other reaches between my thighs, and my eyes close while my mouth goes slack against his as he sinks.

We're frantic breaths of air, swollen lips, making up for missed kisses, sweet sighs, and falling into a space where we only exist. I brace myself on the dresser top as he pushes forward, pressing me into the wall. Pleasure and sadness fight each other inside of me because I know this won't last forever and he'll be leaving me once again, but he forces those thoughts away as he bites my bottom lip and takes me to a place where we're not too young, my family doesn't hate him, and happily ever after is all there is for us.

We laugh and talk about everything until the winter sun goes down, and then we get wrapped up in each other's arms again.

Travis ventures out for some beer, and we drink as we pass a joint back and forth.

"Life going okay for you here?" he asks me as he tokes on the weed.

"I miss you," I reply, picking at the label on my beer.

"Yeah," he says in sad agreement. "I miss you, too, girl."

The weekend passes, and Travis leaves me. Days and nights intertwine and pass with hardly any words spoken between us. I work, go out a few times, and sit in my room listening to records while I lie on my bedroom floor dreaming of a day we can be together again.

April 1974

Spring gives us rain and pretty flowers, and I'm closing up the Bantam Chef when I hear a horn blow. I look out the window, and my heart skips a beat when I see a brown-haired boy getting out. I run to the door and around the building, my pulse quickening when he shows his dimples and that gorgeous crooked smile. I squeal and jump into his arms. He holds me by my bottom while I take possession of his kissable lips.

He pulls away and touches his forehead to mine. "Let's go," he says as I slide down his body.

We take a long drive through the countryside, listening to music and holding hands. He pulls down a dirt road, and I laugh when he turns and drives through an enormous field. He stops and smiles over at me. "This will do," he says, shutting the car off and getting out. I open my door as he pops the trunk, and I see he has our beach blanket. It makes me miss the waves and reminds me of how much life has changed. How far away all of that seems now.

We lie in the field until the stars come out, and we kiss until our lips ache.

"One day it won't be like this," he says in a low voice.

"One day," I reply.

The next day, I'm sitting at the counter at work while Travis strums his guitar out in front. He sits in a chair and cuts up with a few friends he made when he was staying here. They're day drinking, secretly sipping on whiskey from glass Coke bottles they half-emptied and refilled with the nasty stuff. Travis puts down his guitar, and I watch as he walks up to the counter.

"Hey, girl," he says all cool and easy-going.

"Hey, boy," I reply just as casual.

"You wanna get out of here?"

I look at the clock on the wall and see I have twenty more minutes before my shift ends.

"Go on," Sam says. I grin.

"Thanks!" I hit the time clock and exit the building. He stands at his car waiting on me.

"Y'all leaving?" one of the guys asks.

"Yeah, man. Me and my girl need a little alone time." He winks at me and says, "You drive." He tosses me the keys. I fumble them.

"Me?" I ask, surprised.

"Yeah."

I shrug. "All right."

We head down Gray Highway with the music blasting and me behind the wheel. I can feel the power of the car as it vibrates my seat and Travis says, "Hit the gas!" I press the clutch and shift it into fourth gear. We haul ass and Travis leans out the window, yelling and throwing his hand up. I laugh, never feeling such a rush of freedom and excitement. Travis is my wild side, my bad boy, and everything I love in this life.

———

September 1974

With each day, week, and month that passes without me seeing Travis, I'm reminded that life goes on, and that the greatest love story I have ever known might be just that…something that I once knew. I've been going out a lot lately with some of my friends and, believe it or not, I've gone on a date because I can't keep doing this. I've come to the conclusion that sometimes you just have to let go.

———

November 1974

I turn nineteen today, and to celebrate Mama bakes me a cake and we have some family over. I'm walking out of the bathroom when I hear my brother Billy talking with Mama.

"You've got to let her do her own thing, Mama."

I step back so they can't see me and listen to their conversation.

"I don't like her going out like she does."

"But she's not a kid anymore, and if you don't let her, she's just going to do it behind your back," he replies. I could kiss the ground he walks on. Mama is still keeping a tight hold on me, and I'm sick of it. I have been going out behind her back and seeing Travis the few times he's come up here. I hear her sigh, so I walk back down the hall to my room, but then the telephone rings. I nearly twist my ankle running to grab it off the hook.

"Hello," I say as Mama starts walking my way.

"Hey, birthday girl."

My whole body lights up, and I swallow, worried Mama can tell who it is before she even asks.

"It's Shawn Phillips," I tell her. This time her face lights up, because Shawn Phillips is a Phillips, and the Phillips are very wealthy in our small town. She pats my arm and walks on by.

"Who the hell is Shawn Phillips?" Travis says on the other end.

"No one important," I reply. "How are you?"

"Good. I'm trying to get back up there soon."

"It's been so long," I say, stretching the cord as far as it will go so I can talk in the laundry room. I climb on top of the washer and cross my legs.

"I know. Tell me how life is," he says.

"It sucks without you."

"I feel the same."

We talk for a good hour before we reluctantly let each other go. I don't hear from him again until the new year, and after that, nothing.

March 1975

I've had a few drinks on a date I really don't care about as the band plays.

"Wait a minute. You were in a bar drinking? You weren't old enough," Cynthia says.

"But remember this was back in the seventies." I smile. "If you were eighteen, you could drink."

"Ah. Okay. Go on."

March 1975

My friend Sam is swaying to the music, and I turn to my date.

"I'm going to run to the bathroom." He nods, and I get off the tall stool and make my way to the back hall, walking by the cutest boy. My mouth speaks before my brain thinks, and I find myself saying, "Whoa."

He grins at me.

I open the bathroom door and walk in before I can do anything else stupid.

After I wash my hands and check my makeup, I walk back out and immediately see the guy standing against the wall.

"Hey," he says, giving me that same cute smile.

"Hey," I reply, moving out of the way so someone can go into the bathroom.

"You here with anybody?"

"Kinda on a date actually," I say.

He nods and brings his drink to his lips. My eyes follow, and I catch myself smiling because, damn, this guy is cute.

"Is it not going well?" he asks.

I shrug.

"Wanna dance?"

"Why not?"

He pushes off the wall. "John," he says as we walk to the dance floor.

"Charlotte," I counter.

"Nice to meet you, Charlotte."

"Likewise," I say.

"You met someone else?" Maggie asks. "While you were on a date?"

"I did." I laugh. "And he was a cutie," I reply as we take a seat at the bar.

"My date was boring, and I don't think he really cared anyway, so I danced with John and had a good time."

"I just can't believe Charlotte Harris did something like that," Cynthia says.

"I had my moments."

The bartender walks up to us. "What'll you have?"

"I'll take a margarita, this one will have a piña colada, and lavender girl will have a Miller Light," Maggie says, handing the guy her debit card.

He grins. "Coming right up."

We've made it to St. Augustine and grabbed a hotel room downtown, and then walked over to one of the local bars.

I look over at Cynthia. "Have you decided if you're going to see Lit or not?" I ask.

She shrugs.

"This will be your thing," Maggie says.

"What thing?" Cynthia replies.

"The thing you have to do that you've never done."

"What? See Lit? I've seen him before, and I've already done my thing, remember? The fried green tomatoes?"

"I don't think that should count," Maggie says. "It wasn't that big of a thing. You need to take a risk."

"Maggie." Cynthia sighs. "I really don't want to."

"How about this?" I say. "We call up Maggie's friend who told us where Lit is. We can find out exactly where the boat is, and we can just go there and see. We don't have to talk to him or let him know we are even there."

"What do you think about that?" Maggie asks.

Cynthia looks down at the bar, and I see her chest fall. "I guess we could do that."

"Great!" Maggie says.

"So, what's going to be your thing?" Cynthia asks Maggie.

I look over at my friend as she focuses her eyes on the wall of license plates, her expression turning sober, and then she says, "I'm going to meet my granddaughter."

Chapter Eighteen

I look over at Cynthia as she looks at me. "Your granddaughter?" I ask Maggie.

"Yes. I've never met her. My daughter and I didn't have a good relationship when she was growing up. That was her and her father," Maggie says solemnly. "We got into a huge argument after he passed away…" She rubs her fingers over her lips. "God, it was so long ago and over something so stupid," she says as if she's remembering it. "She moved away after that, and a few years later sent me a photo of her child. I was muleheaded and didn't respond, but I've kept that photo in my nightstand, and meeting you two… Well, you've made me think about things. Diane lives in New York, so after we get back, I'm going to fly up and see her. That is, if she'll have me."

"We'll go with you if you want," Cynthia says.

"I think I'd like that," Maggie replies. "We could do another road trip!"

"No scooter!" I quickly say before Cynthia throws it in. She laughs as the bartender sets our drinks down and asks Maggie if she wants to start a tab.

"Yes," she says, not asking us.

"That's settled," I say. "We're all going to take a risk."

"To taking risks," Cynthia says, putting her beer in the air.

We clink our glasses together, and in unison, we say, "To taking risks." And it's at this moment I realize what Maggie meant when she said Cynthia was helping her find her happy also. It seems like we were meant to find each other. Sometimes the big man upstairs really makes you question things, but this time, it seems like He really knows what He's doing.

My girls are tipsy. I'm on my second drink, but it's watered down, so I'm pretty sure I won't be finishing it.

"Tell me who this new guy is," Cynthia says, resting her palm against her face.

"Well, John took me by surprise," I tell them. "I never thought I'd love anyone besides Travis, but I've learned in this life you can love more than one person, just in two different ways. I saw him the weekend after we met, but then I got a surprise visit from none other than Travis Cole."

March 1975

Spring flowers cover the fields as we ride together down old back roads. Lavender and pink as far as the eye can see. I'm with my guy, and he's holding my hand like I may disappear if he lets go.

"You ever think about how it would be if we would have turned left the day we ran away?" he asks, looking over at me. The wind coming through the windows blows my hair across my face, and I tuck it behind my ear.

"All the time," I respond.

"We could have gotten jobs and a little apartment somewhere. Had a blast until we got older and then have those babies you talked about."

My lips lift, but the feeling in my chest doesn't match and I turn my attention back to the road ahead of us. "That sounds nice," I say, feeling melancholic.

"At least we have now," he says.

"Yeah," I agree. "At least we have now." He brings my hand to his lips and kisses my knuckles.

We drive on with the breeze passing through the car, talking about everything and anything, catching up on life, but I leave out the fact I've met John because honestly no one else matters when I'm with Travis. Once the sun starts to sink, we get restless, needing to feel each other skin to skin. We grab a room and get lost. The world floats away as Travis climbs on top of me. I undo my jeans and reach down to remove his belt. He kisses my lips, then he pulls his pants down to his thighs. My fingers run through his hair, and I force his jeans down with my feet. We melt, becoming one like we have many times before.

His lips taste like beer and smoke, but I don't care, and at the moment, beer and smoke are all I want as long as I'm with him.

We spend the night exploring every inch of each other. The only sounds in the room are whispers of *I love you* and *be my forever*. But when the sun comes up, he leaves me with a goodbye kiss and a sad smile.

"We didn't speak for a while after that, and April came and went with me seeing John more and more. Falling for John was something I never intended on happening, but with his cute smile and his fun way of life it was inevitable, so when I was at work and Travis called with John sitting in the room with me, I didn't know what to do."

May 1975

"Who is that?" John asks me.

"It's Travis," I say, holding the phone away from my mouth. He gets a look that tells me he isn't happy because he knows all about Travis Cole.

"What's going on?" Travis asks.

"Umm, there's someone here with me," I reply to Travis.

"Is this someone a guy?" he asks.

"Yeah."

John stands up because he obviously isn't gonna deal with me being on the phone with the love of my life while he's sitting there. I don't blame him, but I can't let him go either.

"John," I say, stopping him. He turns to look at me.

"Charlotte, what the fuck is going on?" Travis says.

"Hold on a second." I put the phone down and walk over to John. "Just give me one minute, okay?"

"You're either going to be with me or be with him. You can't have it both ways, and if it's me, then you need to tell Travis you can't talk to him anymore."

"Okay," I say. "I will."

He sighs. "I'll be outside."

I exhale and look back at the phone. Picking it up, I hear Travis say, "Charlotte."

"Hey," I say.

He grows quiet for a moment, and then he says, "Are you two dating?"

"Kinda," I reply.

He doesn't respond, and I look out the window at John leaning against his car with his hands shoved into his front pockets.

"Is it serious?" he says.

"We've been seeing each other for a couple of months now."

"So it is then," he confirms. I bite my bottom lip and look down at the floor. "Do you not want me to call you anymore?" he asks. I look back out at John, and I feel my heart rip in two.

"Maybe not," I reply.

"No, baby, you ain't doing that. If you don't want me to call you anymore, then you gotta say it."

"Okay, don't call me anymore." *But I'll call you later.*

The line grows quiet, and the silence is deafening, but then Travis says, "Okay." I feel my brow furrow because I wasn't expecting that. "Tell him he better make you happy. Do you hear me?" he says. "That's all I ever wanted was for you to be happy." I cover my lips with my hand, and a tear rolls down my cheek.

"I love you," he says.

"I love you, too, Travis. I always will."

"Oh my God," Cynthia says after she takes a sip of her beer. "Did y'all talk later on that night?"

I shake my head and look in front of me. "No, Cynthia," I say. "We didn't speak again until thirty years later."

"Thirty years?" Maggie spits out her drink, and the bartender looks over at us. "Sorry," she tells him. "My friend just told me some bullshit."

Cynthia giggles.

"Sadly, Maggie, it's not bullshit."

"What happened next?" Cynthia asks.

"John and I fell madly in love," I reply.

January 1976

We sneak in the back room of Mama's house, and I laugh when a drunk John trips over the chair and falls to the floor.

"Shh!" I say.

"Shh yourself," he replies, pulling me down with him and kissing me senseless. He rolls over on top of me, and we do what we've been good at for almost a year now. He takes over my body and tells me he loves me. Our love is like the winds of a hurricane—fast, uncontrollable, and fierce.

I lift up and pull my shirt off while he leans back and undoes his jeans. We sink together, and after we're finished, he looks over at me from the hardwood floor and says, "I don't know how I ever lived without you."

I caress the side of his face and kiss his lips. "Well, now you don't have to." He puts his arms around me and pulls me close, pressing his lips against my forehead. "Let's get off this floor."

We climb onto the bed and pull the comforter over us. I rest my head on his chest and listen to the slow rhythm of his heart. My eyes go over to the neon green numbers on the clock sitting on the nightstand. It's almost two in the morning.

"Charlotte," John says to me.

"Mmm hmm."

"Did you have a good childhood?" he asks quietly. I feel my brow furrow at his question, and I find myself thinking back to old dirt roads and stray kittens. A small smile plays on my lips as I remember Mrs. Tilly who used to live down the road from us in Wayside. I loved that woman, and she loved me.

"I did," I murmur. "There was an old black woman named Tilly who lived down the road from us. She made my childhood special. I'd pick her blackberries, and she'd make me blackberry jam. It's still my favorite. I'd ride my bike to her house almost every day, and she'd say, 'I was wonderin' if you were comin'. I was just a thinkin' to myself *when's that little girl gone come ridin' up to my front porch?*'" I smile at the memory. John doesn't say anything, and I look up from his chest.

"What about you? How was your childhood?"

He moves a piece of hair behind my ear. His voice is rusty and thick like the words are caught in his throat as he says, "I didn't have an easy life growing up." For an extended moment, his eyes remain steady and unblinking as if his mind goes somewhere I've never been.

John's expression holds a mixture of old emotions that he seems to have never recovered from. His eyes grow shiny, and he blinks, seeming to really be looking at me now instead of thinking about faraway painful memories. My heart breaks for the little boy he once was when he says, "My mama sexually abused me and hit me every time she felt like it."

I grow insanely still as anger boils up inside of me. How could a mother do that to her child?

"She was a horrible person and did countless repulsive shit." He looks down as his fingers begin to toy with the small chain around my neck. His body feels rigid underneath me, and there's an uneasiness in his voice as if this is hard for him to talk about. I feel incredibly special that he is sharing this part of his life with me.

"Child Services got called several times, and eventually they took my brother and me and put us in a home." He inhales a deep breath. "We didn't stay there long. My grandmother got us out, and we went to live with her."

"That's good, right?" I ask soothingly as if I'm speaking to a small child.

He chuckles, and his voice turns harsh. "She only got us out because she needed us to work on her farm. Otherwise, she'd have left us in there."

"Oh," I reply. He looks past me, his mind presumably going somewhere else again, so I take his face in my hands and tell him, "John, that's behind you. This is your life now. Here. With me. Do you understand?"

His blue eyes turn back to mine, and I see heartbreak and things no one can undo, but he nods. I kiss his lips and rest my head back on his chest. "I love you, John. We are all that matters now." I feel him lean up and kiss the top of my hair, but neither of us falls asleep quickly.

"That is horrible," Maggie says.

"Yeah." I sigh and take a sip of my watered-down drink. The bartender wipes over the bar with a towel. I look around, noticing that the place is filling up and getting louder. "Our relationship continued to grow more," I say, turning back to my drink. "And a year later, I found myself standing in Mama's house with my family surrounding us as we promised to love each other for the rest of our lives."

"You married him," Maggie says.

"Yes, and we were married for twenty-nine years."

"Twenty-nine years?" Cynthia says. "Wow, what about Travis?"

"Like I said, the day I told him not to call me anymore, he didn't."

"You didn't try to call him?"

"I did a time or two, but I never got through to him."

"Tell us more about your marriage. I mean, twenty-nine years, what happened with y'all?" Cynthia asks.

I sigh. "Our marriage was not an easy one, and over time I saw how John's childhood affected his adult life. We had some good times and we had some bad times, and then we had some really, really bad times. But through it all, I loved him, and I wanted to make our marriage work. Sadly, John let drinking get the best of him for a while, and he got into some trouble with the law. Regardless, we knew we wanted children, but it took us years. I guess that's why I never got pregnant while sleeping with Travis. It wasn't as easy for me as it is for others. But once we finally did get pregnant and had our son William, John got sober and everything was great until William was about two or three. Then John got locked up for something stupid and left me at home alone with a baby.

"Those were some dark times. One night, I found myself sitting on the bed, and Travis' words came to mind. "*Tell him he better make you happy. That's all I ever wanted.*" At that moment, I was far from happy. I was scared, alone, and wondering how I was going to keep the lights on, so I called my cousin Laura, which was Jennie's sister, who just so happened to be married to Travis' brother."

"Damn, it's a small world," Maggie says.

"That it is," I agree. "I called her and got Travis' phone number. She only had their parents' number so I called them. His stepdad answered, and as soon as I asked if Travis was around, he said no and hung up. And that was that."

"Nothing else after that?" Cynthia asks.

"Nope. Not for a long time." A guy moves in between Cynthia and me, trying to get a drink. He looks over at her and grins.

"Can I get you another one of those?"

"Sure," she says. I peek over at Maggie, who has a big cheesy smile on her face. I laugh inwardly and take the last sip of my second piña colada, thinking about times long ago when a guy would buy me a drink.

The evening flies by, and Cynthia is pretty drunk. I've never seen the girl like this, and I'm not sure if it's because she's near Lit and she's anxious or she just wants to have fun. Either way, it's entertaining to Maggie and me. But of course, Maggie is drunk, too, so mainly it's entertaining to me. I did finish one more drink, though, so there's a slight buzz going on my way, too.

"I'm gonna do it!" Cynthia says.

"I've got it right here," Maggie chimes in, squinting her eyes at her cell phone.

"Got what?" I ask. "Put your glasses on," I tell her, lifting them up from her neck. She slides them on, and I laugh because they're crooked.

"The number," she says.

"What number?" I ask.

"Lit's. Woman, where have you been?" Maggie says, swaying in her seat.

"I was in the bathroom, remember? You're going to fall off that thing in a minute."

"Oh, quit your whining," she says, dismissing me with her hand.

"I'm not whining. You asked me a question, dummy."

"Name calling is not nice," Cynthia slurs.

"Give me that phone," she says, trying to grab it from Maggie.

"Wait," I say. "You're going to call him?"

"Yep, because there are some words we need to say."

"What words are you going to say?"

She looks up as if she's waiting for a light bulb to come on in that brain of hers. "I'll figure that out when they come to me." She successfully grabs the phone from Maggie this time and closes one eye. I laugh and so does Maggie.

"Cynthia, you are ten sheets to the wind. You sure about doing this?"

"Yep." She taps the screen with her index finger and puts it to her ear.

"It's ringing." She grins.

We're in the hallway near the bathroom, so it's not as loud. I hear a man's voice. Cynthia's eyes grow wide as her brows draw together. The girl's face turns as white as a sheet.

"Sorry. Wrong number!" She quickly hangs up and squeezes her eyes shut. "What the hell did I just do?"

Chapter Nineteen

The morning comes, and I jump up and grab breakfast for my two hungover girls. A large Coca-Cola for me, coffee for Cynthia with more cream and sugar than actual coffee, and a fruit smoothie for Maggie. A sausage biscuit for me, yogurt for Maggie, and a bacon, egg, and cheese biscuit for Cynthia. I also have headache meds in my purse, so maybe it'll help. I'm not sure what to do about the guilt Cynthia is feeling from drunk calling Lit, but maybe time can work that out.

After we eat and get dressed, Maggie calls her friend, and we find out that Lit is down by the Bridge of Lions, which is literally walking distance for the younger women. Me, not so much. There's my back to consider—and she says not today—so we find a parking spot, and Cynthia keeps her newspaper-framed sunglasses on. She's in a pair of leggings and a long shirt that reads *Coffee Before Talky*. Her purple hair is thrown up into a messy bun, and she skipped makeup altogether today. I'm not sure if she is trying to disguise herself or it's the hangover keeping her from giving a shit.

Archie pees on a post and sniffs around while we search for Lit's boat, which is named *The Cynthia Rose.* Yeah, that little bit of info has kept Cynthia from talking even after her coffee.

"There." Maggie points. I look to where she is pointing and, sure enough, there it sits, bobbing in the water.

We stand, not saying a word, as a young man sprays the deck. He's good-looking. That's easy to see. Tan, dark hair. I jump when I hear a dog bark, and then I see him running full blast right toward Archie.

"Gunner!" Lit shouts toward the dog. I look back at him and see him throw the water hose down. Gunner gets a real good sniff of Archie before Lit lets out a loud whistle. He then takes off back toward his owner, who is walking this way.

"Shit!" Cynthia says. "I've gotta get out of here!" She turns and heads straight back to the car.

"Sorry 'bout that," Lit says, making it over to us. "He loves other dogs."

"Oh, it's no problem. Archie doesn't mind," Maggie says with a sly smile. He smiles back and, whoa, I'm glad my brain thinks more now before it allows me to speak. I see his eyes shoot toward Cynthia's back and then he narrows them.

"Hope we didn't run her off," he says as he puts the leash on Gunner.

"Oh no, she and I tied one on last night, and she's feeling it today," Maggie says.

He nods. "Well, if you're ever interested in deep-sea fishing, give me a call." He slides his wallet out of the back pocket of his jeans and pulls a business card out. "Name's Lit," he says, reaching his hand out.

I shake it, and then Maggie does, too. "I'm Charlotte, and this is my friend Maggie."

"And the other one who's hungover?" He grins.

"Oh, that's Cyn," Maggie says, and I look at her with wide eyes. *What the fuck, Maggie?!*

"Cyn?" he asks.

"Yep," I reply quickly. "We'll keep you in mind if we ever wanna take that fishing trip. Take care."

He nods and rubs his chin. "Good to meet you," he says contemplatively. I yank on Maggie's arm, and we walk back to the car.

"What in the hell was that?" I ask her under my breath.

"I put my foot in my mouth again," she says.

We jump on A1A Beach Blvd, taking the scenic route toward Fort Pierce. We've been on the road for over two hours now, and I can't believe I'm going back. It's been a long time since I've seen the pretty white sand of my teenage years. The ocean stretches out for miles and miles to the left of me, and I take in the view of the crashing waves. I've driven this road several times, some with Travis, and I can almost feel the rumble beneath my seat from the roaring engine of his GTO. The feel of his fingers between mine, and I'd give anything to see that crooked smile and those dimples again.

Cynthia's arm stretching up causes me to look in the rearview.

"My whole arm is numb," she says with a groggy voice. "And I'm sure I drooled a river back here."

"Ewww," I say to her.

She kinda laughs and then yawns. "Car sleep is the best."

"We grabbed you a burger," I tell her. "And there are some water bottles in the cooler or a Coca-Cola."

"Thank God," she says.

"Do you feel better?" Maggie asks.

"Yes, I guess I just needed a nap. How much longer do we have?"

"About an hour or so, because we stopped to let Archie pee and grabbed some food." Maggie hands her the takeout bag, and I hear her pop the top on her drink.

"So, I kinda did a thing," Maggie says after a minute. I look over at her.

"I accidentally told Lit that your name is Cyn." She turns her head and looks back at Cynthia. I glance in the rearview.

"Well, I drunk called him, so it is what it is," she replies over the burger in her mouth. Maggie giggles, and I smirk. Cynthia swallows her food and then starts laughing.

"Good Lord, we are something, ain't we?" I say as I begin to laugh, too. Laughing is contagious, and finding good friends to do it with is a rarity in this life. I'm lucky that I've found these two…but I guess they really found me.

I stand outside of my car as we look up at the empty spot of land our house used to sit on. Holding onto the doorframe, my vision blurs from unshed tears as I remember the day Mama moved us away from here. I was so young and so in love, still, so in love.

I see a girl with hair as straight as the ironing board I used to iron it on—because that was the thing to do in the seventies—running out of the house with tears streaming down her face because she couldn't keep the pain inside. Mama lied to me, told me she would let us see each other just so she could get me home and move us back to Georgia. Till this day that still stings a little, but the joke was on her, because my Travis would have moved mountains to be with me. Sadly, in the end, he didn't have enough strength to hardly move a feather.

I exhale and blink, letting the tears flow and quickly patting my face dry so the girls won't see.

"I wish the house was still here," Cynthia says.

"Me, too," I say sadly. "So many memories inside that house."

"It's a nice spot to have one," Maggie says as Archie lies at her feet scratching his ear.

I still as a familiar rumbling sounds in the distance, and as the train grows nearer, I smile because it almost feels like I'm seventeen again, the house is still here, and Travis Cole is parked down the road waiting to take me on an adventure. God, how I wish that were true.

It's late in the evening now, and Cynthia sits out on the balcony of our hotel room with her typewriter while Maggie and Archie nap in the room. I stare ahead as the sun begins to set, causing the sky to turn beautiful shades of violet-blue and warm yellow. I bury my toes down into the thick white sand and rest my book on my lap.

My eyes look to the water, and a vision of Travis lifting me up and twirling me around plays in my head. Water drops from his strong jawline, and he gently places his hand on the side of my neck. His lips touch mine, and I remember the chills that spread across my young skin.

I sigh and close my eyes, breathing easy as I listen to the calmness of the waves.

The TV plays in the living room, and I hear sounds of laughter coming from William and Elizabeth. I love to hear them laugh, and I smile when I look over at Travis. His shirt is off, and he has his blue jean covered ankles crossed with bare feet resting on our bed. Our bed... For so long, it was a bed I slept in alone. Toward the end of our marriage, John slept in the living room and me in the bedroom…alone. But not anymore. Now I have Travis Cole beside me every night and, God, I wouldn't change this for the world.

I turn my body toward him and run my hand over the small amount of hair on his chest. He looks at me and gives me a small smile. I move closer, reaching up and pressing my lips to the side of his warm neck. My hands have a mind of their own as they venture south, and then I feel his grip onto mine.

"The kids are in the living room," he says.

"We'll be quiet," I reply as I continue spreading sweet kisses over his skin. This time he doesn't stop me, and as we slowly get tangled up in each other, I think, please, God, don't ever let this stop.

"Charlotte,"

"Hmm?"

"Wake up."

"Wake up? I am awake."

"Charlotte."

I hear Cynthia's voice and instantly grow confused. Why is she here?

"Charlotte, the tide is moving in. You're about to be swimming."

I blink my eyes open as a wave of water comes rushing toward my chair. "Shit," I say, grabbing my book and quickly but disastrously pushing myself up just before the wave takes over my chair. Cynthia scrambles to grab it. She laughs as her legs get soaked and I regain my balance.

“Thank God I came when I did,” she says, fighting with the water to pull the chair behind her. “You’d be out there with the fishes.”

I chuckle. “Man, I was having a good dream.”

“I could tell. You were smiling.”

“Well, it was a really good dream.”

She folds my chair up, and I notice the sun is all but gone now, leaving only the bright moonlight.

“I must have been out for a while,” I say.

“You’ve been down here for over an hour. Maggie and I are hungry. I’ve got everything typed up that we’ve talked about,” she says as we make our way to the hotel.

“That’s great. How’s it coming?”

“Good. I’ve narrowed it down a lot, but I’ve got to know more. How does this end? I mean, obviously, he isn’t with you anymore.”

“No, you’re right about that,” I reply.

“I’m worried something bad happened,” she says, looking down at the sand.

“How about we get down to it tonight?”

“Sounds good to me,” she says as I slowly follow behind her young self. I’ve got to walk more.

We sit out on the deck of the restaurant. A small candle rests on the table, its light reflecting off the outside walls of the Seafood Shack. Maggie enjoys crab legs while Cynthia has fried shrimp. I have chicken tenders because I'm not a seafood lover. Maggie cracks a leg, and some flies across the table. "Oops," she says, laughing. "I've never been that good at this."

"I don't see why you want to eat something you have to work to get," I say, tossing the piece of leg back over to her.

"They're absolutely delicious, Charlotte. Have you ever tried them?"

"No, and before you ask, the answer is no. I do not want to."

She huffs and rolls her eyes.

"You two are like an old married couple," Cynthia says, squirting lemon onto her shrimp.

"Sometimes it feels that way," I reply.

Maggie grins, and after a moment she says, "Changing the subject here, but what are you going to do about that boy, Cynthia?"

Cynthia sighs. "I don't know. I guess I need to talk to him. I just don't know what to say."

I look over at Maggie before I say, "Do you blame him for the accident?"

"No," she replies quickly. "I blame myself."

"But you know you shouldn't, right?" Maggie says.

Cynthia looks down. "Yes. I've just done it for so long, that it's all I know."

"What happened that day was no one's fault. It was a freak accident. Things like that happen every day, and there's nothing any of us can do about it. You need to focus on that, and if you don't blame him, and it's clear you still have feelings for him and him you, you need to call him. He's probably still hurting, too."

"Is that why you don't carry a cell phone?" Maggie asks.

Cynthia looks over at her. "Yes."

She nods and continues cracking her crab legs. "Thought so. But you know you can shut that thing off while you're driving. Cell phones are good to have for emergencies. You're a smart girl. You need to have a cell phone."

"Okay, Mom," Cynthia says sarcastically.

"Hey, I just worry, is all. What if you get a flat and are out in the middle of nowhere? You never know about these things."

"You're right," Cynthia agrees. "I may look into it."

"So, are you going to call him?" I ask.

"How about we stop back by on the way home?"

I smile. "I think that's a great idea."

She nods. "Now that that's decided," she reaches for her polka dot bag and pulls her Polaroid camera out, "let's get a photo."

The summer breeze wraps around the back of my neck, causing my hair to lift up as we walk down the pier. Our bellies are full, and my mind is overwhelmed with all the nostalgia this place brings. I tell Maggie and Cynthia about things that happened long ago, and Cynthia captures more photos from her camera. We sit on a bench, and Cynthia props her feet up on one of the wooden boards.

With bright flashlights, people hunt for crabs down below us on the beach. I slide my hands into the pockets of my light jacket as we sit in silence for a while, just enjoying the calmness the ocean brings.

I think back on everything I've told my girls about my life story and realize that the next part isn't going to be as easy to tell. But Cynthia is writing this, and summer is coming to an end so she needs to get it all down. I want nothing but success for her. It's hard to believe that I was so hell-bent on her leaving me alone those first few weeks, and now I couldn't imagine my life without her quirky self in it. I'm glad that she came into my life because I realize how much I needed her and how much she needed us.

People are important. We think that we are better off without them sometimes, but the truth is, without them, we're nothing but empty shells walking around this earth. People give us feelings and a reason to get up in the morning. For most of my teenage years, Travis Cole was my reason to get up, and then my son became my reason.

Since William started his own life, I haven't really had any reason to want to start my day, but these two women have given me a new look on life. Now I have a new purpose, and this time I get up for myself.

Chapter Twenty

After dinner and our walk, we head back to the hotel room and each take a shower before climbing into bed. Cynthia pulls out her pen and notebook, and I get ready to start the last part of my story. With a heavy heart, I recall all the details, from the moment I first spoke to him after thirty years, to the moment I told him that it was okay to go…and once again, my memories play out like a movie on a projector screen, taking me back to a road trip my sisters and I took so long ago…

February 13, 2005

It's wintertime, and I'm thrilled to be away from my home. Well, not away from my son, but away from everything else and everyone else. I spoke with him on the phone before we got here, and he told me he was going out with Elizabeth, the girl he brought to our family Christmas. She's pretty and shy, and I liked her instantly. Especially since I saw the way he looked at her. He never brought girls over to our house, much less around our family, so this was a big deal.

Aunt Evelyn's house was slap full of women. Sisters and cousins from all over. It had been years since we did this, and not only was I happy to be away from my home life, but I was ecstatic to be back in Ft. Pierce, Florida. Aunt Evelyn walks into the kitchen as I'm making a pitcher of sweet tea. I can go without a lot, but never can I go without sweet tea, and this house had none.

"Charlotte, you'll never believe who I ran into the other day."

"Who?" I ask, pouring the hot tea into the pitcher.

"Travis Cole," she says, and I look over at her immediately. "I asked that boy why you two never got married, and you know what he said?"

"What?" I ask, thinking, *you, Mama, and everyone else was the reason why we never got married*, but of course, I keep this to myself.

"He said, 'I don't know. I should have stayed with that girl.'"

A feeling I haven't felt in so long flows through my veins, pouring deep inside my heart, like water from the winding rivers that run into the sea. I swallow and pick up the spoon to stir my tea.

"Anyway, he's a lot older now, but still a good-looking boy."

"Mama," Jennie calls out before she walks into the kitchen.

"Yes?" she says, turning her attention to her daughter. "We're all going shopping. You coming with us?"

"Yes, let me go change my clothes," Aunt Evelyn says. I keep stirring, and after she leaves, I look over at Jennie.

"You know I heard a voice not too long ago that I haven't heard in many years," I say to her.

"You did?" she asks.

"Yes," I reply. "And it's funny that your mama just came in here and told me she saw this person a few days ago."

"Who?"

"Travis Cole."

"You spoke to him?" she asks, wide-eyed.

"No, not really. I was on the phone with your sister a couple of weeks ago, and Travis was over at her house helping his brother, Byron, fix his truck. Apparently, he walked into the house, and Laura told him I was on the phone." I stop stirring the tea and lean back against the counter. Crossing my arms, I look down at the floor, my thoughts getting away from me.

I take a breath and say, "Jennie, all I heard him say was hey. Just that one word, and my mind shot back to…" I shake my head slightly as memories flood my mind.

"Back to what?" she asks. I look up at her, and my lip lifts a tad.

"Back to a time when love was all we knew. It was as if no time had passed. His voice still sounded the same. I could see his walk, even though I wasn't there. I could imagine what his hair looked like, that crooked smile on his lips. I wondered what he looked like at forty-nine. My heart started pounding so hard, I had to sit down," I say with a perplexed smile on my face.

She grins back. "You really loved him, Charlotte."

"Yes," I reply. "Yes, I did." My brow creases, and I run my finger over my lips in thought before I say, "Yes, I do."

I'm putting on my nightclothes when Laura walks into the bedroom Jennie and I are staying in. We've had an evening of shopping and gossiping, and it's been nice to just relax for a bit. I listen and notice she's on the phone when I hear her say, "Yes, she's here." My pulse quickens, and I peek my head out of the bathroom. She looks over at me and smiles. "I've got someone who wants to speak to you," she says as she hands me the phone. My heart starts pounding erratically, and I begin to sweat.

"Hello," I say with a shaky voice.

"Hey, girl." His deep tone causes shivers to run up my spine, and I bite the smile that threatens to cover my whole face so Laura won't see, even though she's grinning like crazy. I turn away from her and move back into the bathroom.

"Hey," I say as all of my emotions go crazy. My mind races with questions. *Where have you been? What have you been doing all these years? Are you married? Do you have kids? If so, how many? Do you still have that GTO we used to ride in so much?*

"How are you?" he asks, breaking me away from the twenty questions going on inside my head.

"I'm good. How are you?"

"Good."

"So, you're back living in Ft. Pierce?" I ask because I had heard not too long after I called his parents years ago that he'd moved away.

"Yeah. You still living in Georgia?"

"Yep, been there since Mama moved us back all those years ago."

He clears his throat, and I look at myself in the mirror. I'm blushing, and I have a stupid grin on my face. I'm so glad he can't see me. I look down at my body and frown. I'm really glad he can't see me. I've let myself go so much he probably wouldn't recognize me now. No longer am I a string bean, that's for sure.

"Are you married?" he asks.

"Yes," I reply and then swallow before I ask, "Are you?"

"No."

For some reason that gives me a feeling of hope. I don't know why, because I'm married, but the fact that he isn't makes me over the moon ecstatic. We grow quiet for a moment, and I walk over to the tub and sit down on the edge. How can this be that I'm talking to the boy I've loved for so long after thirty years? This just doesn't happen in real life.

"Are you happy, Charlotte?" he asks me softly. My eyes peer down at the tile floor, and I cross my ankles as I think over his question. *Am I happy?* I think back on my life and the struggles I've gone through. I come home from work every day to a husband who lives in his recliner, talking to his brother who stays over more than he should. I cook a grilled cheese, say hey to my son if he is home, and then go to my room, eat, shower, and go to bed alone, only to wake up and do it all over again. *Am I happy?* No, I'm not. I haven't been happy for quite some time. My job sucks, my personal life is shit, but there is my son. A small smile plays on my lips at the thought of William.

"I have a nineteen-year-old son who makes me happy," I say.

"Good," he replies. "That's good."

"That night we talked longer than I had talked on the phone in years," I tell my girls as I lie on my side, hugging my pillow. "When I told him William was what made me happy, it was as if that's the answer he wanted to hear. I felt like a teenager all over again, and it didn't stop. God, it didn't stop. It was as if we were a snowball tumbling full speed downhill. It was one of the most exciting times of my life. He told me that he had been married a few times, but none of it ever felt right. And he'd been in and out of jail for petty stuff, just like when he was a teenager. Mason, one of his older brothers, passed when they were in their twenties, and he had no children. I told him that Mama had passed also, and I told him everything about William.

"After that conversation, we exchanged numbers. Like clockwork, he called me every day at the same time. At lunch and then right when I was leaving my hellhole of a job. A few weeks into it, if I missed his call, he'd leave me a voice message and sing, 'I just called to say I love you.' We picked up right where we left off thirty years before."

"What about your husband?" Maggie asks.

I sigh. "That wasn't easy for me to do. I loved John, I did. I wasn't in love with him, but I cared about him deeply. He broke his back some years before and was on disability. He was getting shit money, though, so I basically took care of him.

"I thought about leaving him several times throughout our marriage, but I was worried about what would happen to him. Plus, in our earlier years, he threatened to take William if I left or do something stupid to himself. He was always threatening to take his own life."

"He threatened to take his own life?" Cynthia asks.

"Yes, several times. John was messed up. His childhood did a number on him, and he never got over it. My heart hurt for him, but I was also sick of it all. He knew how to hurt me, and that was by saying he'd take William. I felt trapped, but Travis gave me new hope, William was practically grown, and I knew for the first time in my life, I had to think about me and not everyone else. So that's exactly what I did. I thought about me."

February 2005

I stare at the clock on the wall, waiting for five to hurry up and get here. *Only ten more minutes,* I think to myself. I look to the door when my boss walks in.

"Charlotte, I don't understand this," he says, throwing his hands up. "These numbers don't add up." He walks back and forth, wearing out the carpet. This man drives me up the wall, and I wish I could throat punch him. The numbers are right; they are always right. He is just a dumbass.

"Let me see it," I say to him. He shoves the papers to me. I grab my calculator and do the numbers, like I've already done several times. I know this shit is right, but just to satisfy him, I do it again.

He watches me do the math, and I look up when I'm done.

"Oh," he says. "How did you do that?"

You just watched me do that, I think to myself, but instead of speaking my mind, I explain it to him. He leaves my office with a smile on his face. I roll my eyes as soon as he is out of sight, and then I look back up at the clock on the wall. It's five! I grab my things and quickly clock out. Walking through the office, I say goodbye to everyone and push the glass door open. My phone rings from inside my purse, and I grab it.

"Hello," I say with butterflies in my stomach.

"Hey, baby," Travis says.

"Hey." I open my car door and get inside.

"How was your day?" he asks.

"My day was shit."

"Tell me about it."

And I do. I used to talk to my windshield on the way home, fussing up a storm because I didn't have anyone else to vent to, but now I have Travis, and he always listens and then simply says, *"I'm sorry, baby. That's rough."* Sometimes all a woman wants to do is tell you about her crappy day, and sometimes the only reply she needs is, *"I'm sorry, baby. That's rough."*

"I'd talk to Travis all the way home, and then I'd let him go so I could walk in the house. I'd hurry to my room so I could talk more."

"You talked to him at your house?" Cynthia asks.

"Yes, if John walked in, I'd lie and say I was on the phone with my sister Sophia, Beverly's other daughter who grew up in Indiana. This went on for a good week, and then he told me something that I wasn't ready to hear…or maybe I was…

February 2005

"Stupid people don't know how to drive," I say as I hit the gas on Black Beauty, my Ford Taurus, to get around a car going fifty when the speed limit is sixty-five.

"You need to slow down," Travis tells me on the other end of the phone.

"They need to get out of the fast lane," I reply as I pull down my visor to block the blinding five o'clock sunshine.

He laughs, sending a shiver down my spine. God, I've missed this man. How have I gone so long without talking to him?

"Charlotte," he says after a moment.

"Yes?" I reply as I come to a red light.

"I wanna see you." My heart falls into the pit of my stomach. We've been talking for over a week now. It's like no time has passed between us, yet my appearance says otherwise. I look up in the mirror of my sun visor. Wrinkles and fine lines surround my eyes, and my hair isn't as thick as it used to be. I've gained stress weight, and Lord knows there are other things that aren't the same as they were when I was seventeen. I exhale a slow breath as nerves build up inside my chest, but I know my answer.

"I wanna see you, too." The light turns green, and I press the gas.

"When can we make this happen?" he asks.

"Well, my sister and I are actually planning a trip to Daytona next month. I can stay a day with her and then leave and meet you somewhere."

"I don't want you to mess up time with your sister."

"Travis, I haven't seen you in over thirty years. My sister will be okay."

"If you're sure."

"I am."

"I can't wait," he says.

"I've been waiting for a lifetime," I reply.

"As soon as we agreed to see each other again, my ass went straight to the gym to get a membership. At the time, I worked with my best friend Stella, and she would go with me. We would walk, walk, walk, and I'd tell her about Travis. She was happy for me, and she was the one person I could really confide in during that time.

"Before our trip to Daytona, I had lost thirty pounds in less than a month. I eventually told my sister, of course, and she wasn't too excited that I was leaving her and going to meet him, but I had my mind made up."

"Damn, girl," Maggie says, grabbing her pipe from her bag.

"You can't smoke in here," I tell her.

"I know that. I'm stepping outside. My arthritis is acting up."

Cynthia smirks. "Keep going."

"I think Maggie will want to hear this next part. Let's go out onto the balcony." I get up from the bed, and we make our way over to the sliding glass door. A strip of clouds shades part of the moon, and the ocean breeze spreads over my skin, wrapping around me like a salty warm blanket.

I settle down into the outdoor couch as Cynthia and Maggie take their seats. Maggie strikes her lighter, and the smell of grass takes me back to the car ride with Sophia twelve years ago…

March 2005

I giggle as I pass the joint back to my sister. It reeks of grass in here, and the traffic is horrible as we make our way to Daytona.

"Shit," she says quickly, cracking her window.

"What?" I ask, my mind in a fuzzy daze.

"There's a cop up there!"

"A *cop*?" I ask as panic takes over. My heart begins pounding, and my face starts to sweat. "Throw it out!" I say, hitting her on the arm as I look ahead at the cop. "Throw it out!"

"What do you think I'm doing?" she says, laughing.

"Why are you laughing?" I ask her.

"Because you're making me miss the crack in the window. Stop hitting me."

"Oh," I say, kinda laughing, too, but the thought of two older ladies getting arrested for grass makes my stomach hurt. What will we do? Who will we call?

"He's stopping people!"

"Holy shit, what will my kids think if I get arrested for this?" Sophia says.

"Just act natural," I say, rolling my window all the way down. It's hotter than hell outside, but we've got to get this smoke out. I turn the air conditioner on full blast, and Sophia rolls all the windows down.

"How do I act natural?" she squeaks, her voice sounding higher than normal.

"I don't know. Just don't say anything unless you have to." Moments later, we pull up to the officer.

"Where are you ladies headed?" he asks, leaning down.

"Beach, Daytona," we both say in unison. His eyebrows draw together as his eyes narrow, and I swear I see him sniff. Shit, shit, shit. We're screwed.

"We're headed to Daytona Beach," I say.

He looks up the road before looking back at us a little too long if you ask me. My heart pounds erratically, and I feel like it may give up and crawl up through my throat.

"There's a detour up ahead. Road work," he says. "You two be safe." His lip curves into a smile as he pats the edge of the window. Sophia presses the gas, and we head straight. Neither of us says anything until we are through the detour and away from him. I look over at her. Both hands are on the wheel, positioned perfectly at ten and two. She sits up straight and stares ahead. But then she slowly looks my way, and as if on cue, we both burst out laughing—eyes watering, can't breathe, leg-slapping hysteria.

"Good God," Sophia says.

"We would have had to call Natalie!" I pull the sun visor down and wipe under my eyes.

"I'd rather sit in jail," she barks. "That would have been something. Two older women on the way to Daytona Beach get arrested for smoking grass." She motions her hand as if seeing the words displayed on a television screen. My phone rings, and I reach over and grab it out of the cup holder.

"Hello," I say.

"Hey," my love replies.

I giggle. "Travis, you will never guess what just happened." I tell him all about it.

Then I hear Byron in the back. “Good Lord, you act just like a damn teenager, always on that phone.” I smirk, thinking I feel just like a teenager.

I hear the background grow quiet, and I’m assuming Travis walked away from his brother’s prying ears, and then he says, “I can’t wait to hold you. I mean, I can’t wait for you-know-what either.” He laughs, and I bite my lip to keep from grinning like an idiot. “But just to hold you again. It’s been so fucking long.”

I look out the window as my heart swells and sweet butterflies soar inside my chest. “I can’t wait either,” I say softly. “It has been a lifetime for me.”

Chapter Twenty-One

"Charlotte Harris almost getting busted for weed." Cynthia giggles. "I wonder what William would have thought?"

"William would have been shocked for sure."

"Did he have any idea what you were doing in Daytona?" Maggie asks.

"Only Stella and Sophia knew."

"That must have been tough, keeping all that happiness mostly to yourself," Cynthia says sadly.

"It wasn't easy, and I didn't feel good about it, but my heart knew what it wanted. It had always known…"

March 2005

"I can't believe you're leaving me," Sophia says as I fix my hair and makeup in the hotel bathroom mirror.

"I told you I was before we even came."

"I know, but I didn't think you actually would."

I roll my eyes. "Well, I am." I pick up the hairspray and give my curls a once-over before I apply a little more mascara. I haven't felt this good about myself in a long time. I've lost weight, I've bought a new blouse, but man, the butterflies are going nuts inside my stomach to the point I almost feel sick.

What am I doing? I'm married. I've been married for twenty-nine years.

I have a son, a family. I swallow and look down at the sink. I'm acting like a teenager who has nothing to lose. John hasn't been the greatest husband, but does he deserve this? He has put me through hell, but he has a good heart. He'd give you the shirt off his back, his last dollar if you needed it. Guilt twists inside my gut, and I exhale a deep breath.

"You okay?" Sophia asks me. I turn to look at my sister.

"I'm nervous," I say to her. "I'm having all kinds of doubts."

She smiles. "Charlotte, I don't want you to leave me, but I haven't seen you this happy in years. If he is what's doing this, then I don't think you have anything to be worried about."

I exhale a deep breath again and look back in the mirror. "Here goes nothing."

"I'll be home in a few days," I tell William as I drive to the hotel where I'm meeting Travis.

"Y'all having fun?" he asks.

"Yep," I say, feeling slightly guilty that I'm not telling him the whole truth.

"Okay, well, I'm pulling up to Elizabeth's house," he says as I turn into the hotel.

"Okay, have fun. Tell her hey for me."

"'K, love you, Mom."

"Love you, too, son." I slap my phone shut and put my car in park before I search for the room number Travis told me. My hands are sweaty, and I rub them against the steering wheel, trying to fight the nerves inside my stomach. It's been thirty years. What if he doesn't like what he sees? What if I don't like what I see?

My mind races with random thoughts, and then my heart jumps into play as I think of that teenage boy I fell in love with so many years ago. I think about our endless conversations on the phone these past few weeks and how good it has felt to talk to someone who actually seems to care. No, not seems, who *does* care. Even over the phone, Travis Cole makes me feel loved.

Crazy Atlanta traffic surrounds Stella and me as we make our way to the computer class we are taking. She keeps an eye out on where we are going while I giggle and talk about nothing to Travis on the phone. We've been talking this whole time, and it's amazing that we can stay on the phone like this. We aren't talking about anything in particular, just catching up on all the years we missed out on. He laughs at something Byron says, and my heart swells because that laugh could move mountains. If I died today, I'd die a happy lady, just knowing that's the last thing I heard.

"So, why are you always over at Byron's?" I ask him.

"We're fixing up my old GTO."

"Really?" I ask excitedly.

"Yeah, haven't gotten that far, though. Beer and grass keep getting in the way." He laughs, and I shake my head and smile. Some things never change.

"Okay, woman, you've got to get off that phone. You're supposed to be my navigator." I look over at Stella.

"Travis, I guess I better let you go. Stella needs me to navigate."

He laughs again, and I hear a beer top pop. "That's fine. Y'all be careful, and call me when you get to the hotel this evening."

"Okay, I will."

"I love you," he says to me. I bite my bottom lip and look down; a smile forces its way across my face, and not even biting my lip can stop it.

"I love you, too," I reply before we hang up.

I see Stella's head snap my way. "Did you just say you love him?" She grins.

"I did," I reply. "I've always loved him."

I shut my car off and flip my sun visor down to check my makeup one more time. With a deep breath, I open the car door and step out into the hot Florida air. I adjust my shirt and walk up to the door, pausing for a brief second before I lightly tap my knuckles against it. The pounding of my heart rattles my ribcage, and I take slow breaths to try to control it. *This is Travis,* I tell myself. *The man I've loved for nearly my whole life. Calm down. This is right.*

The door opens, and time stands still. I once thought there's a special compartment in our brain that holds onto precious moments. It saves every detail, so you can always go back and replay it again, and just like the first time I saw him, this moment right here is something I know I'll never forget.

His eyes lock with mine as a flock of birds fly off from a nearby tree and traffic zooms behind me. The wind blows around the back of my arms, giving me goose bumps, and I hear people carrying on farther down the hotel parking lot. My heart slows, my worries fade, and I know this is exactly where I should be.

He's aged, but there's no denying this is my Travis Cole. So good-looking, he makes my mouth water and my hands shake to touch him. He grins, and I could cry because here he is, that beautiful crooked smile and all.

"Come here, girl," he says, pulling me in. He shuts the door behind us, and we stand still. My heart pounds almost painfully against my chest, and I feel like I'm seventeen again. He steps closer, his eyes scanning over my face. "I can't believe you're here," he says, his voice low as though he's thinking out loud. His hand lifts, and he gently runs his finger over my cheek. My eyes close as he places his rough hand against my skin, and I inhale his scent. I open my eyes as he steps us back until I'm pressed against the door.

His forehead goes to mine, and we breathe each other in.

"I've missed you so much," he murmurs.

"I've missed you more."

He smiles and kisses me. He grabs the back of my head, and my hands go to his sides. A rush of heat runs down my spine as my pulse beats uncontrollably against my neck. His kiss is everything I've missed.

Weeks of talking and late-night whispers through the phone have more than built us up for this moment. Years of pent-up need unravel before us as our kiss turns from soft to eager and deprived. Our breathing becomes ragged and uncontrolled. men's cologne and soap. We're desperate and clingy. Hungry for something we haven't had in so long, I'm not sure we'll ever get our fill, but we've got the rest of our lives to try.

I bunch his shirt up with my fingers, pulling upward until he breaks our kiss and lifts it over his head. I quickly start unbuttoning my blouse, only getting a few done before his lips are back on mine. He guides us closer to the bed, and surprising me he rips my blouse open, his hand gripping onto my breast as his mouth goes to my neck. I gasp and close my eyes.

The rest of our clothes go to the floor, and Travis yanks the top comforter off, reminding me of our first time alone together in a hotel room. He doesn't stay away from me long, and within minutes my back is against the cool sheets. He's on top of me, between my thighs, and sinking. I inhale a quick rush of air and slowly exhale as my mouth falls open. The feeling is so overwhelming. I feel a tear escape my eye and roll down the side of my face. He kisses my bottom lip and takes hold of my waist. I link my ankles around his bare back, and we do what time has kept us from for so, so many years. We love like tomorrow will never come, like it's our first and our last. We become one again like we were always meant to be.

"Wow," Maggie says as she looks up at the ceiling from her bed. "Time changed nothing, huh?" she says dreamingly.

I laugh. "Oh, it changed a lot of things. Inside we were the same, but our bodies had changed a good bit. We fell asleep wrapped up in each other that night. Exhausted and fully content. I spent the whole next day with him before I had to leave.

After that, things only got more serious between us. My day would start hearing his voice, and it would end hearing his voice. I kept up with the gym, and I never felt better. William and Elizabeth's relationship grew, too, and I saw that my son was falling hard for this girl. It was clear that things were changing for us all, and they were changing fast.

April 2005

"Are you sure you want to do this?" Travis asks me. It's the afternoon, and I'm leaving the hellhole that is my job.

"Am I sure I want to uproot my son's life? No. Am I sure I want to leave John? Yes. One minute I'm rethinking this whole idea, and then the next I remember why I'm doing this."

"And why is that?" Travis challenges.

"I love you."

"I know," he says softly. I look ahead as I make my way home. My heart is torn in two, my mind scattered. I've been thinking about leaving John for years, but I've always been too scared. Always too afraid of the unknown and of what would happen to him. I haven't been happy for so long, I've literally forgotten how it felt, until Travis. Until he came back into my life and gave me the *strength* to choose my happiness for once. Because that's exactly what this is going to take—s*trength.*

"Promise me one thing," I say as I get on the exit ramp. I lift my foot off the gas pedal when the light at the end of the ramp turns red.

"Anything," he says as I completely stop. I run my hand over the steering wheel and look down at the top of Black Beauty's dash.

"You won't leave me again."

"I promise. I love you. I'll never leave."

I hug my pillow tighter as I think about those words. *"I'll never leave."* I shouldn't have made him promise me that. After all, sometimes we don't get a choice in the matter. Staring ahead as my thoughts run, my eyes land on the clock hanging on the wall. It reads eleven thirty, and I realize how tired I am. Not just physically, but emotionally, too. It's past my bedtime, and I've had enough talk for today.

"You okay?" Cynthia asks me.

"Just a little tired," I say softly.

"Why don't we call it a night?" Maggie chimes in. "It's been a long day."

"Okay," I agree.

Cynthia closes her notebook, and Maggie reaches over and turns the lamp off.

"Charlotte," Cynthia says a few moments later after we've all settled and the only sound in the room is the low hum of the air conditioner.

"Yes?" I say quietly as I stare into the darkness.

"I'm almost scared to find out the end of this story."

I shut my eyes and bring the pillow closer to my chin, as a single tear rolls down my cheek and my heart slightly falters. "I know the feeling," I reply meekly. "Sadly, all too well."

She doesn't say anything else, and soon all that's heard is the air and Maggie's light snoring as I begin to slowly doze off.

I sit on the couch with my video camera as William and Elizabeth decorate the tree. They dispute with each other over how the lights should be hung, and I look over at Travis as he sits in the chair beside the coffee table. He gives me a wink and a grin, and I catch it on camera.

Christmas is around the corner, but I can't think of anything more I would want than this right here. Everyone I care most about in the world is in front of me. Except there's a ball of worry deep inside my chest because life is so unpredictable. Travis clears his throat and pops open a beer.

Music plays from the TV, but it's not Christmas tunes. It's the Allman Brothers, and Travis gets up and starts singing and dancing along. I video the whole time, smiling from ear-to-ear at the sight of him before I move the camera over to the kids.

"You aren't putting the lights in deep enough," William says to Elizabeth.

"Because it's scratching my arms," she argues.

"Well, it's not going to look good if they're hanging off the tree."

Elizabeth rolls her eyes and looks over at me with a smirk. Those two could fuss about anything, but seconds later, they're all doe eyes and laughing. My sister, Natalie, calls this house 'the love shack,' and she's right. This home is full of love. We don't have a lot, but we all have each other, and sometimes that's enough. My camera goes back to Travis as he starts coughing.

"Whew," he says, putting his beer down. "Did it get hot in here or is it just me?"

"I think it's just you," I say as I shut the camera off.

"I'll be back." He walks toward our room. I watch after him before I get up and leave the kids to the tree decorating.

"You okay?" I ask as I turn the corner in our bedroom and see him sitting on the side of the tub in the bathroom.

"Yeah. Throat's just bothering me," he says, and I see the bottle of liquid morphine in his hand.

"This will help, though," he says, smiling.

I walk over and sit on top of the toilet seat, looking down at the floor.

"Hey," he says. "Look at me."

I do.

"It's going to be okay."

"I know," I say, trying to sound reassuring.

He clears his throat again and sets the bottle down on the sink.

"I love you," he says in a singsong voice.

"I love you, too," I reply, grabbing his hand and bringing it to my lips.

Chapter Twenty-Two

I wake up the next morning with Archie scratching behind his ear. I sigh, remembering my dream from last night. Rolling over in bed, I get an eye full of none other than Maggie's behind. She's wearing yellow leggings and touching the toe of her hot pink running shoes.

"I'm going for a walk down the beach," she says, looking at me from between her legs. She flips back up straight and places her hands on her lower back as she bends. "All this car riding has made me fall behind on my exercise," she whispers so not to wake Sleeping Beauty. "Wanna come?"

My stomach growls. *I'd rather eat.*

"You go on ahead," I say. "I'm going to cook us breakfast."

"You going shopping then?" she asks.

"Guess so," I say, tossing the comforter off me. "Want anything?"

"Yeah. Grab me some protein bars, would ya? The kind with nuts."

"Okay, crazy lady."

After I get dressed, I walk out of the room, seeing Cynthia's notebook sitting on the dresser. I look over at her as she continues to sleep, and my curious mind gets the best of me.

I slide my glasses on quietly and flip the notebook open, scanning over words that I've said and little doodles that she's drawn. She has things underlined, notes along the side, dates, and highlighted words. I then flip to the last page and see the supplies needed to dye my hair. I almost forgot I wanted to do this. *Why not grab them now?* I softly rip the page and place the notebook back down before I exit the room.

Once I make it to the store, I grab bacon, eggs, sausage, and bread and, of course, butter and my beloved blackberry jam. Breakfast has always been my favorite meal of the day, and I just realized it's been a while since I've cooked it.

After I check out, I make my way over to the beauty store I spotted before I parked the car in the shopping center. I walk inside and am greeted by a woman with a shaved head and hot pink bangs.

"Can I help you?" she asks me.

"My friend wrote me out a list of things I needed to get," I tell her as I take it out of my purse. She looks it over.

"Your friend going purple?" she asks.

"Nope. She already is," I reply. "I'm doing it, too."

She smiles. "Sweet. Let's find these items then."

Once I get back, I unload the bags and start cooking. Cynthia wakes in the middle of the bacon frying, her lavender locks a tangled mess.

"Man, that smells good," she says.

"It'll be ready shortly."

She stands up and stretches her arms out. "Where's Maggie?"

"She went for a long walk. Catching up on her exercise."

"Ah," she says as she folds up her bed. "I'm gonna shower really quick."

"Oh!" I call over to her and take the hair dye stuff off the counter. "I bought the supplies."

She smiles. "Let's do it after we eat."

"Okay, I'm ready."

I look at the wall as Cynthia blow-dries my hair. She trimmed it, too. Turns out, she's pretty good at this stuff. I guess she's been doing her own hair for so long, she's become an expert. Maggie looks in on us in the bathroom and smiles.

"It's amazing," she says excitedly.

"Hurry up," I tell Cynthia, and only a few minutes later, she shuts off the dryer. She grabs the curling iron and wraps the ends a few times before giving it a spray over.

"Check it out," she says. I hesitantly turn toward the mirror and gasp.

"Oh my." It's lavender, not dark purple, and some of my gray shines through, mixing in with the lilac shade beautifully.

"I made it more of a strong highlight, so your hair would have some definition."

"I think it looks amazing." I look at her and smile. "Thank you."

"You're welcome." She starts to put up everything, and I can't stop looking at myself in the mirror. I feel younger and hip. I've always had the same hair color, a deep brown and then gray. But now I have soft lavender, and I love it. I look up and see Cynthia has her camera. "Smile," she says. I do.

"Girls, this is our last day here," Maggie says. "Let's go have some fun."

"I'm down," Cynthia says.

"Okay, I can show off my new hair." I stand up. "And I've done my thing, so it is now on you two." I point at each of them.

"I'm ready," Maggie says as we walk out of the bathroom.

"I'm kinda ready," Cynthia says.

"You better be," Maggie counters. "That boy ain't gonna wait on you forever."

"Maggie," I scowl.

"Just saying."

Dressed in a pale yellow sundress with a tiny blue belt around her waist, Cynthia hits the golf club, and we watch as the ball shoots up the ramp. Her bright red lips and the way her hair is styled make her look like a pin-up girl. She's beautiful, and she doesn't realize it. We chat about this and that as we make our way around the putt-putt course.

"Did you play this as a kid?" Maggie asks after Cynthia sinks another hole in one yet again.

"Actually, yeah," Cynthia says. "My nanny would take me to the local entertainment complex and I would play by myself, so I got a lot of practice."

"Your nanny?" Maggie questions as Cynthia retrieves her ball.

"Yeah."

"Your parents didn't take you to do things?"

"No, my parents and I didn't have much of a relationship. They worked their lives away."

"Can we sit for a moment?" I ask, spotting a bench. "My back is starting to give me a fit."

"Sure," Cynthia says. We flop down, and I sigh as I bend, trying to relieve my aching back. Old age only brings more problems. I have to take pills in the morning and the evening, but there are some things a pill can't fix and that's these growing old pains. When you're young, it's growing pains. When you get my age, you add a word in that sentence. And the damn doctor appointments are endless. I see him more than my own family.

"Would you tell us more about what happened with everything?" Maggie asks Cynthia, interrupting my thoughts about old age. "I know you're a private person, but I think we have gotten pretty close over these weeks, and I'd like to know more about Lit, your parents, and the accident if you can talk about it."

Cynthia squints her eyes toward the blinding sun, and I see her slowly inhale. "A few weeks ago, I would have told you no," she says, looking down at her blue tights and picking a piece of fuzz off. "But you're right. You two have become very important to me, and I know now that what happened that day wasn't anyone's fault." She looks over at me. "You have opened up so much of your life to us." She looks back at Maggie. "And you have told us about your past with your daughter. I guess it's only fair I share my story with the both of you, too.

"Four years ago, on my seventeenth birthday, my parents surprised me with a Range Rover. I didn't want it. I felt like it was a way for them to get back into my good graces. They were never around. The only one who was, was Lit. He was not only my boyfriend, but my best friend.

"Anyway, my folks and I got into a fight, because along with the Range Rover, they gave me empty promises about cutting their hours at the hospital and spending more time with me. I told them to keep the Rover. That it was too late. I had grown up, and they'd missed it. My mom was a beautiful woman. Blonde hair, blue eyes, and every time I looked in the mirror with that same blonde hair, it just reminded me of a time when I screwed up. When I took my parents' life," she says, looking down.

"Is that why you dye it so much?" Maggie asks.

"In the beginning, yeah," she tells her. "After the fight, I took off that night with Lit, and when I came back, my dad was sitting at the kitchen table waiting on me. It surprised me, because usually they'd already be back at the hospital. He told me he was serious, and that he was sorry he'd missed out on so many years. I learned in that moment, that for the first time ever, their promises weren't empty.

"My folks and I took off with no plans. I drove my new car, and Mom oversaw the radio. It was like we were getting to know each other. I realized on that trip that not only had they missed out on me, but they had missed out on each other as well. We spent a few days doing stupid things like looking at the world's largest this and the world's tallest that.

"We made memories on that trip. My dad tried to eat a five-pound hamburger for bragging rights and a free T-shirt. Mom let me have a margarita. She said life's too short, and she wanted my 'first' drink to be with her.

"Lit even met up with us for a few days, and my parents went off and did their own thing so we could do ours. We camped out on the beach. We had a tent, but Lit wanted to sleep under the night sky, so we opened my sleeping bag and laid it down on the sand. I curled up next to him, and we counted stars until our eyes closed.

"We decided to head back home a few days after that with a glove compartment full of old Polaroid photos we'd taken and sun-kissed skin." She looks over at me. "See, I used to take photos, too." I smile, and then she sighs and looks away as I see her throat move when she swallows.

"We all have moments we regret. Things we look back on and think, *why did I do that? If I would have just done this differently and not said that.* Regret is one of those silent killers. I was driving," she says softly. "The light ahead of me was green, and my phone was in my lap. Mom and Dad were talking about going on a trip on his boat in a few weeks. He'd bought it the summer before, and we had yet to really do anything with it.

"My phone chimed, and I looked down. The light was green, but how was I supposed to know the driver of an eighteen-wheeler had dropped his coffee in his lap and he was trying to clean it off? How was I supposed to know he didn't see his light was red? Well, I would have known if I hadn't looked down at my phone. I would have looked both ways, even though that light was green. But I didn't. I looked at my phone.

"It was so quick and so loud. The sound alone made my ears ring. He hit the passenger side—the side they both were sitting on. I was told they were killed instantly. I busted my window with my left shoulder and head. Broke my right arm and was cut up badly from the glass. But they were killed instantly." She shakes her head, and I rub her back.

"When I got out of the hospital. I went to see the car. I got out the photos and found my cell phone in between the seat and console. Lit was just telling me he missed me and to call him when I got back in town.

"The funeral arrangements were made, and I said goodbye to my parents and the life I knew. I said goodbye to the boy who loved me through it all. I crushed his heart right when I needed him the most. When all he wanted to do was be with me." Cynthia toys with her bracelets and exhales.

"We had no idea," Maggie says, looking over at her with sad eyes.

"Yeah, well, how could you?" she says, biting her bottom lip and twirling her thumbs. "I haven't been very forthcoming about my life."

"I'm so sorry about your parents, sweet girl," I say to her.

She sighs. "Me, too."

"I now feel like more than ever you have got to talk to that boy. I can't imagine what he has been thinking all these years," Maggie insists.

"That's why I'm so afraid to reach out to him. I did him wrong."

"But that was long ago. Sometimes time changes feelings, too," I say.

"Yeah, and he used to love me. What if he hates me now?"

"Girl, he named his boat after you. The boy doesn't hate you," I argue.

She looks down and shrugs. "Maybe you're right."

Maggie pats her leg. "We've lived longer. We're always right."

Cynthia grins as I push myself up from the bench, saying, "Let's go eat some good lunch and get ready to leave."

Chapter Twenty-Three

The moonlight shines through the small cracks of the hotel curtains, and I look at the clock on the bedside table, noticing that it's only five a.m. Last night, we had a nice dinner with no talk about the past. We were just three women, having a few drinks, talking about everyday things, and it was nice. But today we leave, heading back to North Caronia and our homes. This has been a fun trip going down memory lane, but all good things must come to an end eventually, and my girls have some things they need to take care of.

They are still fast asleep with Archie lying at Maggie's feet. I silently get out of bed and change out of my pajamas before I brush my teeth, and then I quietly pack up my things. It's closer to six now, so I hurry out of the room and make my way down to the beach.

I take a seat once I reach the hotel beach chairs and wrap my light jacket around myself. It's not cold really, but there's a strong breeze that gives me chills. Staring ahead at the wonder that is the ocean, I watch as something insignificant to most takes place before me. A glimpse, so slight, of fire brushes its hello against the horizon, blasting warm colors over the ocean. It holds promises of a new day, a fresh start. We tend to take this for granted, most of us. Thinking that it's a given right, but it's a gift.

The waves tumble expectantly against the waiting shore, and seagulls scurry about to catch what's left over after the waves descend. I sit, gazing with wide eyes as the sun continues to rise slowly as though someone is pulling it up by a string, yet there is no string to be seen. It hangs alone in a vast sky, turning the once cool blue into a vivid painting of tangerine and blood red. It's a sight, and I watch until it's completely light and there is no darkness left.

———

We pulled into downtown St. Augustine almost three hours after we left Ft. Pierce. The ride was quiet with me taking a nap and Cynthia in her own world, probably stressing over talking with Lit after so long. I pray this goes well for her. The streets are busy, so we have to pull around a few times before finally finding a parking spot. We put some coins into the parking meter and make our way over to the docks. *The Cynthia Rose* is sitting where it was before.

"You okay?" I ask, looking down at Cynthia beside me.

"Not really," she responds. "I feel like I may throw up."

"Take a breath," Maggie says. Archie sits at her feet.

Cynthia inhales, and then with a strong exhale, she steps forward. "I'll be back," she says to us.

Cynthia Rose

With sweaty hands and a stomach full of knots, I make my way down the dock toward *The Cynthia Rose*. My shoes echo against the aged wood, and I try my best to calm my nerves. I look around before I take a step onto the boat. It rocks underneath me, throwing off my equilibrium. Steading myself, I walk to the only door I see. Taking my lip between my teeth, I whisper a silent prayer and knock.

A bark from behind causes me to jump. I turn to see Lit walking my way. The dog, Gunner—I believe is his name—runs to me and starts sniffing my feet, wagging his tale ninety miles per hour. I bend down and pet his head.

"Hey, Gunner," I say.

I hear a whistle, and Gunner turns and makes his way back to his owner, who is looking at me with narrowed eyes. *Shit.* He's shirtless, sweating, and wearing a black snapback backwards with gray jogging shorts. I swallow.

"Cynthia?" he questions in disbelief.

"Umm, hey." I wring my fingers, nervous and unsure of what to say.

"What are you doing here?" he asks, walking closer and scanning his eyes over me. "How did you…" He stops himself, his expression changing from confusion to understanding. His eyebrows lift, and his mouth opens slightly.

"Cyn. The older women that Gunner ran to the other day. That was you walking away."

I clear my throat. "Yeah, it was me." I curl my toes in my wedges. *Come on, Cynthia. Say something else!*

"Can we talk?" I ask.

"Can we talk?" he repeats, his eyebrows creasing. "You wanna talk now?" His expression changes quickly from surprised to guardedly angry. He steps closer to me, Gunner following behind. I'm standing at the entrance of the boat, and he walks right up. "You going to move, or you wanna talk right here?" I move to the side so he can step up. As he passes me, I catch a hint of cologne and sweat. *Man.* I said one day he would be all man, and now here he is.

He walks to the door I knocked on earlier and opens it. "Come on," he says, gesturing for me to go in first. I glance back at Charlotte and Maggie and find them sitting on a nearby bench. They quickly turn their heads away from us when I look. As nervous as I am, I can't help the small laugh that comes up my throat as I walk to where he is.

"Something funny?" he asks.

"It's nothing," I reply. I step past him into the small room. I take in the helm chair and all the knobs and gears. Windows line all four walls, and there's a bench seat across one. A door leads down below, and I assume that's where he lives.

"Nice boat," I say, taking a seat. He sits in the captain's chair and rests his foot on the bottom bar.

He nods.

"I never pictured you a fisherman."

"I never pictured you one to run away." *Oh, we're getting right down to it then.*

I exhale. "Lit, I didn't run away. I moved away. You knew that." I notice his body tense up, and Gunner lies down beside him.

"Whatever you want to call it," he says, his voice sounding cold.

"I had to go."

"Yeah, you had to go, but you didn't have to disappear."

"I thought it was best."

He quickly stands up and walks over to me. I move back as his hand loudly slams above me and he leans in. "I called you more times than I could keep track," he seethes, his teeth bared. "I fucking tried my best to find you!" I flinch at his raised voice and swallow at his proximity.

He moves back and lifts his hat off his head, running a hand over his buzzed hair. He tosses the hat into the wall and scrubs down his handsome face in frustration. His hands go to his hips, and he stares out at the other boats.

"I would have moved with you if I could," he says more softly. "I would have left everything to be with you." My eyes go to the floor, and my heart pounds in my ears. *He loved me even before I knew what love was. I had never felt it before, not from my parents, not from the nannies they hired, but Lit. I felt it from him, and I pushed it away.*

"You left me without so much as a glance back," he says, and my eyes shoot up because that's just not true. I looked back. Boy, did I look back, but I was messed up.

"We were so young, Lit."

"Yeah." He nods his head and looks over at me. "But love is love. And I fucking loved you."

My eyes dance around the four walls that surround me. *Loved.* But this boat.

"What were you hoping to get out of this?" he asks.

I bite my lip. "I don't know."

"You don't know? You have no idea?" He looks skeptical.

I peer down again. "Forgiveness, maybe? To see if you were okay." I swallow and focus back on him. "To see you again."

He ignores the last sentence. "Forgiveness?"

"Yeah."

"You gotta say sorry first, baby."

I push myself up from the bench seat and walk over to him, looking him directly in the eyes so he'll know I mean it. "I've never been sorrier," I say, and my wall crumbles. My emotions come full force with him standing before me. He was always the best-looking boy in school to me, not only on the outside, but where it counts—deep on the inside. My eyes water, and I try with everything in me to keep the tears from falling, but one slips and he notices. I quickly wipe it away, embarrassed for getting emotional.

"How long has it been since you've done that?" he asks.

"What?"

"Cry."

I shake my head and shrug. "I don't know," I say, disconcerted.

He nods once as though he figured that'd be my answer. "Well, I forgive you," he says. He walks over and scoops up his hat, placing it back on his head carelessly. "So you can go."

I look down and fold my arms, my heart falling to the pit of my stomach. This is what I was afraid of. This feeling. *Rejection. The same thing you did to him? Yeah. That.*

"Okay," I say. I take a step toward the door before I look back. "By the way, I live in North Carolina in a small town called Sea Harbor." I continue to the door. "Take care," I mumble as I step out, not caring to shut it behind me. I make a beeline for the dock and walk as fast as my wedges will allow. Maggie and Charlotte jump up from the bench.

"Cynthia?" Maggie says, looking at me with concern. I told them this would happen.

"He wants nothing to do with me." I wipe the tears away from my face as they look at each other.

"I'll go and tell that young man a thing or two!" Maggie says as she starts to pull Archie with her. I hold out my hand.

"Don't, Maggie. It's okay. I deserve this. What? Did we all really think he was just going to forgive and forget? Just come back into my life as though I didn't leave him like garbage on the side of the road?" I shake my head and look up. "Not everyone gets a happy ending. I mean, look at you two." I exhale and stare up at the sky as a small airplane flies above us, a banner trailing behind advertising a local restaurant. "Let's just go home," I say, defeated.

Chapter Twenty-Four

Charlotte Harris

We're less than halfway home now, all of us in a mood because things didn't work out the way we wanted them to with Lit. And honestly, Cynthia's comment about us not having a happy ending kinda stung a little. But mostly, I'm puzzled about Litton. Why would the boy name his boat after her if he wants nothing to do with her? I think he just needs some time to think, and I'm praying he'll come around. Cynthia is more crushed than she lets on, hardly eating anything when we stop for lunch, but we let her handle her emotions the way she sees fit. She stirs from the back seat, and I look up in the rearview, seeing her grab her notebook and pen from her pink polka dot bag.

"Wanna finish this story?" she says with a tired voice, opening her notebook and resting it on her lap. She pulls the pen top off with her teeth and crosses her legs.

"You sure you're up for it?" I ask.

"It would be a welcome distraction."

I nod in understanding. "Okay, where were we?"

"You made Travis promise not to leave you again."

"Oh, yes." I look ahead at the road and think back on my memories of that time, trying to pull out the important parts. I've told her so much, and I'm sure she won't be able to put all of this in the newspaper. She's got a big job to do with narrowing it down already. "I left John on April 15, 2005. It was not a good day. He was devastated, but he caused no scene. He sat in his recliner and stared mindlessly at the TV as my friends and family helped me move my son's and my things out of the house. The look on his face broke my heart, because despite his behavior over the years, I never wanted to hurt him. John was a good man; he just got a shit start, and it stayed with him. But I knew this was what I needed to do. For me, for Travis.

"I just hate that my son had to witness his dad hurt so much, even though he wasn't the best dad. Regardless, it crushed William. He was torn, and I could see it. He wanted his mom to be happy, but he didn't want his dad to be sad because he loved him. It was a difficult time. As a parent, you never want to see your kids hurt, especially if it's because of something you did.

"We moved into a little three-bedroom singlewide trailer. It was just a tin can, sitting on a piece of land with another singlewide nearby. It wasn't pretty, it wasn't ideal, but it became my heaven on earth. Not too long after we moved in, Elizabeth joined us. She was having issues at home, and I remember one night she stayed over. I told them not to sleep in the same bed together, but I woke up only to find they didn't listen to me.

"Pissed me off. I thought what would her parents think? But if I learned anything from being a teenager in love, it's that kids are going to do what they want. And if you don't approve, they'll just do it behind your back. So, they did what they wanted. They were both smart, so I trusted them to be careful, and they still don't have children till this day if that tells you anything," I say. "But boy, do I want them to!

"It was just us three for a little while, and I would leave the kids on Fridays and take my ass straight to Ft. Pierce, Florida. Travis and I would spend the weekends together, and then I'd head back to Georgia, until the time came for Travis to meet my son. He was nervous as hell about it, but I knew it would all be okay. Travis was the love of my life, and if I loved him, I knew William would, too. Plus, everyone liked Travis. He was just a likable guy.

"The first time he came up, I remember he had to pee so bad that he insisted we pull over on the side of the road. He'd said, 'I can't meet your boy and then tell him I need to take a piss.' I laughed at him, but he was serious, so I had to pull over."

Maggie looks over at me with a smirk. "I don't think I blame him on that one."

"What was it like having him in your home? I mean, with your kid there and Elizabeth? I know you had to feel like you were dreaming," Cynthia says from the back seat.

I grin and look toward the road. "It was everything to have him there with me. I felt like my life was complete. We stayed up all night talking and I had to be at the hellhole the next day, but I didn't care. I took a shower and drove straight there with a smile as big as Texas on my face. Not even my asshole of a boss could have ruined my mood that day."

Maggie laughs, and Cynthia asks, "What did William think about him?"

"My son is a nice guy, so he wouldn't be an asshole even if he didn't care for Travis. But they shook hands, and that was that. They hit it off immediately, because they both had a love for music. The next time Travis came up, he mentioned that to William.

"He'd said, 'Your mom tells me you love music and used to play the bongos in a band.'

"'Yeah,' William replied. 'But I haven't learned the guitar yet.'

"'Well, I know a little.'

"'Really?' William asked with a slight smirk on his face.

"'Yeah, go get your stuff, man. Let's play some.'

"William went and got his bongos and guitar that John and I bought him for Christmas one year. Travis walked to our room and grabbed his twelve-string, and after that, the two would sit up all night. Travis took time with William, and eventually, he taught him how to play that guitar.

"Some nights we'd all be in the living room and I'd just watch in adoration as Travis would tell William, 'Use this chord here, and strum like this. You got it. That sounds good, man.' He'd laugh as he was playing, and he'd be the one who messed up. He'd say, 'I'm fucked up.' And then right after, 'But fuck it, I'm home.'

"He was so patient. John was never patient and would get fed up if William wasn't getting something fast enough for him, so if possible, it made me love Travis even more seeing him like that with my kid."

"He sounds like a really great person," Maggie says.

"Yeah."

"How long did he come back and forth?" Cynthia asks.

"Only a few times, and then finally, he moved in…"

August 2005

"I got a bunch of shit I don't need," he says, throwing his things into a suitcase.

"Bring whatever you want. We'll make room." I watch him as he takes things from his dresser and brings them over. I can't believe this is happening. I swear, sometimes I feel like I need to pinch myself. My life is amazing right now. I'm finally happy again. I'm finally back with Travis.

After we get the car packed, Travis says goodbye to his family and we hit the road. We've got a good drive ahead of us, but this is the best trip home I've ever taken, because this time, I'm bringing him back with me for good.

"When we got to Georgia and unpacked, Travis popped open a beer and that was that. He was home. Over the next few weeks, I was floating. Every day I got to come home to Travis Cole, my soul mate, the one I was supposed to spend my whole life with, and we had the rest of our lives to do so. I'd never been happier, and that was the downright truth." I smile and adjust my seat belt as I turn a little in my seat to move my stiff back. "We might have to pull over and stretch in a bit," I say.

"That'll be fine with me. I gotta pee," Maggie says.

"Get off at the next exit," Cynthia throws in. "I could use some coffee. Continue," she tells me.

"We fell into a routine," I reply. "But." I sigh and lift my heart-shaped necklace from my neck, rubbing it between my thumb and finger.

"But what?" Maggie asks, and I look over at her. She lifts a brow before looking back at the road.

I remember my place. "But troublingly, that dang cough and sore throat was still an issue, so around October he went to this little doctor that took patients with no insurance.

"He didn't really do any tests or anything. Just gave him some throat medicine and sent him home." I shake my head. "So we continued with life. I'd get up and go to work, and he'd have supper cooked when I got home. Our stove went out, so he had to cook on a griddle, but man, he cooked a mean breakfast on that thing. We would watch TV and curl up together, and every night I was thankful that I could fall asleep in his arms. He was planning on getting back to work, but we were waiting for his car."

"His car?" Maggie asks. "The GTO?"

"That's the one." I smile. "His brother was hauling it up for us, and they were going to work on it and get it back running so he would have a ride."

"Man, I'd love to see that car," Cynthia says. I smile to myself. Maggie gets off the exit, and I see the sign for gas stations to the left.

"Can you get a coffee from there?" I ask Cynthia.

"Yep, I'm down with being in control of the cream and sugar."

Unfortunately, the stations are farther down than we thought, so we lose some time, but after we stretch our backs and Maggie and Archie use the bathroom, we climb back in the car and head back toward the interstate with a cup full of cream and sugar for Cynthia. I really can't wait to sleep in my own bed. We pass by a house that has a lit-up neon sign that reads *Psychic Readings.* It makes me think of a woman I spoke with long ago.

"I remember a friend of mine, Sara," I say to the girls. "She told me about this psychic lady who worked with her. She walked by her desk one day and saw a photo of her husband.

"'Are you happy?' she'd asked Sara.

"'Yeah,' she'd replied. And then the lady started telling her crazy stuff about her husband. Turned out, he was a nut, and she eventually left him. I had always thought he was odd. You know how you just get a feeling about people sometimes?

"Well, anyway, I'd said, 'Maybe I should give you a photo of Travis to give to her. See what she says.' I did, and Sara showed it to her. She then called me and told me the lady said, 'He is so in love with her. He would do anything for her. She's going to be happier than she has ever been, but there is something looming over them that has to do with his throat.'

"I said, 'Yeah, we've been going to this small-time doctor because Travis doesn't have insurance, but he hasn't done anything.'"

"Oh, that's weird how she knew about his throat bothering him. I've always wanted to see a psychic," Cynthia says.

"Those kinda people freak me out," Maggie throws in. "I don't think you're supposed to know the future."

I chuckle. "Yeah, but sometimes they bring you peace of mind."

"And sometimes they tell you shit you're better off not finding out."

"Anyway," Cynthia says with an eye roll, "where were you?"

I look away from the rearview and smirk. "I believe I was going to tell you about Labor Day weekend before Travis started going to that doctor. It was one of the best times we all had as a family. We ended up going to my sister Sophia's house in Indiana. Travis and I took my car, and the kids came a day after. Now, even though Travis was forty-nine, he was still the same Travis, and he still liked to smoke grass and drink beer."

"You know if they got any pot here?" he asks me as he tosses his cigarette into the fire pit. I can tell fall is in the air, and I'm grateful for this warm fire. Sophia overhears him.

"My son Ryan does, but don't let my other son Ethan know about it. He'll have a fit. Come on," she says, and we get up.

"William," Travis calls him over as we're walking toward the house.

"Yeah?" he says.

Travis coughs and rubs his throat. "Wanna come hit this with us?" he says after he clears it. William looks back at Elizabeth.

"Baby," he says, and Elizabeth walks over. "Let's go."

"You still got that cough," I say to Travis. He's been doing that since our ride home from Ft. Pierce.

"Yeah, just a dry throat. I can't seem to get rid of it."

"Maybe we need to get it checked out," I reply.

"Nah, it'll go away." He gives me a wink as Sophia grabs her son out of the room.

"They wanna smoke," she whispers. Ryan looks back at his friends and Ethan. Ethan has a game controller in his hand and stares straight at the TV, ignoring us. Ryan signals one of his friends to come on.

We sneak around the house, and I giggle because this is ridiculous. We are hiding from a teenager, but somehow it makes me feel like a teenager, and the sweet nostalgia has me clutching Travis' hand and whispering I love you *in his ear before we all get stoned.*

"Time passed by in our little love shack. Travis and I enjoyed late nights talking while the kids went out and had their fun. Sometimes they'd come home arguing up a storm, and I'd want to go in there so bad, but Travis would say, 'Leave them be. They'll work it out. They always do.' Still, I couldn't stand arguing. I'd lived through so much of it over the years. But he was right. They always worked it out, and within minutes we'd hear them laughing and cutting up again.

"We had so many good times in that little trailer. Travis always had the front door wide open, Guns N' Roses blaring through the whole house, and a fire outside in the yard. We'd go visit his sisters and brother, too, and that's just what they all did. Bonfires, drinks, and grass.

"As time passed, I noticed Travis' throat situation wasn't getting any better. If anything, it was getting worse. I grew more and more concerned, and the night came where he finally did also. We went to the emergency room at two in the morning. By this time, it was November. The leaves were changing quickly, and the weather became super chilly.

"I've never been a fan of fall. The plants and trees die away, and the weather turns cold. I hate being cold, but sadly, the weather and the dying plants were about to be the least of my worries."

November 20th

We sit in the tiny white room waiting for the nurse to come back with the X-rays. This is the first time he's had them done. That doctor he's been going to hasn't done shit.

"I'll sure be glad when we figure this mess out," Travis says.

"Me, too."

He smiles and reaches over to grab my hand, pulling me up onto his lap. I laugh. "They could come in here any minute."

"Let them come." He presses his lips to mine, and then we hear a loud knock on the door. I scramble out of his hold as he chuckles. "Come in," he says.

A little guy walks in with a smile on his face. "Well, the good news is it isn't cancer," he states. "Because cancer doesn't hurt."

I look over at Travis and smile. "That's great news."

"Yeah," the nurse replies. "But we still aren't sure what's going on. We suggest you go to an ear, nose, and throat doctor." He hands Travis a card. "This is the one we recommend."

We leave the ER at four a.m. I'm exhausted and so is Travis. We walk into the house and hear the hum of Elizabeth and William's fan, signaling that they are asleep, so we head back to our room. The glow of the bedside lamp illuminates the small bedroom we share, and I flop down onto the mattress.

"Oh, I'm glad I'm off work tomorrow, but I do have to clean the office."

"One day you won't have to clean all of those offices," Travis says. "You deserve a break, and I'm going to make sure of that." He takes off his shoes and lies down beside me.

"I don't care how many offices I have to clean as long as I can keep coming home to you."

He smiles that Travis Cole smile. "Let's finish what I started at the ER."

We arrive at Dr. Blackwell's office a week later. It's cold, and we hurry inside to check in. We only have to wait a little while before the nurse calls us back. She asks Travis a few questions and then leaves us when the doctor walks in.

"Mr. Cole," he greets, reaching his hand out. "I'm Dr. Blackwell." Travis stands and shakes the doctor's hand.

"Nice to meet you, Doc. Wish it was under different circumstances," Travis replies. I kinda smile, because he does.

"So, your throat's been giving you some trouble," he says.

"Yeah, it's been hurting for a while now."

"I see you smoke and drink," the doctor says as he washes his hands and then grabs his light.

"Yeah, man," Travis agrees, giving me a sideways glance.

"Open up for me." Dr. Blackwell clicks on his light. Travis complies, and the doctor peers down his throat. He then stands back and shuts the light off. "It's cancer," he says nonchalantly, like he didn't just say the worst word on the fucking planet. My heart. It shatters. My stomach twists, and my pulse quickens. "Squamous cell carcinoma. Throat cancer."

Travis looks at me, and I see it in his eyes. *Worry.*

"I want to take your tonsils out and see what we're looking at here," Dr. Blackwell says. He goes on about other things, but my mind only focuses on Travis, who still looks at me. We speak with our eyes. In mine, I pray he sees hope and it's all going to be okay. It has to be. We just got back together. It's going to be fine. In his, I see *You okay? Don't worry. I love you.*

We walk out of the office hand in hand, neither of us saying anything. But my mind is screaming, *How could this happen? How is this possible? Could the universe really be this cruel?*

We make it to the car, and Travis pulls me by the hand, making my chest touch his. He stares into my eyes, and I see it. I see it all. *Regret, sorrow, worry.*

"I'm so sorry, baby," he says, looking down. My chest shakes, and my eyes fill with tears. "I would have never come back. I would have never…" His voice trails off as he lifts his head. His golden browns look at mine, and my tears fall. "If I had known this was going to happen, I wouldn't have gotten back in touch with you."

"Travis," I cry. "I wouldn't change a single second. Not one." He presses his forehead to mine before embracing me, and we stand in the parking lot. Me with a tear-streaked face and unanswered questions. While he stands strong, holding me up, and I can't help but think it should be the other way around.

Chapter Twenty-Five

November 23, 2005

Today is my birthday. I'm fifty. The big Five-O. I'm a year older, and just the day before yesterday my life was everything I'd always wanted, and now it's crashing in around me. After I hang up the phone with Travis, I sit in my car and ponder about things. *We can't find each other and him leave me again like this. That just can't happen. Maybe when he gets his tonsils removed, they'll see that it's not that bad. He'll get treated for it, and it'll be gone.* I mindlessly rub my thumb over the top of my phone as I talk myself up. *Yes, that's what's going to happen.* I shake my head. *No need to worry when we haven't even heard anything yet. It's going to be fine. It'll all be fine.*

I tell myself this over and over as I get out of the car and make my way into the hellhole. I open the glass doors and turn the corner.

"Happy birthday!" the whole office shouts. Even my boss. I'm stunned, and then I see the sign above my office door.

Here's to fifty! Your best year yet!

And I can't control it. I burst into tears and cover my face. Stella runs over to me. "Charlotte, what's wrong?" She grabs my shoulders and urges me to walk, so I do straight to my office. I sit down, and she shuts the door.

"What is it?" my best friend, the woman who stands by me, asks with bunched eyebrows. Unlike my family, who isn't speaking to me because of my recent life choices. My eyes go to my desk in front of me. A photo of the kids from their first Christmas together, little whatnots that say positive things about life. I sigh and stare at the photo of him. My vision blurs, and tears fall down my cheeks. *I just don't understand.*

"Charlotte?" Stella says. I look up at her, my chest heavy with pain.

"It's cancer," I say, forcing the word out.

"Cancer?" She shifts her head back in disbelief.

"Yes, we just found out Travis has cancer." I grab a tissue from my desk.

"What kind of cancer?"

"Throat." My voice cracks, and I shake my head as more tears fall.

"My God," she breathes. I put my face into my hands, asking God *why?* Why would He let this happen? Someone knocks on the door.

"Girls, we need to get back to work," our boss says.

Stella rolls her eyes. "Fucking prick," she mumbles. She walks over and sits down. "We're going to get through this," she says. "Travis will get through this, because you're my best friend and you deserve to be happy. I fucking demand it."

Travis has the surgery a week after my birthday, and as soon as they get the results, we are called into the surgeon's office. We sit, waiting, nervous, praying, and then the doctor comes in. She pulls up her little black stool and takes a seat while we both stare at her.

"I'm sorry," she says. "There isn't much we can do. It's too far-gone. With chemo and radiation, he probably has a fifty-fifty chance."

My eyes go to the floor, and I shake my head in disbelief, and still, my brain keeps saying, *He's gonna be okay. This is going to be okay.*

"We'll fight it," Travis says. "I'll fight this motherfucker."

She nods and says, "I'll set you up with an oncologist."

"So, she did, and we got him on Medicaid. He started seeing the doctor for radiation and chemo every week. His family was a Godsend. His half-sister and he were never close, and like I already mentioned, one of his older brothers had passed, but his two sisters and Byron took turns staying with us because I still had to work and clean offices.

"They would take him to his appointments when I wasn't able and stay with him at the house just to keep him company. But regardless of our shitty situation, we still enjoyed each day the best we could, and I swear to you, if you didn't know he was sick, you would think he was just as fine as anyone without cancer. Travis acted the same, his eating changed, of course, and he lost weight, but he smiled like he was gonna live forever. He was the strongest man I'd ever known.

"On Christmas Day, we four sat in the living room and gave out gifts. I recorded everything on my camera back then. I'm not sure why, though. I guess maybe deep inside somewhere I wasn't so optimistic. I wanted every moment captured to look back on. Just in case, ya know?

"That January, Travis had to have surgery for a feeding tube, because he had gotten to where he couldn't eat as well. The radiation was killing his throat, and he already didn't have much of an appetite, but he was still able to eat if he chose. This just made it to where he didn't have to."

The girls are quiet as I tell all of this. Just listening to my every word and soaking it up. "I know this all sounds terrible," I tell them. "But I promise you, we had a ton of good days."

"I just don't know how you dealt with it," Maggie says, reaching over and touching my hand. "I knew something happened, but I had no idea it was all of this, Charlotte."

"I never told you." I shrug. "But about the good times. We traveled to his sister's house in Waycross. The kids, too. We grilled out, sat by the fire, and listened to them all tell stories. Everyone smoked and drank, and I marveled at how much they all loved their brother, but like I said, Travis Cole was a likable person…not just likable, though. Travis Cole was a man to love…"

February 2005

We sit around the warm fire as Travis strums his guitar. Everyone sings along softly to the Allman Brothers' song he's chosen to play, and the fire crackles and pops in the afternoon sun. Elizabeth mindlessly stares at it, and William watches Travis' hands. His brother and sisters laugh and enjoy their drinks, and I just relish being beside him. Nothing is better than family. To me, there's no greater joy than being surrounded by people who love you for just being you, and I know this man beside me loves me for everything I am and everything I'm not.

He sets the guitar down a few moments later and drinks his non-alcoholic beer. He said he just has to have the taste even if he can't have the fun part anymore. The alcohol burns his throat now, and he's also given up cigarettes. But not his weed. That helps with the pain anyway, so I don't argue. His niece sits in a plastic chair across from us, as her cousin sits beside her.

"Uncle Travis, have you ever built a porch?" she asks him.

"Yes, several," he replies.

"Have you ever got arrested?" she asks. He looks over at me with a small smirk, still as handsome as he was when we were teenagers. He will always, always take my breath away.

"Only a couple of times," he replies with a smile.

"Ever raced a motorcycle?" the other one asks Travis.

"Once, and I almost killed myself," he says, chuckling.

"What about you, Ms. Charlotte. You ever raced a motorcycle?"

I laugh as I hold the camcorder. "Can't say that I have."

The kids grow tired of playing twenty-one questions, and they get up from their chairs, leaving behind notebook paper with scribblings and crayons with the wrappers torn off. I do a take around the yard before landing on Travis. He looks at me and smiles, giving me a wink at the same time.

"I love you," I tell him from behind the camera.

"I love you, too," he says softly.

April 2006

I walk in as Travis is putting his shirt on. It's doctor day, and for a moment I just stare. I haven't realized how much weight he's lost until now. His ribs are showing, and his stomach is sunken in. He looks up at me, and I smile. "You about ready?" I ask.

"As ready as I'm gonna be," he replies, sliding on his blue jean shirt. He gives me a wink. I walk over, and just because I can, I kiss him softly. He pulls back a tad, and I stare into the same golden brown eyes I've always loved.

"I wish I could marry you," he says, and it breaks my heart. We know that's not possible. If we get married, he loses his Medicaid, and he can't do that.

"One day," I say.

He nods and says, "Well, let's get on with it."

We're going in for a PET scan, and it's either unclear news or bad. I feel like that's the only news you get from these kinds of places. But we stay hopeful, and I keep thinking, *It's all going to be okay.*

Chapter Twenty-Six

The next day I leave work, and my car won't go into gear.

"Nothing's working," I tell Travis.

"Call a tow truck and get home. We'll figure it out."

Turns out, the transmission went out in Black Beauty. To say I'm disappointed would be an understatement. I love that car. We go to the Ford dealership not too long after that and try to pick me out another one.

"It's too slow," I tell Travis. "I want a V8 like Black Beauty."

"It's not too slow. You don't need all that motor. You drive too fast as it is."

"That's just the way I drive."

"I need to know you're going to be safe." And I realize what he's saying. My lip quivers, and I try to swallow the tears that threaten to come up.

I clear my throat. "Okay," I say softly. "I'll get this one."

A few days later, the doctor calls and says they need to see us. Travis' PET scan results are in.

We walk into the room, hand in hand like always, and wait for the news. I pray. God, I pray. Travis kisses my knuckles and tries to keep my mind off of why we are here. He's always doing that, trying to keep my mind off of the reality of our situation, but I sometimes wonder what his mind is thinking about all of this. I don't bring it up, though.

When the doctor comes in, I know what she's going to tell us before she even speaks a word. It is all in her expression. The way her lips are in a firm line but slightly frowning. Her eyes are soft, and she links her hands in front of her resolutely.

"It's spread."

I feel as though someone has stabbed me right in the chest. I have trouble finding air, and my whole world collapses right before my eyes. *It spread.* My mind can't comprehend this. Spread. We did everything right. We came to the appointments. We did the fucking chemo. Anger and sadness battle each other inside my head. Pain and utter agony wrap around my heart, squeezing the life out of me.

"The chemo isn't working," she says regretfully.

Isn't working. The one thing that's supposed to help isn't. I look up at her, and without even thinking, I ask, "How long?"

"Two to four weeks, we're not sure." I watch her mouth move as she starts saying things about hospice, and I look over at Travis as it finally hits me. We aren't going to win.

That night, when all the world is quiet and fast asleep, I lie awake beside him. I always relish in the feel of him next to me. I love sliding my feet over and rubbing them up his once strong calves and back down to the heels of his feet, so I do that over and over. I hold his hand while he sleeps, full of meds to help with his pain. I kiss his back, and I breathe him in more than a million times, because I know, one day soon, I won't get to do it again.

I wipe the tears away from my face and stare out the window beside me. Trees pass us by, and I hear Maggie sniff, but none of us say anything. Because there's nothing to say. It's sad. And that's just it. It's fucking sad.

May 2006

It's Friday evening, and I'm curled up beside him in bed, as we watch nothing important on TV. The small lamp casts a yellow glow in the room, and I look over at the dresser it sits on. Yellow bottles line the top, filled with a different pill for a different problem. I look away and set my eyes on the TV screen, thinking how I missed the good day he was having because I had to work, and that reminds me. "I've got to go get Elizabeth," I tell him.

"Yeah, it's about that time, isn't it?" He uncrosses his ankles, only to cross them again. "You know, I want something good to eat."

I look up at him in shock because he never eats anymore. "Really?"

"Yeah, like Chinese or something."

"Okay." I grin, and he gifts me that crooked Travis Cole smile, dimples and all. Even through all this, it's still there. I lean up and kiss his lips.

"I'll be back shortly." I sit up and stand, grabbing my cell phone, before I walk to the door.

"I love you," I say, turning around.

"I know, baby. I love you." He gives me a wink. I walk out but look in the mirror, seeing him sitting on our bed. He's wearing that same blue jean button-down shirt, and he's resting back on the pillow, closing his eyes. I take a photo with my mind and promise to always keep it.

Once I grab the food, Elizabeth and I head home and talk about her and William. They broke up, but she needed a ride home from work, and I don't mind because she's like the daughter I never had.

"I hope y'all work it out," I tell her as we pull up to her parents' house.

"Yeah, me, too. Tell Travis I said hey."

"I will. Love you."

"Love you, too."

Once I park the car in the driveway, I head inside with the food and put it on the counter. "I'm home," I say in a singsong voice as I walk into our bedroom. He lies on his side, looking at the TV.

"I got your food."

"I'm sorry, baby. I just can't eat it right now," he says, looking back at me.

"That's okay," I tell him, noticing his mood has changed. It worries me, but I take off my day clothes and grab a quick shower so I can lie with him. I'm just happy to be beside him. I don't care if he eats the stupid food or not.

"He started going downhill quickly after that. They say you get better before you get worse. Guess that explains his great mood," I say gravely.

May 2006

I jump awake and gently place my hand on Travis' side of the bed. It's empty, and I see the glow from the bathroom light under the door. Tossing the covers off me, I look at the clock and see it's the middle of the night.

"Travis?" I call out as I walk around the bed to the bathroom door. It's cracked, and I can see him on the floor. "Travis." I open the door, and he stares in front of him, void of emotion. "Let me help you."

"Give me a minute. Just give me a minute," he says, breathless.

"Okay," I respond worriedly. I put the toilet seat down and sit. My eyes go to the floor, and I say nothing. This is hard for me to see, but as hard as it is for me, I know it has to be even harder for him. Travis Cole has always been a strong man. My bad boy from Ft. Pierce, Florida. But this fucking cancer has stolen his strength. It's stolen everything.

"Come on. You can't stay down there," I plead because I can't take seeing this anymore. He looks at me and nods.

"Okay," he says as he reaches for the countertop, gripping onto the edge for support, but I know I'm in this alone. He has nothing left in him. I put my hands under his arms and lift with everything I have. It almost kills my back, but I know it would hurt his pride if I called William for help, so we make it work and he finally stands on weak legs and I get him to the bed. He lies down with a grunt, and I feel so helpless. I pull the covers up over him and kiss his forehead before I walk back to my side and lie down. He doesn't move, and I don't sleep.

"I don't think it's the cancer. I think something else is wrong," I say to his sister, Ryanne. It's the next day, and he hasn't moved since last night's fall. "He keeps saying he has to use the bathroom, but he can't." I'm anything but easy at this moment. My thoughts are running wild, and I just don't know what to do.

"He may be blocked. He's on a lot of medication," she says.

"I'm just worried. I mean, what if this is something they can fix, ya know?" I walk a hole in the floor as I pace back and forth, looking in on him and then back to the living room.

"Let's call the ambulance," she says. I lean against the doorframe of our bedroom and watch him sleep. He looks so fragile. He hardly slept last night, and I didn't get a wink.

"Let's just wait a little bit," I say to her. "He's finally resting."

The clock on the wall reminds me that hours have gone by, and he isn't getting any better. I'm getting more and more worried, and I'm ready to call the ambulance.

"I love you," I say softly, looking down at him and running my fingers over his palm.

I look up when I hear a knock on the door, and Ryanne tells someone to come in. I then hear Elizabeth's voice, and I get up from the bed. "I'll be right back. Elizabeth's here." He doesn't respond, only lies there staring ahead.

"Hey," I say quietly as I walk out. "Did William call you?"

"Yeah," she says. "How is he?"

"Not good," I reply with tears in my eyes. She bites her bottom lip, and I see the tremble in it. Reaching her arms out, she embraces me, and I grip her back. Everything is going to shit, and I hold on for comfort to the only daughter I've ever had. When we break apart, we both wipe our cheeks, and I take an unsteady breath. She looks toward our room, and for a moment she peers down. I lean against the wall and cross my arms. My tears are unstoppable; my heart is shattered. I'm broken, this home is broken, and cancer has torn my world to shreds.

I see her swallow, and she steps forward, walking into our bedroom with hesitation. His reflection in the closet door mirror shows him lying across the bed. The look on his face says he isn't here, but his heart still beats, his lungs still take in air, and as long as that's happening, I can do the same. We said no to hospice, and I just don't know what to do right now as I watch her speak to him.

"Travis," she says with a soft voice. She clears her throat when he doesn't respond. "When things get better," she continues, sitting down on the bed, "you and I will get those old fishing rods out. We'll throw a line down at that pond you, William, and I always talked about visiting but never got around to." I look up to the ceiling, praying for God to give me some strength.

"We'll go on a warm day." Her voice shakes, and I look back as she wipes under her eye before turning her head toward me. Tears stain her cheeks, causing her makeup to run. When he mutters a response, she turns her attention back toward him and reaches for his hand. He doesn't move when she squeezes it, and what he mumbles is not understandable. "I love you," she says, and she stands up and walks over to me. She shakes her head and hugs me again. "I'm so sorry."

"Me, too." I struggle to get the words out, feeling like something is stuck in my throat.

I'm mad that she and William aren't together right now, comforting each other when they need it the most. I'm mad at how cruel the world can be, and mostly, I'm mad at God. Why would He do this? Why would He bring Travis back to me only to take him away again?

When Elizabeth leaves, I sit down on the couch and stare toward the door, my mind trying to figure out what to do here. I look up when William comes out of the back hallway. "Mom, can I talk to him alone before you call the ambulance?" he asks.

"Of course," I say to him. He walks to the back room and shuts the door, but it doesn't close all the way. I know he needs this moment, but I can't help but get up.

"When William gets done, I'm calling," I tell Ryanne as I lean against the hallway wall.

It's Saturday night, and I hear the ambulance pull up outside. I call down the hallway to William's bedroom, "They're here." I open the door for them to come in. They have a stretcher and ask me where he is, so I tell them. I follow as they make their way toward our bedroom, my heart barely beating because this is the moment I've been dreading. It feels like there's nothing I can do now. I've prayed more than anything, and it hasn't worked. Travis is still dying, they are still taking him, and I'm still helpless.

Once we make it to the hospital and they get him settled in, I sit and listen to all the machines he is hooked up to. Different beeps coming from different ones. I hold his hand in mine, looking over every wrinkle, every line, memorizing them in fine detail. Ryanne walks into the room and gives me a small smile. "You should eat something," she says.

"No, I don't want to leave him."

She nods and takes a seat in the empty chair. We don't speak, just sit and watch as the machines keep Travis alive and comfortable. For now.

The night passes with me fading in and out of sleep. He's no better today, and I haven't left his side but to use the restroom.

"Mom, you have to eat something," William says.

"I'm just not hungry."

"But you need to eat. Come on. Let's go down to the cafeteria." I look back at Travis and exhale. "He would want you to eat," William urges, and I know he's right. I look back at Travis' brother, Byron, who showed up this morning.

"I'll be right here with him," he says. "Go on and eat something."

I nod. "I'll be right back," I say to Travis as I get up. I kiss his hand and let William take me down to the cafeteria.

William and I take a seat after we get our sandwich and bag of chips. I open the bag and slowly take a few bites. My stomach growls, but it's a struggle to get this food down. I feel sick, and my chest aches. William makes small talk, trying to get my mind off the situation, but nothing is working. The smell of the hospital is too strong, the feeling inside my heart is too painful, and I just want to be back up there with him.

"After this, I'm gonna head home to shower, and then I'll be back," he says.

"Okay," I mutter.

"Mom?"

"Yes, son."

He has tears in his eyes. "I'm sorry this is all happening."

I have tears in mine. "Me, too."

We sit for a moment longer, and then he slides his chair back and stands. "I'll be back," he says. I nod and pick up my half-eaten sandwich. "I'll throw this away. You go on back up there."

"Okay." I stand up as he walks around the table, embracing me, and I almost feel my knees give out. I sniff and wipe my face when we pull away.

"Be careful," I say.

"I will. Love you."

"Love you, too."

I exit the cafeteria and walk the halls of the hospital toward the elevators. Photos of flowers hang on both sides of the stainless steel doors. I push the button, waiting for the thing to ding and take me back up to ICU. I feel empty, drained, and in so much pain, I'm not sure how much more of this I can take. But I'm not the one who's dying, even though it feels like it.

When I walk back into the room, Byron is sitting there talking to him.

"I'm sorry," I say, stepping out.

"No, come on back in." He clears his throat, and I can tell he's been crying. "I'm sure he'd rather you be here than this blubbering old boy." I give a weak smile, and he gets up from my seat. He takes the other one across from me, and I pick up Travis' hand, linking his fingers with mine.

"You know he really loves you," Byron says. I look over at him, wanting to know more.

"I remember when we were all teenagers, the way he'd light up when you called, and the way he acted when y'all started speaking again after so long. Witnessing a love like that is rare," he says, looking over at his brother. "But I got to see it, and you got to live it." My eyes blur, and I sniff, trying to rein in my tears.

"But why does it have to be over?" I ask, wiping my nose. He shakes his head.

"Everything has an expiration date. Eventually, we all fall."

I look back at Travis and bring his hand to my face. My tears roll onto his fingers, and I close my eyes as I silently cry.

It's later in the afternoon, and I'm laying my head beside him on the bed. I hold onto his hand and run my finger up and down his arm, looking at the tattoos he got when he was a younger man. William stands looking out the window in his own world. I look up when the doctor comes in.

"Mrs. Cole," he greets, and my heart skips a beat at the sound of that name. How I wish it were true. How I wish we could have married and I had his last name. He checks the machines and does something on the computer before taking a seat in front of me. "How are you?" he asks.

I swallow and sit up. "I'm okay." He nods and looks over at Travis before looking back at me.

"At this point, there's really nothing else we can do," he says, his voice full of sympathy. I narrow my eyes. "Would you like us to take him off the machines?"

"No," I say in disbelief. *Why would he ask that?* "There could still be a chance," I add, anger building inside of me. *Why would they give up on him?*

He gives me a look of sympathy but says, "Ma'am, there's no need for him to be on all of this medication anymore. We'll keep the blood pressure drip in and the pain meds going so he'll be comfortable."

I look back at William, and he says, "That's up to you, Mom."

My eyes go to the floor, and then I slowly turn my head toward Travis. "This is it," I mutter quietly. I stare at his face and the rise and fall of his chest. I think about the first time I saw him and how handsome he was. I think about the way my heart felt as his golden brown eyes sparkled in the summer sunlight. That was one of the best days of my life because it was the day I met him. Today is the worst day of my life because I'll remember it forever as the day I started to let go of the man I love.

It's day three in the hospital, and I sit with my feet propped up in the other chair. The machines are off now, only the blood pressure drip and his pain meds continue. The nurse walks in and adjusts his blanket while giving me a sympathetic smile.

"Ma'am, would you like the chaplain to come in? I know some people like to say a prayer before the end."

I sigh. Those words. *The end.* I hate them.

"Yes, I would," I answer. She nods and exits the room.

An hour or so later, we all stand around Travis, his two sisters and his brother, William, the chaplain, and me. I hold one of Travis' hand and his sister, Ryanne, holds his other. The man says words about healing and asks God to be with all of us in this time of physical, emotional, and spiritual need. He prays for God to help us cope with the challenges we are facing, to comfort and encourage those who love and care and whose lives have been unsettled and disrupted by illness. He asks God to remind Travis that he is walking with Him right now, to remind him that He loves him no matter what he is going through.

The chaplain keeps talking, and I open my eyes, looking down at my love. No words can describe the pain I feel; no prayer can make this go away. It is done. Everyone says amen, and it's just a whisper past my lips because I've never felt farther away from God as I do right now.

It's day number four in the hospital. Travis is still holding on. I stare at the clock on the wall as time ticks by too quickly, and then a thought hits me. He wanted to die at home. *At our home.* I jump up and run into the hallway, hearing William call my name, but I need to find a nurse or a doctor.

"Mrs. Cole?" someone says from behind me. I turn to look at the nurse who keeps checking on Travis.

"He wanted to die at home," I say, panicked. "That's what he told me."

"Okay, ma'am, well…umm…" She looks like she is unsure of what to do.

"I need to get him home!" I say to her.

"Okay, let me go get the doctor, and we'll see what he says. Just hold tight for me." I watch her scurry away, and I bite my fingernail anxiously. As I walk back toward the room, I see William standing at the door.

"What's going on?" he says worriedly.

"He wanted to die at home, son. I want to get him home."

"Okay," he says. "We'll see what the doctor says." I nod and sit down again as William remains standing. We wait for what seems like forever before the doctor comes in.

"I hear you're wanting to take him home?" he says to us.

"Yes. Please," I say.

He exhales. "Sadly, Mrs. Cole, Medicaid won't cover the ambulance ride back."

"I don't care. I'll pay for it."

He gives me a small smile. "Ma'am, if we take him off this blood pressure drip, he won't make it home."

My eyes close, and I feel tears fall down my face. "But he wanted to go at home."

"I'm so sorry," he says.

I feel William's arm wrap around me, and I realize he's bent down. "Travis wouldn't want you to have to worry about all of that, Mom."

I sniff and nod my head. "I know. You're right. He never wanted me to worry about anything."

I sigh and wipe my face. "Ma'am, we would like to suggest moving him to a quieter room."

"What do you mean?" I ask.

"It's called the transition room. It will be quieter, less people walking around the halls."

"What about the blood pressure drip?" I ask.

"If you want to know his blood pressure, the nurse will be happy to take it for you at any time."

"And his pain?"

"We'll keep him comfortable."

I take an uneasy breath and search the ceiling for an answer. I know in my mind we've lost this battle, but my heart is having a hard time coming to terms with that. I'm just not ready.

"I know this isn't easy," he says. "But I do believe it's what's best at this point."

I nod my head, knowing he's probably right. "Okay."

"Okay," he repeats. "We'll have someone come and get him." He exits the room. I rub my hands over my face and cry.

After a while, two young boys show up, and the nurse disconnects him from the machines. Travis is out, no longer conscious, and I watch as the boys move the bed and begin to push him out of the room. I stand and follow, but they go so fast I can hardly keep up. They hit bumps, and I hear Travis grunt. They treat this move like it's nothing, just another patient they have to wheel down to the transition room as they talk and cut up, but this is the love of my life!

"Slow down," I say loudly. They both look back at me. "You're going too fast. You may hurt him." They look guilt-ridden and then do as I ask.

After they get him settled, they leave us alone, and I talk to him. I tell him I love him and that some of the best moments of my life have been when I was with him. I kiss his hand and his fingers, and I lay my head down beside him. There's a window in here, and I look toward it, staring at the midnight sky. The stars are hardly visible, but I know they're there. I listen to his breathing, and before I know it, I've fallen asleep.

I jerk awake, and my eyes go to Travis. His chest still moves, and I exhale a relief. I rub my eyes and look at the big clock on the wall. It's three in the morning, and I stand up to see if I can find the nurse, but she walks in just as I turn around.

"Hey," she says.

"Hey, can you check his blood pressure?"

"Of course, honey."

I stay standing as she puts the cuff around his arm and the stethoscope in her ears. Her eyes go to her watch, and she gives me a sad smile before she tells me what it is. It's low…so, so low.

"Thank you," I say.

"If you need anything, just call me. I was glad to see you getting some rest," she calls out as she walks toward the door. I watch it shut behind her before I walk to the window and look out. I watch as a lone car or two rides down the road. Probably late night parties, drinking, and driving. It takes me back to when we were teenagers and all those parties we had by Taylor Creek Bridge. God, what I would do to go back, if even for a day. I look up to the sky and shut my eyes.

"I know I've been angry, but God, please let him know I love him more than I've ever loved anyone. Please let him know."

His family visits a little the next day. We chat lightly about nothing important until they decide to head home. His sisters kiss his forehead, and Byron grips his hand. I tell them bye and promise to call later. The silence in this room is deafening sometimes, but it is better than all those machines, I guess. I prop my feet up and rest my eyes when I hear someone come through the door.

"It's just me," William says as I turn to look.

"What do you have there?" I ask.

"I thought he'd like to listen to some music." He takes the small radio and places it on the table beside Travis.

"I think he would, too." My lip lifts a tad at my son's thoughtfulness, and my heart does, too, because in the little time Travis was a part of his life, William really got to know him. He switches it on, and it plays lightly beside his bed. William takes a seat, and we both sit in silence, just listening to the radio as I also listen to Travis take small breaths.

The afternoon passes too quickly, and he's still holding on. I study his face and keep hold of his hand. I think back on the last couple of months and how hard he has fought to stay with me. Chemo only tears a person down while it's trying to fight the cancer. I know there had to be moments when he was sicker than he let on just so I wouldn't worry. I hope that wasn't the case, but if I know him, it probably was. Sometimes, I wondered if he wished he could have been somewhere else so he wouldn't have had to pretend to feel good.

"No one has ever loved another person as strongly as I have loved you, Travis. No one ever will," I whisper as the tears fall down my face. My vision blurs, and I put my head down on the bed. My body shakes as I sob, and I hope that he knows how much I love him. I hope he knows being with him again was everything to me.

The bright moon shares its light with the small lamp in the vast room as the radio still plays. William walks out of the bathroom, and I can tell he's been crying. He clears his throat. "I'm going down the hall for a minute, Mom," he says. He wipes down his face and says, "I wish Elizabeth were here with us." I stand up and hug him tightly, realizing he's not only upset about Travis, but he misses her.

"I know," I say. I feel his body shake, and I embrace him harder as my tears begin again. We stand holding onto one another. Him missing his love because they chose to end it, and me missing mine because of something neither of us could control.

"I love you, son," I say as he lets go.

He rubs his eyes and says, "I love you, too," before he exits the room.

I wrap my arms around myself as I sit back down and reach for Travis' hand, bringing it to my lips. His chest shakes, and tears pour from my eyes as mine shudders, too, but not in the same way. Mine trembles because my heart is barely holding on from being broken. His shudders because it's barely holding on to keep him alive.

I look over his handsome face and think of all of the happy times we've had together. My love, my life. I met this boy when

I was seventeen, and I've never loved anyone more. I'll never love anyone more.

I sniff and grip his hand in mine. "I know you promised that you would never leave me again." I cry as I try to get out the words. My whole body shakes, and I wipe my face. "But it's okay if you need to go," I whisper, my voice full of agony and sorrow. I watch as his chest rises and falls. It takes a moment for it to do it again, but this time it jolts painfully, and after it rises no more.

I think about how they announce time of death in movies, and my eyes go to the clock on the wall as I say to myself, "Time of death: 12:07."

Chapter Twenty-Seven

"My son and I rode home from the hospital that night with the windows down and 'Sweet Child of Mine' blaring from the truck's speakers.

"'That's Travis saying goodbye,' I told William. 'He loved that song.'

"When we got home, I walked in the living room and saw Elizabeth sitting on the couch. 'He's gone.' I wailed as I held his clothes tightly to my chest. I walked back to our room and lay down on the bed, gripping onto his clothes for dear life. I sobbed with William standing at the foot of the bed and Elizabeth sitting on the end. I wept like a baby."

Maggie pulls over because we're all crying and undoes her seat belt. She gets out of the car and walks around to my side. I'm sobbing as though it just happened. She opens my door and pulls my arm. I stand, and she wraps me in a hug. I hear Cynthia's door open, too, and I feel her arms around me. We stand, three very different women, on the side of the road, hugging each other tightly as cars pass by and tears fall from our eyes.

June 2006

Endlessness lies ahead of me. As far as the eye can see, nothing but deep blue. The ocean is a wonder. It holds secrets with no way to tell them. It's where one can find peace or where one can get lost if they choose to or not. It holds life and death; tears and laughter. It captures moments from long ago, grasping onto time like only it can.

Here I stand at the edge of it all as the warm water washes over my bare feet, wave after expected wave. Shutting my eyes, I let sweet memories take over my vision, and my breathing becomes uneven, because it's not fair.

"It's not fair!" I scream out. I clench my fist and dig my nails into the palm of my hands as blood pumps wildly through my life source. My knees, after standing so strong, buckle and I fall to the ground. I beat the sand with my fist repeatedly.

"It's not fair," I whimper as I look at the sand through blurry tears. Scrubbing my hands down my face, I'm torn between praying my frail heart can survive all this unbearable pain and praying that it won't. I wipe the tears from my jaw as I blink my eyes open and look ahead.

Still… there's the ocean, unaffected, yet my whole world has changed. I push up from the ground and dust the sand off of myself. Today was a bad day. I've had a lot of those lately, but I take them as they come.

Leaving the private beach and making my way back to the house we've got for the week, I walk in and head to my bedroom. I take a seat on the bed and look at the box of keepsakes he kept beside our bed at home.

I brought everything with me up here. I needed to get away and think about things, so I thought *why not North Carolina?* The kids refused to let me be alone, though, so they rented the house with me, but they've given me my space. They got back together, just like Travis said they would. I lift the box and notice the number to that psychic my friend Sara knows, and I think about the funeral…

Sara comes up to me and hugs me tight. "I'm so sorry, Charlotte." I'm a mess, of course, as I stay near his casket. "I wanted to tell you something," she says softly. "Remember my psychic friend?"

I think for a moment because my mind just hasn't been right these past few days, but then I remember. "Yes," I say, rubbing the tissue under my eye.

She nods. "Well, I didn't tell you everything because you were just so happy."

"What?" I ask. "What was everything?"

"After she said that about Travis' throat, she said that you would be happier than you'd ever been. But to enjoy every day because he wouldn't be around long."

I close the lid to the box and grab his shirt. I put it on my pillow and let the tears fall until exhaustion finally takes over.

———

July 2006

"Okay, Linda. I'll talk to you later." I hang up the phone and walk into our bedroom. I love talking to Travis' sisters because they remind me of him and they understand. I'm alone in the house, and I sit on his side of the bed and look down at the dresser. "I miss you so much," I say. "I just don't know how to move on." My eyes go to his box, and I lift the top, seeing that number again. With the phone still in my hand, I figure what can it hurt? Sara gave me the psychic's number the day she told me everything and said the woman told her I could call anytime.

I flip my phone open and punch in the number. It rings, and I hold onto my heart necklace that contains some of his ashes.

"Hello," a woman says.

"Hey. My name is Charlotte. I'm Sara's friend, the one who gave you the photo to look at."

"Yes, I know who you are," she says it as though she was expecting my call.

"I don't mean to bother you, but Sara said I could call."

"Of course. I was sorry to hear about his passing."

"Me, too," I say. "So, what can you tell me?"

"He is sitting on the bed right beside you." I instantly get chills, and my eyes shoot to the spot beside me. Tears form in my eyes, and I reach my hand over, placing it on the comforter. "He loved you so much, Charlotte. He wasn't supposed to live as long as he did, really only a month or so after the new year, but he held on because he was worried about letting you down again."

Tears fall down my face, and I shake my head. God, the pain he must have been going through. How scared he must have been. He never showed it, though. He was always worried about me.

"He keeps telling me that you drive too fast. He's worried and says you need to slow down." I can't help but laugh through my tears. "He said he loves you and that he is fine."

I look over again and rub the comforter. Maybe I can be fine now, too. Maybe…

Chapter Twenty-Eight

Cynthia prepared the story and turned it in three weeks after we came home from our road trip. She offered to let me read it, but I knew she would do our story justice, so I chose to wait until it was published. Maybe I was getting a little ahead of myself, but I had all the faith in her.

Maggie has talked me into taking walks with her every day, and I've promised to cut back on my sweet tea drinking if she promises to cut back on her many alcoholic beverages before five. It's working out okay, but we'll see how long it lasts.

I talk with my son on the phone every evening, and the week before *The Sea Harbor Journal* announces their winner, which just so happens to be Cynthia Rose, he tells me Elizabeth is pregnant. To say I'm excited would be a damn understatement. I'm ecstatic.

Happily, that's not the only good news I have to share. Litton Daniels got his act together and showed up in Sea Harbor two weeks after we got home. He and Cynthia have been inseparable, and there's talk about him moving his fishing business here. He's a good kid, and in a way he reminds me of my Travis.

I'm looking online at baby clothes when I hear a knock on the door. Putting my computer to the side and taking my glasses off, I stand and see Cynthia.

"Hey," I say, opening it for her to come in. I look behind her and see Lit in the car. I give a wave, and he waves back.

"I don't need to come in," she says. "I just wanted to drop this off for you." I look at the newspaper she's holding out for me. I take it and slide my glasses back on to look at the cover. A Polaroid photo of Travis and me sits in the top left corner, and I look back at her.

She wrings her hands and looks down before she says, "Charlotte, what you two went through." She sighs and shakes her head. Her eyes focus back up. "No one should have to go through that. I cried a lot toward the end of writing this because your story touched me so deeply, just as it's going to do many readers. Basically, you're my hero."

I chuckle. "I'm not a hero, Cynthia." I gaze down at the paper again, scanning over her words before I look back up at her. "I'm just a woman who loved a man with everything I had, even after he took his last breath."

As the day slowly comes to an end, I sit on the beach in my Adirondack chair with the paper on my lap. The sun starts to sink, and for a moment I take it all in, just enjoying the view and the calmness of the ocean. I inhale before I slide my eyeglasses on and look down at the paper. Running my hand over his face, I smile a little. "I miss you," I whisper. My eyes move to Cynthia's words, and I begin reading.

"Charlotte Harris had always been a woman of many titles. Some being a daughter, a wife, and then a mother. But in the summer of 1972, a seventeen-year-old brunette beauty with freckles spread across her shoulders embraced a new title. Charlotte became a keeper of someone's heart, and that heart belonged to Travis Cole...

Chapter Twenty-Nine

A little over a year after our trip to Ft. Pierce, Cynthia, Maggie, and I took a road trip to New York. It was long, but it was pretty cool to see through the windows of the GTO. That's right. She's been sitting in my garage for twelve years. I paid someone to fix her up after we got back. She looks just as good as she did way back when Travis and I took her down old country roads and got lost in each other.

Maggie bravely took the steps of the little brownstone her daughter lived in, and when she knocked on the door, a little blonde-haired beauty answered it with her mama standing right behind her. They hugged, and it was as if time had never passed between them. You see, Maggie had already called and apologized, so that trip was strictly a reunion.

I sit in my chair as the summer sun sinks in the evening sky. My grandson lies on the blanket beside me. Cole has blue eyes like his mama and dark hair like his daddy. He's the most beautiful thing I've ever seen, and my heart finally feels full again after so many years of feeling half-empty.

I'll always, always long for Travis Cole. That will never stop, but I have a lot of love around me to keep me going every day.

Cynthia sits in the chair beside me with her shades on top of her rainbow-colored hair.

"You know, you were wrong when you said I didn't get my happy ending," I say to her. She looks over at me with a raised brow. "I didn't get the ending I was hoping for, but I'd say this one is pretty good."

She smiles and grabs my hand, squeezing it with hers. "Can I ask you something?"

"Of course."

"Did you ever find out what William said to Travis? You know, when he wanted to talk to him alone?"

I look toward the beach at my son and daughter-in-law. They have a drink in their hands and stand knee-deep in the water, side by side. My mind goes back to the day William asked to speak to Travis, and I hear his broken voice speaking to him again…

I stand close enough to hear, but not to intrude.

"Travis, I just wanted to say thank you. Thank you for coming back and making my mom happy," William says. He's quiet for a moment before he continues. "You've been more like a dad to me in the short time you've been with us than my dad ever was." His voice cracks, and I look down, tears falling from my face. "Thank you for all that you've done for me. I love you. I wish I would have told you sooner."

Cynthia sighs. "I wish I could have known him."

"Me, too," I say, looking ahead as the sky turns a crisp cool blue.

"What happened to John?" she asks a moment later. I look down, remembering I never told them about John. Just so much devastation with Travis, and then we got home and got back into our daily routines.

"After I left him, we still spoke every now and again because of our son, and he had seemed to move on with his life. He was even dating someone new, but John was still troubled." I pause and gaze ahead as the waves crash against the shore. "John had a lot of demons," I say sadly. "And the day came when he no longer had to fight them. He passed a year after Travis."

"Oh my God."

"Yeah, both of the men I loved dearly left this world way before me. I was heartbroken, of course, but more than anything, I was worried about William."

"You've been through so much," she says. I sigh and look down at Cole.

"They say what we go through makes us stronger, but sometimes I don't know."

Cynthia kinda laughs. "I know what you mean." We sit in silence for a while, just enjoying the ones around us and taking in the view of the setting sun. A man runs down the beach, and Cynthia says, "Let's get this guy to take a photo of us." She quickly grabs her Polaroid camera and stands.

"Everyone get together," I say. "We're going to take a photo." William and Elizabeth come up from the water, and I grab little Cole. Maggie holds her grandbaby while her daughter adjusts the little yellow hat she has on her head. Lit waits for Cynthia, and Marty wipes the sand from her legs.

"Everyone ready?" Cynthia asks as she runs back over to us.

William looks down at me. "I haven't seen you like this in a long time, Mom." I pull him in for a hug and kiss Cole's head. We all stand side by side, and as the man takes the photo, I smile, thinking, *being happy is a choice, no matter our circumstances*. Travis Cole chose to be happy, even though he was going through one of the scariest things of his life. He chose to be happy for me. Cynthia looks over at me after the photo is taken.

"So, tell me," she says as we walk back to our chairs. "If you knew then how it all would end, would you have gotten back with him still?"

I look down, pondering her question. I think about my life. Every special moment I have saved, every tear that I've cried, and every laugh that I've had—they've all led me to here. Yes, I'm without Travis, and that still stings, but look at all I do have. A small smile plays on my lips, and I look back at her and say, "If I'd known then what I do now, I'd do it a million times over. Just to be with him."

The End

Hang out, talk books and other fun shenanigans in her reader group: The Paige-Turners

A Note from the Author:

When I thought about writing this book, I was cleaning windows at work. The line, "It was the summer of 1972," popped into my head and I immediately sent my mother-in-law a text and asked her if I could write about her and Lloyd AKA Travis. She gave me the honor of doing so.

For years, I'd been saying her story was something that needed to be told. I mean, it's almost unbelievable, right? Two young people fall in love, everyone tries to keep them apart, time and miles finally do, and then they get back together thirty years later! Only for him to find out he has cancer and then pass away a little over a year later. But that's the thing. It happened, and I was a witness to the end.

I had the honor of knowing Lloyd Lacy, or as you know him, Travis Cole, and let me tell you. He was a man to know. Free-spirited and kindhearted. The love they had for each other was undeniable and something to see.

We didn't have much in that singlewide trailer, but we had love. We had each other, and we still do. Even though Lloyd is no longer with us, he is mentioned all the time, and he lives on in my mother-in-law's heart.

Sometimes it's the little memories that mean the most. My mother-in-law holding that video camera, Lloyd singing and laughing, my husband and him playing the guitar together. I can always look back on those memories with a smile on my face.

Lloyd, you left us too soon. You are missed daily, and I hope wherever you are, we will see you again.

Acknowledgements:

Mama C., thank you for letting me write this story. I will always cherish the many nights we sat and talked about the past. We cried, we laughed, and we made memories.

Lloyd, thank you for coming into our lives and making them brighter. I hope I made you proud, and I hope you still get to listen to your music.

Thank you to my girls, Crystal, Monica, Julie, and Kelley, for always being eager to read whatever I'm working on.

Thank you to my best friend, Collins, for always being so supportive and someone to talk to when the world is driving me crazy.

Thank you to my beta readers:

Julie Healey-Vaden, I thank God for Sarasota and meeting you. My life is better because of it. Thank you for your words of wisdom and your honesty. You tell it like it is, and I really love/hate that about you. ;) I think you may be my Fairy Godmother.

Lily Garcia, thank you for always being so kind, and thank you for your words of honesty on this story. I'm so glad you took a chance on my writing!

Julie Gustafson-Monk, thank you for falling in love with my words and staying with me after *Chasing Fireflies*. I know that book means a lot to you, and that makes my heart smile.

Thank you to my husband, Billy, who encourages me to work harder, who takes my dreams just as serious as his own. I love you, and I thank God every day for making our paths cross thirteen years ago.

Thank you to my editor, Paige. You have been a Godsend. Thank you for always being honest and making me be my best.

Thank you to my family. You may never read my books, but I know you're proud.

And, of course, to my readers. Without you, I'd just be a girl who writes. With you, I'm an author. Thank you from the bottom of my heart.

Until next time—Paige P. Horne